Always
WILL

Always
WILL

a novel by

MELANIE JACOBSON

Covenant Communications, Inc.

To the Barbies, as is fitting for a story of best friends

Acknowledgments ❤

So many of the same people go with me on this journey every time, even though we all should know better. I love them for climbing on the bandwagon anyway. For Kenny, who makes it all possible. For my kids, who are patient when I have to work. For my critique partners, Brittany and Kristine, who tell me how to make it better. For Ellissa, Ranee, Rachel, and Christina, who gave great feedback. And for Skip and Joan, who are always giving me the best spaces to work.

Chapter 1 ♥

I SHOVED OPEN WILL HALLERMAN'S apartment door and grinned. Widely. Then I stood there until he looked up from the bar of soap he was whittling and rolled his eyes. "That's gloat face. Go ahead, Hannah. Spill it."

"It's her. Your dumb girlfriend is the laundry bandit of building H."

That made him set down the soap. He was roughing out a sinuous shape. I could already see the curves forming. "That'll be amazing in cocobolo wood," I said.

"Maybe." He didn't even glance at it. "Still have some design elements to work out before I think about wood. Shelly isn't dumb," he said, returning to my accusation.

"You're right. She's too smart to steal clothes that I would recognize. But she's a thief. I saw her raid a washing machine. She sorted through it and picked out what she wanted. That's bizarre, Will. Who goes shopping in other people's wet laundry?"

"Why are you assuming she was stealing? Why would she do that with someone watching her? Maybe it was her own washer and she needed something in particular."

"She didn't know I was watching. I staked out the janitor's closet and peeked at her through the shutter slat things. She went over to the machine where *my* clothes were washing, dug out my favorite bra, and stuck it in her dryer. Proof. Your weirdo girlfriend is a laundry bandit."

"The woman who staked out a janitor's closet is calling someone else a weirdo. You get that there's some irony, right?" But he slumped in his seat, and I smiled.

I had him, but I pushed the point anyway. "I'm sure if I got a search warrant, I'd find my white shorts plus a whole closet full of other people's clothes in her apartment. Sucks for anyone who's the same size as your girlfriend." I dropped into my favorite easy chair but not before considering a victory lap around his living room first.

"You're sure it was your bra? Maybe you forgot which machine you were using."

It was my turn for an eye roll. "It was hot pink with black polka dots. Kind of distinctive, so, yeah, I'm sure."

Will's eyebrows lifted. I had no trouble interpreting that. Every one of his expressions read like simple declarative sentences to me. I'd been studying his face obsessively since I was thirteen years old. I spent my teenage years becoming an expert on it, on the way the planes and angles intersected, the exact degree at which his cheekbones curved under his hazel eyes, the scar near his hairline where he'd gotten stitches after my brother, Dave, had accidentally sliced Will open with the ragged edge of some reclaimed tin they were using to roof their treehouse. I'd worried for days after the accident until I was sure he hadn't gotten lockjaw; only then had I finally been able to sleep at night, knowing the love of my life was alive and well and free to continue not taking notice of me.

By fifteen, I could extrapolate his mood on the strength of a single twitch. And not once did any of his twitches or smiles or frequent blank stares into the middle distance ever show me what I had wanted to see more than anything: that he was madly in love with me. So even though those hopes had flamed out back when I was seventeen, my skill set was still very much intact. And that lift of his eyebrows just now meant he'd never once considered that I wore hot-pink, polka-dotted bras.

Seventeen-year-old Hannah would have been thrilled to plant the image in his brain. Eight-years-sadder-but-older-and-wiser Hannah knew Will was running a computation in his head: *Hannah = Dave's kid sister who isn't even in training bras, is she?* Therefore, the polka-dot bra variable must be ignored as not fitting in the numerical set.

"Remind me," I said, wading back to the present. At least Will never minded my fade-outs. His mind wandered even more often, working through difficult engineering problems, pondering the mysteries of the universe, and so on. "What do I get for winning?"

"Can we suspend the gloating and focus on the fact that I'm the real loser here?" He winced as soon as he said it, his mouth opening to snatch the words back, probably, but I was all over it.

"Yes, you are, dummy. King Loser. I think I'll make you a beauty-pageant sash to wear around the complex for a week so everyone else knows too."

"Funny. And you can't make me. Those weren't the stakes."

"Too bad. But I'll settle for Tetris nachos." The precisely stacked nachos were the kind of thing only a brilliant mind like his could come up with, each mouthful a perfectly balanced blend of pico de gallo, carne asada, sour cream, guacamole, black beans, and his genius addition: smoked cheddar.

He groaned. "I'm not sure when I can do it. I've been working on a new sensor suite for the satellite's navigation system, and I—"

I held up a hand to stem the tide of excuses. I knew it was a two-hour project for him since he fried his own tortilla chips and grilled the steak himself. "You'll do it tomorrow so we can eat them during the Rangers game."

He sighed. "Okay. But don't you feel bad exploiting me when I'm in the middle of a breakup?"

"You are?"

"I will be by tomorrow. It's not like I can date a laundrynapper. There's weird, and then there's unbalanced."

"Should've listened to me when I told you not to date her two months ago."

"You tell me not to date everybody I date."

"Have I been wrong yet?"

He wore the same expression he got when he ran into math he couldn't do in his head—the kind other people couldn't do with a calculator and a tutor. The look cleared after a moment. "Nikki Gaines," he said, smug triumph underlining his answer.

"She was pretty great," I conceded. "But I was totally right that you guys shouldn't have been dating. You were all wrong for her."

His head dropped back against the sofa, and he stared up at the ceiling. "There have to be normal women out there. Right? Or am I doomed?"

"You don't need normal, drama queen. That would be the worst thing for you."

"I don't know what I need."

Me, Will. It's always been me. It was an old habit to fill in that blank for him. But I'd been pushing that thought out of my head every time I'd had it for the last few years, and that habit had gotten pretty strong too. "You need pizza, I'm betting."

"It's the answer to everything." He picked up his phone and tapped it a few times, his pizza app already letting the local delivery place know that he wanted his usual meat monster on pan crust delivered ASAP. "Send." He dropped the phone. "I wish dating were that easy. Punch in what I want and the right girl shows up."

"I don't think it's legal to find women that way outside of Vegas."

"You're on one tonight, hmm?" He straightened and fixed me with narrowed eyes. "This whole modern-dating thing is riddled with system inefficiencies. There has to be a better way than bumping into someone at the mailboxes by your house and hoping they're normal when you ask them to lunch. Or when they're alone in the laundry room and think no one is looking."

"System inefficiencies" was a red flag. Any time that phrase came out of Will's mouth, it meant he was about to fix a problem, and sometimes the search for a solution could preoccupy him to the exclusion of everything—including Texas Rangers games and Tetris nachos—for weeks.

I scrambled for a way to divert him, but before I could utter the words, "Look, Kate Upton's on TV," his eyes lit up and extinguished my hope. He'd thought of something. And whatever it was, he would think of nothing else now.

"Internet dating."

I relaxed. "Be real, Will." We'd had this conversation a billion times, like every time an online dating ad aired during game time. He had always insisted that dating that way was as inefficient as regular dating because it took the same amount of time and money to dig down and find the crazy.

"I'm being real. I'm going to figure out a way to game the system and bypass the inefficiencies."

His eyes glazed over. That meant he'd already gone down a wormhole of algorithms that would make my head hurt. Sure, I could understand them if I wanted to. But I didn't. Sometimes, though, listening to Will's complex theoretical analyses was the only way to get his attention. I took a deep breath. "In nonmath terms, can you sketch out your basic idea for me?"

He turned his head toward me, but it took another half minute for his eyes to focus. "I need to study all the different sites, figure out which approach each one uses and what kind of people sign up for them. I'll weed out the sites that attract a high proportion of psychos, like the mainly hookup sites, and focus on the rest. I'll develop a matrix of what I'm looking for, comb through profiles for keywords—"

He grabbed a takeout menu and a pen from the coffee table and scribbled as he talked, his words barely keeping up with his scrawl. "I'll assign point values for different positive attributes and subtract for negative qualities. This is going to—"

"What kind of negative qualities are you talking here?" I had to break in. He'd never looked at the world through the same lens as anyone around him; there was no telling what he'd single out.

"Cats."

"Your hatred of them is unreasonable. It's not their fault."

"Want to trade allergies?" he asked, finally giving me all his attention.

"No." I was only allergic to walnuts, which I didn't like anyway, and my reaction was a scratchy throat. Cats made Will look like a superstrain of hay fever had tried to kneecap him.

"It's not only the allergy thing," he said. "Women with cats are afraid of being alone. They have a higher rate of being clingy."

My jaw dropped. "Can you back that up with data?"

"It's logic."

I itched to grab the remote and give him a hard thump on his skull with it. "What about women with dogs?"

"They, logically, are looking for protection. That makes sense for females living alone."

"What about females living with roommates? Or females with little dogs, the kinds that fit in purses?"

He shrugged, lost in his head again.

"Will! Make Benadryl your friend, suck it up, and let the cat prejudice go. What other requirements do you have?"

"She must be educated, driven, financially independent, physically active, and pretty."

Check, check, check, check, and check, I thought but said nothing. I dug my fingers into the throw pillow sitting on my lap and pressed it down as hard as I could to keep myself still. "What about funny? Smart? Kind?"

"People describe themselves that way all the time. I'll give self-analysis less weight. But having an education is a good objective indicator that they'll be both smart and driven, so that gets more weight in the point system."

As much as I wanted to point out all the flaws in his logic, I kept quiet, the hard knot in my chest easing for the first time since he'd announced he was going to take his search for love seriously. He'd never get it right if he went down the road he was mapping out for himself, and that meant I had more time to brace myself . . . The same way I'd braced myself again and again with each new relationship he'd paraded in front of me since his first girlfriend, Sarah Lancey, when he was sixteen. That had only lasted two weeks, but I hadn't taken one quality breath that whole time.

The knot never went away entirely. A pebble-sized spot lived somewhere in the middle of my chest, made up of pure worry, with cancerous tentacles trying to creep outward. "Why now?" I asked, vomiting out the question that fed the worry. "You've done all right dating. Why not let it happen when it's going to happen?"

He set his pen down and stretched, and I stole a glance at the lean muscles extending from the short sleeves of his Dallas Mavericks T-shirt. "You and fate," he said, standing to ruffle my hair before wandering to his fridge. "You'll never give up the idea of soul mates, even after all of your boring boyfriends."

Of course not. I figured out mine when I was thirteen. How could I not believe? All I said out loud was, "That's not an answer to the question. Why now?"

He retrieved a sports drink—blue, always blue—from the fridge and held it up. I shook my head, and he leaned against the counter, opening the lid and taking a long swallow. It was stupid how sexy that looked. It was second nature to notice and equally ingrained to never let that reaction show on my face.

"I'm twenty-eight," he said. "It's time."

"Is that an algorithm somewhere too?"

"I've been thinking ever since the wedding. Dave is happy. I wouldn't mind that." He scrubbed his hand through his hair, and the caramel-colored strands tangled like unset taffy. He needed a haircut again. He always needed a haircut. For a guy who held an infinite number of complexities in his brain at any given moment, he had a habit of forgetting things like trips to the barber.

"I kind of want that, what Dave has. It looks like a better option than stringing together four to eight dates with someone before it unravels. He got it right. I should definitely be able to get it right."

I shook my head at the competitive vibe in his words. *It has ever been thus*, Grammy would have said if she were still alive. Mostly it was healthy competition that drove my brother and Will to push themselves harder and to do better. And they genuinely cheered each other's successes. But there was no doubt that every success created a new goal for the other one.

I had a difficult time drawing my next couple of breaths as I realized I hadn't dodged this bullet after all. I'd feared this all the way through Dave's engagement and marriage last year, but when a few months had passed and Will still seemed more interested in his work than in a wife, I thought this must be an area where Will didn't feel the need to catch up.

Looked like he was having a delayed reaction. I took a breath to make sure I still could, careful not to sound like I'd been punched in the gut. But that was what it felt like. He was serious. I could see it in his face. And for the first time, I wondered what would happen if he brought the right girl home instead of the long line of wrong ones who had passed through over the years.

He wandered back to the sofa and plopped down. I popped up from my easy chair. "I'm going."

"Why? Pizza's not here yet."

"Seriously? I never eat the pizza you order."

"But one day you'll stop being stupid and you will."

"It's not stupid to take care of yourself."

"It is when taking care of yourself means eating rabbit food."

"Congratulations to you for being some weird biological anomaly, but the rest of us can't live on carbs, fat, and sugar indefinitely and not blob out."

"You're in great shape. You're paranoid."

I did my best to ignore that so no color would creep into my cheeks. Not that he would notice, really, but if anything would give me away, it was my lame blushes. My cheeks stayed cool, and I raised my chin a notch. "The person in this room who was not named Heavy Hannah in high school should not talk. At all."

"First, you were never heavy."

Lie. I'd lost fifty pounds between my senior year of high school and sophomore year of college.

"Secondly, high school kids are idiots. Who cares what they called you? Probably they'd say Hot Hannah now anyway."

Heat flare, solar level, in my cheeks before I could fight it down. I hid it by stooping to straighten the *Smithsonian* magazine on his coffee table to align with the *Sports Illustrated* next to it. "I literally have to run," I said into his tabletop as I waited for my cheeks to cool enough not to betray me. "There's always a creepy guy on the lake trail if I wait too much longer."

This time it was Will who shot straight up, and I bit my lip, realizing I'd made a very dumb miscalculation.

"What creepy guy?" he demanded. "Someone been bothering you? Where? I'm coming with you."

"Shut up," I said, pushing against his chest until he sat down, savoring the fleeting feel of his solid pectorals beneath my palms. They were as hard as the rocks he'd spent years climbing to sculpt his chest and shoulders to perfection. And his legs. His legs . . .

I caught myself before I could wander too far off into day-dreams. "No one has bothered me. I don't like the way he looks at me, but I don't like the way he looks at any of the women who run past him. And if he did bother me, I could handle him."

Will's jaw set, and his arms crossed, a sure sign that he was about to dig in on the subject. I headed him off, whipping my phone from my back pocket. "I'll keep this set to speed dial you the second I catch a whiff of Creepy Dude in the vicinity. Then you can come glare him to death. Good enough?"

"No."

"Make it good enough, Will. I'm going running. Enjoy your pizza, and don't worry about me. Worry about your internet-dating algorithm." That was all I would worry about while I ran. His sudden focus on the project unnerved me, almost literally—

as if my nerves were unstringing and no longer capable of holding me together like they should.

Running this evening would be about outrunning that feeling, not calorie burn or heart health. It would be about pounding back the anxiety trying to pluck at me, every foot strike against the lake path an effort to chip away at the knot that kept growing.

"Give me some of your drink," I said, reaching over to pluck it out of his hand for a fortifying sip before I took off. He jerked it out of my reach and caught my wrist with his other hand, toppling me into his lap. Knowing what was coming next, I cursed myself for setting myself up for it, even as I managed to twist and land on my behind and not face-first into a sofa cushion.

"Will!" I hollered and tried to squirm away, but he pinned me to his chest with those well-defined arms, and I decided to curse them too. As if he were holding a sleepy puppy and not a full-grown woman who was straining against him, he leaned over and set his Gatorade down. "Will, no!"

But he lifted his free hand, folded his knuckles under, and delivered a noogie.

I wanted to kill him. For three seconds, I considered doing it. But years of experience taught me to endure it and he'd go away faster.

He let me go, and I dug my elbow in hard while leveraging myself to my feet. "Bye, loser," I called over my shoulder.

"Don't go away mad," he yelled.

I slammed the door as an answer. I'd made it ten feet down the hall to my place, three doors down, when Will scooped me up from behind and held me against his chest, with my feet dangling above the ground. I'd resented every short girl Will had ever dated since very few guys were tall enough to keep my toes from touching the ground in a maneuver like that. I'd resented all the petite little things he'd fallen for over the years, wishing I could shoo them away like flies to go circulate among the much larger pool of men who would work for their height. Even though I was five nine, Will had me by a good six inches.

I cursed every one of those inches between him and me now as I tried to make contact with the carpeted hallway, but Will had me locked. I wasn't in the mood for this. I skipped the pleading that I usually dragged out for maximum Will contact when he had me pinned and went straight to my surefire release option: I yanked on a tuft of Will's arm hair. He yelped and let go, backing up so quickly I had to windmill for a second to catch my balance.

"That hurt." He rubbed his arm and scowled at me.

I scowled right back. "You are not the boss of me. If I want to go away mad, I can go away mad."

"At least I know you can handle yourself against the creepy lake dude. Seriously, let me come run with you."

"You're too slow."

"Nice, Hannah."

"You'd be faster if you trained too, but I'm not slowing down for you. You're taking this keep-an-eye-on-me thing too seriously." I started toward my door again.

"I promised Dave when he left—"

"I know what you promised him. It was nice of you. But I think he meant you should help me change lightbulbs or get stuff off tall shelves, not monitor my jogging."

"That's not what I'm—"

"Ooh, look, pizza guy is here," I said without turning around. I knew he'd check behind him anyway. He was kind of Pavlovian about his pizzas. I slipped into my apartment and shut the door, waiting a moment to see if he would give up. He did. Of course he did. It wasn't like I was going to trump a pizza.

Chapter 2 ♥

THIS IS FOR REAL. THIS is for real.

My feet pounded in time with the words a half hour later even though I was doing my best to outrun them. If I managed to push away the chant for a few yards, the expression on Will's face intruded, the image of the light his eyes caught when he was deep inside a new idea.

He had a crazy-smart brain. I did too, but Will was . . . beyond. And if he'd decided to take this seriously, to follow Dave's lead and settle down, he'd solve the "system inefficiencies."

I kicked up my speed, fueled by impatience. Why should I even think of it as bad news? I'd talked myself out of being in love with Will at least two hundred times since high school. I'd thought for sure the last talk I'd had with myself had actually gotten through.

But, then, why had I been so determined to prove that Shelly was the wrong fit for him? And pretty much every girl before that?

Because I'm a liar, I admitted. *Liar, liar, liar.*

Ugh. This was not much better as a beat for my footfalls.

I checked the running app on my phone and veered toward a lakeside cement bench when I hit the three-mile mark. I dropped onto the seat and stretched my legs in front of me, leaning down to touch my toes and enjoy the gentle pull on my hamstrings. After a minute, my brain quieted enough for me to straighten and look out at the water.

I punched out a text. I was going to need Sophie for this.

BND broke up with PS. "Boy Next Door" was my code for Will with my best friend since elementary school. *PS* was Psycho Shelly. Obviously.

But you don't care, right?

I laughed at Sophie's quick sarcasm. *Nope. But now he's got a Project. To Get Married.*

Uh-oh.

I'd no sooner read the words than Sophie's name lit up my screen on an incoming call.

"He's getting married? I thought you said he just broke up with someone."

"Technically he hasn't broken up yet, but he will. I caught her stealing my bra. So she's crazy, but she has good taste. It was my favorite bra."

"So weird. Explain the marriage thing," Sophie said, undeterred. I loved that I had every bit of Sophie's attention. We'd bonded in fifth grade when we'd both put NSYNC stickers on our folders. She'd proved her friendship when my parents died in a car wreck two years later, and she'd held me together through seventh grade until I could bear to interact with people again. My aunt Cindy had moved in to raise Dave and me after that, and while she was well-intentioned, sometimes she was misguided, too strict about some things, and too lax about others.

Dave was too protective *all* the time after the accident. Sophie's house and family had been my refuge. And her bedroom had been where I'd confessed all the ins and outs of my doomed love for Will. Almost all.

"He mumbled something about wanting what Dave has and online dating and gaming the system, and then he got the look."

"Ohhh."

"Yeah. I don't know what he's planning, but he's never talked about dating like this before."

"I wouldn't think so. That dude has always been about who falls into his lap." She paused for a moment. "Well, mostly. Present company excluded on account of he's an idiot."

"Whatever he's planning, it'll work. It always does. It sounds like he's going to mathematically find the perfect girl for him. And you know him and math."

He'd tutored both of us through college calculus, even though one of us always broke down in tears before the end of the session. Not because of him. Because *calculus*. Blerg.

"So basically you're freaking out," Sophie guessed.

"I don't know what I am," I said. "I feel like I've been on the verge of permanently losing him for years, which is stupid. You can't lose what you don't have. But this still feels different." I sighed, frustrated at the loops my thoughts were following without getting anywhere. "Maybe it's because the bombshell is brand-new."

"Bomb metaphors," Sophie the English teacher said, sounding relieved. "Let's go with that. You're shell-shocked. Maybe you're feeling like it's blowing all your chances with him to kingdom come. But I think something else is happening."

"You're going to drop a bomb on me?" I said, cracking myself up.

"No, but I think that's exactly what you need to do with him."

We let the words hang while I tried to figure out what Sophie meant. But it could have been a thousand things, so I gave up.

"What kind of bomb do you see me dropping?"

"I think you need to pursue the nuclear option."

"I'm nodding like I know what you're talking about, but, really, I have no idea."

"Tell him. Tell him how you feel."

Right. One of the few secrets I'd kept from Sophie was that I *had* told Will how I felt once. When I was seventeen, I'd confessed my feelings for him through a panic attack while fighting back nausea. And he'd done exactly what I'd feared; he'd laughed at me. Not in a mean way, as if I were an idiot for thinking he would ever like me. But in the way adults laughed at kids who did something cute and then sent them off to play again. He'd dismissed my feelings as a kid crush.

He saw the three-year age difference between us as a generation gap. For me, that three years had narrowed the older we'd become until it was invisible. But he still saw me as an honorary kid sister, and the gulf between us was as big as ever on his side.

"I'm not going to tell him how I feel. After he finishes letting me down easy, he'll give me pity looks, and then while I crawl back to my place to die of humiliation, he'll be ten steps behind me, trying to feed me chicken soup to make me feel better because he promised Dave he'd look after me."

"So? How is that worse than if you say nothing? What happens at the end of that road if you're right about this new plan of his?"

"Me crying in my apartment, and he doesn't bring me chicken soup because he doesn't even know."

Sophie let my conclusion hang there, and it drifted in front of the lake sunset like a hazy cobweb of unsolvable problem fibers I wanted to swat away. But touching it meant getting more tangled up.

"I don't want things to change," I said. "I love spending entire lazy Saturday afternoons on his couch, playing Mario Kart with him. If I say something and it messes it all up, it ruins that. What if he feels like he can't drop by my place anymore to raid my bookshelves and talk about what we read? Or what if he quits talking to me about his carving? *Sophie.*"

"*What?*"

"What if I don't get Tetris nachos ever again? I would die."

"At least you're joking about it."

"Only so I don't cry." I stood and hit the trail again at a brisk walk. "Maybe I'm wrong, anyway. Maybe I misread the situation. Maybe he'll get distracted by something else."

"Maybe," Sophie echoed. "But you've never called me this freaked out before. You need to get more details before you lose it, okay? What do you call it at work?"

"Gathering requirements." It was what I'd been doing for the last year as a project manager in the IT department of a big life sciences company; I steered a small team of software developers through the deadlines upper management needed them to hit to develop new websites for their different products. I had to see the bigger picture and figure out the pieces it would take to deliver what my bosses wanted.

"Do that," Sophie urged. "Find out exactly what this is. But if your gut instinct is right, and Will really is trying to hunt down the future Mrs. Hallerman, you need to decide whether you want to hold the train of her wedding gown while she walks down the aisle to marry him or stick out your foot to trip her as she passes."

"Nice one."

"Nope, totally flawed analogy now that I'm hearing it. You need to figure out if you even want it to get that far, because if you don't, you're going to have to trip him on his way out of the front door to his first date."

"I want things to stay how they've been." I heard the whine in my voice, but Sophie wouldn't judge me for it.

"Really? You want *nothing* to change? That's the central conflict in the story of your life, girlfriend. Think hard about it."

"I don't think I'll be able to think about anything else. I'm going to run home, shower, and go see where his head is at."

When we hung up, I tucked my phone away and finished out my last two miles in a personal best time. I almost, but not quite, outran my thoughts. But it was worth it. By the time I reached the last block before home, I'd planned my approach to figuring out what was going on with Will.

Chapter 3 ♥

WILL'S APARTMENT DOOR FLEW OPEN right as I reached to open it, and Shelly barreled straight into me before we both took a step back.

"Sorry," she muttered before pushing past me and heading for the stairs. I watched her go, wondering if I'd just seen my polka-dot bra walk off too. I shook my head and stepped into Will's place. The sound of a cable news channel came from the TV, but he was digging in the fridge. Again.

"You break up with her?" I called.

He jumped and whirled, another energy drink in his hand. "Yeah."

"What'd you tell her? That she was a dirty bra thief?"

"I thought she stole your clean one."

"Ha."

"I didn't mention the laundry issues because I wasn't sure how to explain how I knew without sounding like I was stalking her or ratting you out for lurking in the janitor's closet while she sorted her colors."

"Sorted my colors, you mean? So what did you say?"

"I went with it's not you, it's me."

I plopped down on his sofa. "Usually that's true. You're a real gent for saying so tonight when it was most definitely her."

He grunted and dropped down beside me and handed me a drink of my own.

"So what now?" I asked when he didn't say anything else. "Grow a beard and hide from women forever?"

"Nah. I told you I've got a plan."

My stomach clenched. "I was gone less than two hours, and you dumped your girlfriend plus put together a plan for getting yourself married off? You don't mess around."

He pulled his laptop from the end table on his side of the sofa and slid it onto my lap. "I got this finished before Shelly came over. It's the first iteration. I'll do some A-B testing and see how it plays."

Cragen Life Sciences used A-B testing when we were rolling out a new product to see which marketing approach generated more customers. We'd use two different website designs promoting the same thing and see which one got more traffic. One of my first projects after my promotion had been overseeing the build on one of the A-B websites for a cream that lightened liver spots. But what faced me on the screen now was a gloriously un-liver-spotted picture of Will with some bullet points about his personality beneath it.

Engineer at Jet Science Labs
Hazel
Tall
Athletic
Jazz
Rap
Sports, mainly baseball
Lord of the Rings, Star Wars, the smart superhero stuff
Comic books
Pizza
Smile, cloud
Cats

Long walks on the beach

"What is this?" I asked, looking up from the list.

"It's all my stuff to cut and paste into the profile things they want you to fill out when you join a dating site," he said. "That way I don't have to re-type everything."

"I get that hazel is your eye color and you hate cats, but what does 'smile, cloud' mean?

"That's what's important to me in a woman. First I'm attracted to her smile, but it's everything she has stored on her cloud— music, movies, e-books—that decides if I stick around."

"Ah. And long walks on the beach? You've been to the beach twice in your life."

"I need to put things in there that women like." He pulled the laptop back but kept the screen angled so I could see him highlight "comic books." "I figure I have to let women know certain things up front, like about my comic-book collection. That one hasn't gone over well in the past, so I'll put it out there and let that filter some candidates out right away."

Candidates. Like he was filling a job.

"But I don't want to filter everyone out right away, so I have to put other stuff in there that women like. And you all like walks on the beach, right?"

I wrinkled my forehead. "I guess if women live by a beach they'd like walking on it. But I don't think it's a major requirement for Dallas women. They're probably more worried about whether you like to go on long walks through the Galleria."

"That's cynical," he said. "You're not like that."

"I'm not like most women," I retorted, a point I'd tried and failed to make for years with him. But the urgency to make him *get it* was spiking to a level I hadn't felt in years. I worried the tension would show on my face. He'd already come up with more plan specifics than I'd expected. "Why is rap on the list?"

"That falls under stuff I hate and dealbreakers."

That made more sense. "You've already put a lot of thought into this."

"Not really. I barely started working on it."

"You think twice as fast as other people. That's like four hours of thinking for regular humans."

"Minus an uncomfortable twenty-minute conversation with Shelly, it's really only three and a half hours." He smirked, and I reached over to deliver a light smack to the back of his head, a long-standing code that meant it was getting too big.

"Anyway, I'm going to spend all day on this tomorrow, and then it should be ready to go."

"What? Your list?"

He tapped a few keys on the laptop, and the screen filled with code. "No, this."

I didn't have to study it to know the code would be clean and elegant. If he ever got tired of rocket science, he'd make a killer programmer. "I should have known you got more than a list done."

"I'm writing a program to crawl the top three dating sites and sniff out the profiles for the women who are the best match for me. Then I'll program each site to send them a personalized greeting."

"Wait, you're going to have a computer program automatically send the exact same prewritten message to everyone that it identifies as a match for you? That's not what personalized means, genius."

"When you say it that way, it sounds so calculating." He grinned and punched a fist in the air. "Success. No more messy trial and error."

If it had been anyone else laying out this plan, I would have found it plain depressing, a cold way to approach what was supposed to be the wild, messy plunge of falling in love. But coming from Will, a sense of dread gripped me.

He'd never taken a serious approach to dating. Sophie's characterization of him dating whoever fell into his lap wasn't really wrong; the tall, athletic frame and hazel eyes he'd made into bullet points caught women's attention regularly. And if it wasn't that, it was the slightly too-long, sun-streaked gold hair that fell into his eyes until I sat him down in his kitchen and trimmed it the way I used to for Dave.

So, yeah, women were always around, always trying to snag him. The really blonde, tiny ones generally succeeded. At least for a few weeks at a time. But if he came at this from a totally different angle, maybe he would find totally different women. And that could lead to a totally different outcome, where there was no built-in two-month expiration date on the relationship. Well, "relationship." Will hadn't mastered the long-term thing since college. Then again, he hadn't wanted to.

And now that he did . . .

With a shudder, I remembered Brooke. I had known there was something different about her from the moment Will had brought her over to show her off, and he'd been lost to me, even as an honorary brother, the whole time he'd been in the Brooke Vortex, as Dave called it. Will's whole life had been nothing but Brooke and how smart she was and accomplished she was and funny she was for that whole year until she'd graduated from college—and Will—and moved on to New York and a glamorous career.

Dave and I had picked up the pieces. Or tried to. It had taken six months for Will to go on another date, and ever since then, it had been an unbroken stream of bright, shiny, fresh-faced beauty-pageant runner-ups who lost only because they weren't ruthless enough to win. Nice. So nice. He dated such nice, vanilla girls.

And strangely, I'd been okay with that. There were no Brookes among them, and as long as there were none of those, Will was safe. And I could breathe.

But not now. The code filling his screen—the neat, precise rows of slashes, brackets, and asterisks—spelled success. And doom. Because once he deployed it, it would work. He would figure out he'd been dating the wrong women for years, and suddenly he'd have an unlimited supply of the right ones.

Sophie's words flashed through my mind. *Drop the bomb.*

Maybe it would work. Maybe he would see me in a new light, and we would have a happily ever after. Or maybe he would laugh and give me another noogie.

Or worst of all, maybe I would get Will at a polite, uncomfortable distance, only seeing him when Dave moved back from Qatar and we both showed up for barbecues at his place.

"Hannah? Join me on Earth. It's nice here," Will said, his fingers flying over the keyboard.

"What are you doing now?" Every single thing he did in this plan felt like a nail pounding into a coffin, the one that would bury my hopes and dreams of the day Will realized he'd always secretly loved me. The inside of my head echoed the pounding. I grimaced. Sophie would be ashamed of me for coming up with such a hackneyed cliché. Although she'd probably give me back some points for using *hackneyed*.

I thought about how the words would sound coming out. *I'm madly in love with you, Will. The crazy crush I've had on you since I was thirteen never went away. It just turned into something else, like trading Tootsie Rolls for Godiva chocolates. So, how do you feel about that?*

No way. The words, or any version of them, would choke me before they ever got out of my mouth. But my stomach percolated with a weird mixture of dread and certainty. And possibly greasy-pizza smell. It was do something or lose Will for real. And I couldn't lose Will for real. So then what?

Ruin his plans, for one thing. It was the only decent thing to do.

I looked down at my clothes, my baggy running shorts and dingy T-shirt. Step one: change while I figured out steps two through a million, if need be, to derail Operation Find a Bride. "I need to go change," I said. "I'll be back in a few minutes."

"Why do you have to change?" he asked, glancing over. "You look comfortable."

Frumpy, more like. Will's women always looked pulled together. I needed to go that route too. "I don't want to stay in my sweaty clothes, that's all. Give your brain a break while I'm gone. I think you're going about this all wrong, and I have an idea of how to tweak it when I get back."

"Like what?" he said, his tone offended.

"Tell you when I get back," I repeated. I had to think of the answer first.

Chapter 4 ♥

I TOOK MY TIME MEANDERING down to my apartment door. It took all of thirty seconds. I stripped off my running gear and considered my closet, trying to figure out the right thing to put on while 80 percent of my attention went to figuring out Find-a-Bride Sabotage. I wished I'd done more Internet dating so I could tell Will all the wrong things to do, but for now I'd have to rely on stories I'd heard from friends about their mishaps. And I couldn't do anything too obvious, or Will would figure it out in a second.

What I needed was to design the perfect profile for him so he'd think he was getting the women he liked, but they'd actually be the kind of women he'd lose interest in quickly. And then I'd have to step up my game. I'd always been the right girl for him, so there was no point in changing things about myself. But I'd have to figure out how to draw his attention to me in a good way, to make him see that I was what he needed, not another pocket blonde. I had to make sure he had dates so miserable that being with me was a refuge.

I'd trailed along once on a post-college graduation trip he and Dave had taken to the Bahamas, where they'd swum with the sharks. It was one of the few times I'd seen Will genuinely nervous, but with Dave jumping into the water without any fear, Will wouldn't back down from diving in too. It had taken the guide, a grizzled dive master named Roger, who was incredibly patient, to get him there, talking him through every bit of the process: the design specs of the underwater cage that would protect him from the sharks, the exact genus and species of the chum they were using to draw the sharks, the science of their dive gear.

Only after the guide had nailed every answer did Will's shoulders relax, and he'd dropped into the water without another word. I'd followed right behind him, and we'd been rewarded with a spectacular view of reef sharks.

I'd be his Roger *and* his shark cage, the person who made everything okay, who made it so he could breathe, and the defense against the predatory women who would come after him for all the wrong reasons, not for the qualities only years of knowing him would reveal.

I winced. Sophie would flunk me for that metaphor too.

* * *

I walked back into Will's place, and his eyebrows rose. "You going somewhere?"

"Just here."

"Why are you dressed up?"

I looked down at the yellow knit dress I had agonized over choosing. "This isn't dressed up. It took about as much energy as pulling on a T-shirt and flip flops." Granted, they were bejeweled sandals. But at the most basic level, I was wearing a T-shirt and flip flops.

"But I have to make you nachos, and you always spill when you eat them."

Thanks for making me feel twelve again, dude. "I'm not that hungry. I'm taking a rain check. I'm going to demand them on a day when it's super inconvenient for you to make them."

"Of course." He grunted. "You had ideas for my profile?"

"Let me look at it again." The second he posted his picture, it was going to be game over unless I planted some red flags to make his potential matches think twice—but only the potential matches he would like. The rest of them I wanted pinging him in droves. Annoying, whiny droves. Like gnats. That he wanted to flick away.

"I think the main thing here is that you want to tell the truth about yourself, but you want to tell the best version of the truth you can," I said, pulling out my cell phone and tapping the camera. "You should avoid putting stuff like 'rocket scientist' out there and save it for a first date."

"Why wouldn't I say that straight out? That's what I've spent the most time being."

"Yeah, but telling someone you're in the sciences, especially astrophysics, will give them the impression that you're analytical and detached. Besides, you know the joke: how do you know someone is a rocket scientist?"

He sighed. "He'll tell you. Fine. We'll save it for later dates. But I *am* analytical. That needs to be there. I need someone who can handle the fact that I believe in logic because . . . logic."

I played out the possibilities. Something like that could draw equally hyperanalytical women. If they had a fun streak, that was bad news. A highly logical person who also had a sense of adventure was exactly what Will needed. That was me in a nutshell. If he got someone who was as analytical as himself but who wasn't fun, that would be ideal. Will would convince himself for a few dates that he *should* like Miss Logic before the boredom would win out, but those few dates would buy me time.

It was a gamble worth taking. I'd screen the candidates for anyone whose hobbies were fun and convince Will that those matches were a bad choice.

All right, phase one: The Logical Match. Let it begin.

"Let's put up your profile picture. We need something that shows you looking like a thinker so you'll attract smart women."

"I'm not exactly rolling in the selfies."

"It's kind of weird when dudes are." I waved my phone. "I'm a genius problem solver. Smile, but do it thoughtfully. It needs to look candid, like someone snapped it for you when you didn't know they were taking a picture of you. Act like you're looking out a window and thinking about something cool that makes you smile a teeny bit."

"This is stupid."

I marched over to him and grabbed the front of his T-shirt, pulling on it hard enough that it forced him to look up at me. "I'm the boss. Do it before I make you put on fake reading glasses."

He didn't even bat an eye at the manhandling. That's how it went when people were so used to each other. I let him go, and he sagged back on the couch. "Also, you need to change your shirt."

He dropped his head back against the sofa and groaned. I ignored him and hurried down the hall to his bedroom, yanking open his closet door to find something better for him to wear. He couldn't wear a sports jersey *and* a thoughtful smile. He'd look like a laid-back guy with interesting secrets, and all kinds of mystery-loving, spontaneous women would come out of the woodwork, which was exactly what I didn't need.

His closet smelled like him, the faintest hint of his cologne hanging in the air. Once a guy from accounting had walked past me, and I'd gone weak in the knees. I spent fifteen minutes trying to figure out why the middle-aged man with a borderline comb-over had affected me like that until he had walked back the other way and I'd realized he wore Will's cologne. Potent stuff.

I took longer to choose a shirt for Will than I really needed to. I liked being in his room. It was so Will. His spare room was a monument to frat boy whimsy, the inside full of an intricate fortress made of empty Gatorade bottles. This room reflected a guy who had some taste. He'd painted the walls a dark gray and picked black furniture with black-and-white bedding in a geometric print—it probably soothed his engineering mind to be surrounded by all the square edges of the blanket's print, the furniture shapes, and the pristine hospital corners he made his bed with.

I reached into the closet. All he needed was a plaid button-down, something in a baggy cut, not the trendy slim style. I pulled a shirt from the back. Boxy, drab plaid. Perfect.

"Here." I walked back into the living room, where he'd turned the TV back on to look for a game. "Put this on, and look thoughtful. You can even stare at the game and pretend you're thinking about something important." I flicked a glance at the screen. "The Lions are losing. That should be enough to make you smile."

He sighed and stood to pull his T-shirt off. I mourned the rippled-ab view that disappeared button by button as he put the new shirt on.

"So what do you want me to do again? Sit here and grin like an idiot?"

"Watch the game and smile," I said.

He heaved another sigh.

"Careful, Will. You're going to fog up your windows with all that heavy breathing."

He shot me a dirty look before switching his gaze back to the TV.

"Good. Now smile."

He grimaced.

"You look like I'm torturing you."

"You are. This is dumb. Can't I use the picture from my work badge?"

Absolutely. It was unflattering. But I shook my head. I was saving that baby for when I tried to get him to draw in the women looking for a reliable, serious guy. Will was reliable until he disappeared into one of his projects. And he was serious then too. But that all went away when he emerged, problem solved and ready to blow off steam on some nutjob adventure.

Will's post-project adventures were some of the best times I'd had hanging out with him and my brother. That thrill-seeking was another side of Will the ladies of the Interwebz would not be meeting if I pulled this off.

"Just forget I'm here, and smile," I ordered again.

This time it looked like his sixth- through ninth-grade yearbook photos where he'd clearly been uncomfortable flashing his braces for the camera.

I dropped beside him on the sofa and flipped through the channels until I found a *Mythbusters* marathon playing. "Have you seen this one?"

He nodded.

"Good. Now think about how you'd redesign the experiment."

He rested his elbows on his knees and watched as the redheaded Mythbuster explained the design of the propellant they were using to test their hypothesis. Will's forehead furrowed for a second, and I moved off the sofa to the adjacent armchair where I could get a better shot. Then I waited. As the TV guy ran through the physics of their predicted outcome, the furrows in Will's forehead deepened.

Wait for it . . . there. His forehead smoothed, and I poised my finger over the camera button. He leaned forward, and a small smile appeared as he corrected the trajectory in his head. I caught the picture I needed right before he sat back, satisfied that he'd figured out the right way to set up the test.

"I'm e-mailing this to you. Hand me your laptop so I can pull it up and post it."

"You want me to give you my laptop with access to all my password-protected accounts so you can dig into all of it and post stuff?"

"Yeah. When have you ever had a secret from me anyway?"

He looked stumped for a minute, then grinned. "There's definitely some stuff I've kept from your tender, young ears. Stuff you're never going to be old enough to hear."

I refused to even think about what that meant about women, about past relationships. Instead, I focused on shaking another one of his pet ideas about me. "Tender, young ears, my right elbow."

Will grinned. "That was a good Aunt Meryl." Meryl was actually Grammy, who had died when I was in high school. We'd grown up going out to her house in Waxahachie on weekends to fish or ride ATVs, and Will had usually sat right next to Dave in the back of Mom's Forerunner, itchy to get to the bass pond. He'd called Grammy his Aunt Meryl because he'd said she looked like Meryl Streep, and it had stuck. As had a lot of Grammy's country expressions that Dave, Will, and I all still used with each other.

"Thanks. But my point is that I'm not that young."

Will shrugged and looked like he was going to disappear into the rest of the *Mythbusters* episode.

"You know the last three girls you've dated have all been younger than me, right?"

His head whipped toward me, his face startled. He didn't say anything, only narrowed his eyes for a minute as he stared at me before he shrugged and mumbled, "That's weird."

"You're the one who's cradle-robbing."

"Shut up," he said, a smile creeping in. "Every last one of them is out of college. It's not cradle-robbing. I meant it's weird that they all seem older than you. More life experience, probably."

I wanted to throw the laptop at his head. They definitely had *different* life experiences, namely not growing up next door to Will their whole lives so they weren't family to him. "I'm not as young as you're trying to make me, Will, is my point. Now check out your profile."

I shoved the laptop back at him, waiting for him to check the final result of his phase-one profile: Will, Master of Logic, the guy who would attract incredibly intelligent but boring women.

"You sure this is the way to go?" he asked, looking up. "I feel like I come off kind of dry."

"You come off as a serious thinker, who doesn't need to date anyone who would carry a dog in her purse or think a quarter hour means twenty-five minutes." I grinned when he winced at the memory of the girl from last year I referred to. "Should we leave figuring out what women want to you, the guy in his gym shorts, watching a *Mythbusters* marathon, or me, the actual woman?"

He shook his head but hit "post" without arguing, sending his profile out to a worldwide web of potential dates.

I took a deep breath. Operation Find-a-Bride Sabotage was in full effect.

Chapter 5 ❤

THE NEXT DAY AFTER WORK I pushed open Will's door in time to swipe his phone from his hand.

"What did you do that for?" he asked, staring at his empty palm.

"You were about to order pizza, right?"

"Maybe not. Maybe I was going to call my mom."

"You were ordering pizza. You're still in work clothes, which means you were going to order pizza, change, sit on the couch, and wait for dinner to show up."

"Fine, I was ordering pizza."

"Change, make sure you put on running shoes, then we'll have dinner."

"I don't want to run."

"It's because I'm faster than you, right?"

He gave me a "whatever" look. "You're so lame. Fine. We'll run."

I didn't bother to hide my smile. Will didn't have any hang-ups about losing to a woman, but it would gall him to let any trash talk go unchallenged. "You know you're super predictable, right? All I have to do is say I'm going to beat you at something to get you to do it."

"That's not true."

"Really? How come you're about to go put on your running shoes?"

He dropped onto the sofa. "I'm not."

"I know. Because you hate losing."

He shot up off the sofa and headed down the hallway, shutting his door on my laughter.

"Meet you back here in ten," I yelled.

I headed back to my place and changed into shorts but hesitated over my choice of shirt. Normally I threw on one of my old college T-shirts, but this time I slipped on the dark purple tank my old UT roommate, Katie, had sent me for my birthday. She'd explained something about the fabric being high tech, but at the moment, I only cared that it did me more favors than my usual raggedy running gear.

I backtracked to Will's and found him dressed in shorts and a worn-out Cowboys T-shirt. He stood at the sink, filling a water bottle, another full one already on the counter next to him, and I admired the view for a minute, his broad shoulders sloping into well-defined arms. He turned when I shut the door, then he capped the bottle he held and tossed it at me. "One for you."

It was one of the things I loved about him—he was always taking care of me in little ways. I just wished it wasn't because of his big-brother mind-set. I caught the water but held up the squeeze bottle I'd brought with me. "Thanks, but I'm covered."

"Not really. Since when do you go running in shiny space clothes?" He eyed my fitted tank top like I'd literally stepped off a UFO.

"Since Katie gave it to me for my birthday. It's not even shiny," I said, suddenly self-conscious when I'd felt super cute only minutes before. It was the same stretchy-looking stuff most athletic clothes were made of, not shiny at all.

"It's shiny compared to this," he said, plucking at his T-shirt.

"Well, it's not a space shirt. Wait, maybe it is. According to Katie, it's made of polymers and microbial fiber weaves. But I like it. It's comfortable." I smoothed it out, even though it was designed to fit so it would never wrinkle. But self-consciousness always made me fidgety with my hands, and they wouldn't stay still.

"Sorry," he said. "I sounded rude. I meant that I'm used to your Longhorns shirts, and now I feel like a slob. I didn't mean to make you feel dumb. But I'm going to look like a real hobo running beside you out there. You look good."

"Beside me?" I repeated, hoping the heat in my cheeks at his compliment didn't actually make them pink. "You'll be a mile behind me and fading fast." I willed the heat to die down. He was only saying it because he was trying to make me feel better. But he'd commented on my appearance for a second time in the last couple days, and it was a start.

He straightened and headed toward the door. "Put up or shut up, Becker. Let's hit the trail."

An hour later, he was panting right behind me as I reached the bench that marked the end of our five-mile run.

"You were holding back for me," he said, dropping his hands to his knees and drawing a deep breath.

"You did all right," I said. "You kept up."

"Yeah, but I'm dying," he said around a couple of gasps, "and you're not even winded."

"Ohhhhhh, is that why you're bent over like that? Because I deflated your ego and now there's nothing to keep you upright?"

I shrieked as he grabbed me and hauled me against him to pin me again. "Don't poke the bear when he's way bigger than you," he said over my giggles. I reached up and tugged on his arm hair, and he let go. "Ow!"

"Dear bear, don't toy with the mouse when she's a dirty fighter," I said, grinning.

He reached over and tousled my hair. "You've never been a mouse."

I smoothed my hair back, tucking an escapee from my ponytail behind my ear and trying to hide the tremor in my hand. Why was it shaking? Hurt. His words hurt. "I've lost fifty pounds. When do I get to be a mouse?"

His deep-thought wrinkles appeared before his eyes widened. "I wasn't talking about size. I meant disposition. Like that you've never been quiet as a mouse?"

"Wait. Now I'm giant and loud? Does that make me Bigfoot?"

"I mean you're not quiet, like timid. And why do you keep fixating on your size?"

Ha. Said the guy who dated tiny blondes.

"You're a fine size. A good size," he said. "And you're not loud. But you're not mousy."

I crossed my arms. No more letting him wave away situations with "You know what I meant," implied or otherwise. "If you get to be a bear, and I'm not a mouse, then what am I? I want to be a cheetah."

"You can't be a cheetah."

"You aren't the boss of what animal I am, dummy."

"Maybe not, but I picked to be a bear first, and bears are in the forest. Cheetahs are in Africa. Why would a cheetah and a bear be hanging out in a metaphor together?"

It was hard not to laugh at the childishness we were slipping into. Will was fighting a smile. The telltale twitch at the corner of his mouth gave him away.

"Stop interrupting," he said. "You have to be a forest animal. And since I'm a bear, you must be a—"

"Deer," I said. "I want to be a deer."

"Not a deer. You're a fox."

I had my phone out of my armband before it even dawned on him what he'd said. I held it up and clicked record. "Repeat that, Will. I want it on tape, forever, that you said I'm a fox."

"You're a fox," he said and then heard it and burst out laughing.

"That's totally going to be my ring tone for you now, you saying over and over that I'm a fox."

He shook his head and started on a slow jog toward our apartments. But he didn't argue that I was a fox, and I floated home behind him.

"See you in a few?" he called when I passed his door.

"Make it thirty, and come down to my place with your laptop. I'll make you real dinner, and we'll see if you got any matches yet."

"It's barely been a day. Of course there aren't any matches."

"It's cute how much you don't know," I called over my shoulder as I opened my door. "My place in thirty; laptop or no dinner."

When he walked in a half hour later, he had his laptop under his arm, and the stir-fry I had thrown together was almost done. I'd pulled on my favorite jeans and a silky top, going for casual sophistication. The important part was the sophistication.

He set his laptop on my coffee table and sniffed. "What is that? It smells good."

"Eye of newt. It's the next big thing after Paleo and South Beach."

"So, chicken?"

"Chicken," I confirmed. "Plus healthy stuff that grew in the ground."

"Weird."

"Shut up. Let's see your matches."

He opened his laptop and squinted at his inbox. He had perfect vision, but he always did that squint when he was about to dive into something new. "Seven," he said, and surprise laced his voice.

"I was right, right, right," I sang while I did a touchdown-style dance in the kitchen. But I couldn't fully enjoy the moment. A pit of worry opened in my stomach. What if there was a perfect match for him in those seven? I mean, *seven*. It was one of those lucky numbers. Maybe it meant something that it had shown up as a bundle of seven. A touch of nausea bubbled up. Why couldn't it be a meaningless number like—

"Eight. Another one just came in. This is crazy."

"And I'm . . ." I trailed off so he could fill in the blank.

"Right. You're right. And that wasn't obnoxious at all."

But I didn't care about his eye roll because my stomach had cleared up when I realized that the seven matches wasn't a sign. I was going to have to rein that in quick though. I developed a bunch of superstitions around Will when I was a teenager, like if I smoothed my ponytail in front of my left shoulder he would give me his special smile, or that for every one of his discarded gum wrappers I could rescue from the trash can, it would equal a date he'd ask me on when I turned eighteen and graduated high school. It was tricky to get the gum wrappers out of the garbage without getting caught and having kids accuse me of being a trash digger or, worse, getting busted by Dave or Will wanting to know what I was up to. So each wrapper I got required a lot of effort, and to my smitten fifteen-year-old brain, that kind of risk and effort should have translated into a date when I was old enough, for sure.

When that didn't happen at eighteen, I pushed the deadline to twenty-one. When I turned twenty-two, I finally threw away the dozens of gum wrappers I'd been hanging on to.

That was young, dumb Hannah, the girl. Older, wiser Hannah, the woman, had a relationship track record and a life that looked like an adult's from the outside, and I didn't feel like slipping into stupid schoolgirl habits.

I turned back to the stove and gave the skillet a few good shakes, letting that substitute for the shakes I wanted to give myself. "Time to eat," I said, scooping up two heaping bowlfuls of stir-fry and depositing Will's in front of him.

He shook his head at it. "It looks pretty, and it smells nice, but there's a part of me that is sad every time I'm eating something that isn't pizza."

"It's all the same stuff you'd find on top of your pizza," I pointed out. "Peppers, onions, protein. It's just tasty chicken protein instead of greasy pepperoni protein. Now eat, and let's look at these girls. Show me candidate numero uno."

He pulled up honeygirl42. Her message said, "Hi. I saw on your profile that you like jazz. I love it too. I'd love to know what else we have in common." It was hard to concentrate on honeygirl42 with Will's shoulder brushing mine every few seconds as he breathed.

"She's cute," he said.

"Pass." Girls who liked jazz fell into two categories: pretentious and boring or quirky and interesting. Pretentious and boring jazz lovers were totally safe to date Will, but they did not name themselves honeygirl. She had to go.

"Why? She looks like a good fit."

"Nope. She named herself honeygirl42. How boring are you to be the forty-second person to think of that screen name?"

"But she's cute."

"Remember that thing where we're going to listen to me because I'm the actual woman here and therefore understand women better? It's time to do that thing now. Really. Pass on her. You can always come back to her later." *He most definitely could* not *come back to her later. Or ever.*

"Fine, Hanny. You pick. Let's see what you got."

Part of me loved hearing his nickname for me. He only gave nicknames to people close to him, and I liked being in that circle.

I scrolled through the remaining matches and stopped at the fourth one, a plain-looking woman with the handle "janeingit." I had to think about that one for a long time before I could see it: Jane-ing it. As in a joking reference to herself as a Plain Jane? If so, it was too clever and made her a threat.

Contestant number five looked like a much better bet. She was also ordinary looking and had the screen name Dallasgirl. Boring. I read her profile, looking for any flashes of humor that might send up a red flag, but she was still as boring as her screen name by the time I finished. But she liked jazz, and she was going to be one of the pretentious jazz fans. "Perfect."

Will quirked an eyebrow at me after he skimmed her info. "Really? Because I don't see it."

"Why? Because she's not a supermodel? Don't be that guy, Will."

"Whatever," he said, giving me an absent-minded bump with his shoulder, our shorthand for knock it off. "It's the whole package. What are you seeing in her profile that makes you think I should start here?"

"Look at her message. She says you look like a thoughtful guy, and she's a thinker too. She says maybe you should trade ideas sometime. Come on. You know an idea-driven person is going to make for fascinating conversation. There's no way you're going to run out of things to talk about. You should go for this. The whole point is to do something totally opposite your usual dating pattern, right?" I pointed at the screen. "Meet totally opposite."

"Fine." He yanked the computer onto his lap. "Tell me what to say, Girl Whisperer."

"I think you're going to have to meet a lot of women to find the one." Mainly because I needed to buy time by sending him out with lots of women who were absolutely wrong for him. "So I think if you're serious about wife-ing it up, you need to be efficient and get to the date sooner than later so you don't spend time getting to know someone online only to find out you have no chemistry."

It was the exact opposite of how I would do it myself. If a guy couldn't make me laugh or think, any physical chemistry we might have might as well be sparklers in a rain gutter. But I didn't want to risk him building a good foundation with any of these girls before he met them. Nothing would ruin my plans faster than him finding something real. I was his something real. "You should probably come up with a standard cut-to-the-chase open, like an invitation to lunch right away or something."

"How about, 'The nerdy side of me believes in chemistry. Should we just cut to the chase and see if we have any over lunch?'"

"Wow. I had no idea how badly you really needed my help. I'm so embarrassed for you."

"You just lost all future nacho privileges."

"I take it back. That was pretty genius, but you should probably try something like, 'I believe in chemistry—let's skip the IMs and just meet.' I even kept your science joke."

"You're kidding."

"Yes."

He hauled me half onto his lap, holding my arms hostage while he demanded, "Loser says what?"

All I had to do to free myself was say, "What." It was a joke Dave and Will had played on each other and me a hundred times. A thousand, even. But it didn't feel good to be so close to his fresh cotton scent, the strong bars of his arms confining me. Not like this. "Let me go," I said.

Will kept me right where I was. "Loser says what," he repeated.

I shoved against him harder, squirming to be let go. When his hold tightened, I reached up and grabbed arm hair again, yanking and not feeling the least bit bad when he sucked his breath in and released me. "Geez, Hannah. Relax."

I pushed myself up from the sofa and stormed to the kitchen for a drink and a chance to calm myself. I took three long swallows of water before I felt like responding. "I'm not a kid anymore, Will. You can't just manhandle me like that. You should grow up and knock it off."

"All right, all right," he said. "Didn't know it bugged you so much."

If he'd looked offended or hurt, I might have kicked him out of the apartment. Instead he said, "Hey. I'm sorry. Really."

"Don't worry about it," I said, setting my empty glass on the counter. "I don't care if you tease me, but maybe don't do it like I'm twelve, okay?" This whole balance was much harder to walk than I'd thought it would be. This was so confusing. I sat back down beside him and latched on to something I was more sure about. "You should tell her that you're a spontaneous guy and would like to meet her over lunch instead of through a computer screen."

"Sounds good to me," he said, turning back to the screen to type out something to Dallasgirl, then clicked back to his matches. "Who else?"

"Uh . . . Don't you want to see how it goes with Dallasgirl?"

"Yep. And a few others too. We're doing this on an efficiency model. It's already Tuesday, so I want to set up at least three dates this week. Next week we can shoot for five."

Even the thought of trying to keep track of so many women made my head spin until I saw how to spin the situation itself to my advantage. "Let's check out the rest of these profiles. But remember that women appreciate honesty, so be open at some point during each lunch and let them know you're dating several people."

"Wouldn't that make you mad if a guy said that to you?"

It would put me off and make me think he was tone deaf and kind of cocky. So basically it was the perfect thing to tell him to say. "It would make me mad if I found out he wasn't honest about playing the field. Definitely tell them." His look suggested that I was trying to redefine the theory of relativity. "Doubt me if this fails. Until it fails, believe me. Deal?"

"Deal," he said, shaking his head like he couldn't believe he was agreeing to this. That made two of us.

Two more women had sent him messages since we'd sat down, and after throwing them into the pool, we fished out one who struck me as adventurous to the point of craziness and a pretty girl whose snoozefest of a profile made me sure she would bore him senseless with discussions about her collection of mailbox photos. She liked mailboxes. A lot. She was the perfect girl for Will if I didn't want him to fall in love. With anyone besides me, anyway.

I leaned back against the sofa, exhausted. It wasn't even the running that had wiped me out. It was trying to manage Will. And I had a bad feeling the anxiety gnawing at my insides like a tiny but persistent termite was guilt, not fear of loss. Because I'd just thought of a synonym for *manage. Manipulate.* And if that was the right synonym, it made the termite hungrier.

Chapter 6 ♥

"AM I MANIPULATING HIM, SOPHIE?" I wailed into the phone.

"Hello to you too. What are we talking about?"

"Will," I said.

"Right. Don't know why I asked. Are you manipulating him?"

"I called you so you could tell me."

"Define manipulate," she said, sounding like she was breaking down the SAT word of the day with her eleventh graders. "Are you making him do anything he doesn't want to do?"

"I'm nudging him to go on dates he wouldn't normally choose."

"But that's what he wants, right? I mean, that's why he decided on this whole online dating marathon?"

"No, he wants to get married."

"Right, but if he were dating his usual type, he wouldn't get married, would he?"

"No," I said, uncertain because I could feel myself getting caught in the web of her brilliant English-teacher reasoning. "He'd get bored."

"So by pointing him toward women outside his usual, you're increasing his chances of finding someone he could marry. Right?"

"No! I don't want him to do that! I want him to see that any girl he picks that's not me is the wrong girl."

"Then you're manipulating him."

"But I don't want to manipulate him!"

"Then you're helping him expand his dating pool to improve his chances. *Right*?"

"Right. Yes. That's what I'm doing. Thank you? I think? I can't tell if you made me feel better or not."

"You totally feel better. I've got a stack of essays longer than my arm waiting for me. Forsooth, I must needs go grade them."

"Fo' shizzle." We hung up, and I stared at the phone, trying to feel through the confusing emotions scrambling my brains. No matter what Sophie said, I probably was manipulating Will. But was there such a thing as benevolent manipulation? It was for his own good. It's not like I was going to make the women he met act a particular way. Everyone had their own free will there.

I wasn't making him do anything either. He could disagree any time he wanted to. I wasn't holding anything over his head. Yeah, I'd promised him I'd help him find a wife, and that was exactly what I was doing. I just understood him well enough to know who that wife should be and the roundabout way that I hoped, prayed, and wished would bring him to me.

* * *

You're 0 for 1.

I stared at the text from Will like it was the winning Powerball lottery numbers. He must have finished lunch with RealChillPill, the one whose profile suggested she was the least chill woman ever. That was the first lunch date that had worked out. She'd liked his description of himself as "spontaneous." Leigh, as her name turned out to be, appeared not to be the woman for Will. I'd never been so happy to have a losing score. Grinning, I tapped out some pseudo encouragement. *I could go 0 for 99 as long as I'm 1 for 100. You just eliminated a variable. That's a good thing.*

A minute later, he called my cell phone. "Nothing about that date was a good thing." His irritation rumbled out of the phone.

He was almost a baritone, and the vibrations of his voice tickled my eardrum and sent a shiver down my back.

"What went wrong?"

"The selection process, apparently. I'm all for adventures or whatever, but this Leigh person takes it to a whole new level. Five minutes after we sat down, she suggested blowing off the pho place and catching the next Greyhound bus out of town."

"Aw, but you love pho."

"Stop it. I can hear you trying not to laugh."

I let the laugh out. "Why did she want to catch a bus?"

"I don't know. She thought it would be fun to catch the first bus leaving, ride it for a hundred miles, and see where we ended up. She said even with gas station snacks, it would still cost less than a steak dinner to have an adventure."

"She's right."

"I like a different kind of adventure," he growled. "And then she got this pitying look on her face when I said I thought I'd better go back to work. The bus thing I could maybe overlook, but trying to separate me from pho, plus being condescending? Pass."

"Did you really think you were going to knock it out of the park the first time at bat? This is field research. We'll look at key words she had in her profile that should have been a clue and filter out anyone else who uses them."

"All right," he said, and I could almost hear the circuits humming in his brain. "Tomorrow is the other end of the spectrum, the quiet-ish one."

"Dallasgirl?"

"Her name is Leslie. I'll let you know how it goes."

"Can't wait." Especially not if she tanked as badly as Leigh had.

* * *

CALL ME.

The message came in halfway through the Leslie lunch. I dialed immediately, worry making my hands clumsy. Will had never sent me a panicked text before.

"What's wrong?" I demanded as soon as he picked up after the second ring.

"Hey, Dave. Is something wrong?"

"What? You told me to call."

"You're kidding. She did? Is everything okay? Can I do something to help?"

"Will, what are you talking about?" I asked, but I was figuring it out on my own pretty quickly.

"Whatever you need, buddy. Hang on." He spoke to someone else for a minute. It sounded muffled, like he had his hand over the phone, but I still caught, "Sorry . . . Emergency . . . Take this . . . In a minute."

Thirty seconds later, he was talking to me again, only I couldn't hear any ambient restaurant noise. "O for two, and this one is so bad I'm hiding in the men's room. I need to splash water on my face, or I might resort to clawing it off."

"Uh, why?"

"I need some way to keep myself awake, and so far pinching my leg under the table isn't working. If I have to stick this out much longer, I might move on to stabbing myself with a fork."

"Why are you so mean?"

"Why are you picking bad dates for me?"

"Let's not talk about us. Let's talk about Leslie. What's the problem? Is she not cute?"

"Remember how she said she likes jazz? It's more like she likes to talk about it. But only so I know how much she knows about it, not in a she-loves-it kind of way. And she likes acid jazz. Which is noise. So I'm listening to her talk about noise. And that's becoming its own kind of noise. It's very meta." He paused. "I feel like I'm trapped in an artsy short film about the futility of existence."

It was a full minute before I could stop laughing enough to speak. "So it's zero for two. No big deal. That means I've got ninety-seven more chances to find you the right match. I totes got this, yo."

"I don't think so. If you strike out a third time, I'm going to have to reevaluate your technical-advisory capacity on this project. I might need to scrap your input and try a new data set."

"Right now, you need to go back to your date."

"And inform her that the emergency we're discussing is going to call me away from lunch? Permanently? Don't mind if I do."

I snorted. "I'm going to doubt all motives of all guys from this point forward."

"Have I not been telling you to do that for years?" he said. "Men are fine except for the ones who want to date you. Those men are dogs, and you should stay far away from them."

If only that was coming from a place of jealousy. "I'm really glad I didn't start going on dates until college and you boys were far, far away."

"Probably a good thing," he agreed. "Gotta go handle Miss Acid Jazz now."

"Good luck."

"What I really need is a good exit. I'm not kidding, Hanny. Number three better be a major improvement."

Oh, she wouldn't be. Not if I could help it.

* * *

Strike three. You're out. No more picking for me.

You're kidding. I can't believe Letterbox was a bust.

We are so talking about this after work.

Only if you catch me. I'm going on a run.

Have I mentioned I hate running?

Have I mentioned I hate listening to you whine?

Oh, it's on, H. I'm going to be right on your heels. Whining.

Not so much. You won't have the breath for that.

Mean but true. See you 6-ish.

* * *

He pounded on my front door at six sharp. I opened it to find him in another worn-out T-shirt.

"Let's go," I said, stepping into the hallway and hoping he noticed my new running shirt. It was a lemon-colored tank top, and I loved it. He didn't say anything though. Maybe he was afraid I would start lecturing him about polymers again.

We'd barely hit the sidewalk for a warmup jog to the lake before he started in. "You know how you thought that Letterbox's fascination with mailboxes suggested an intensity I might understand?"

I'd made up a pretty great theory about how her ability to elevate what other people found mundane into an art with her photographs suggested that she saw the world in a deeper way and could connect with Will's super-smart brain. "Not so much?" I asked, keeping my tone bland.

"Not at all. There is literally nothing more to it than that she likes mailboxes. It's like how some people collect salt and pepper shakers. She collects pictures of mailboxes. She doesn't have any deeper thoughts about them."

"Maybe she was too intimidated by you to articulate them. Maybe she has some sad backstory about the destiny of the letters that do and don't arrive in them. Maybe there's some tragic letter she received—ooooh, or, better yet, never received in her past, and that's why she loves them."

I could feel his measuring gaze on me, but I kept my eyes on the sidewalk. "No," he said, finally. "You would think that way. But not her. Your brain is full of possibilities. Let me put it this way. We went for sushi, and I asked her what she wanted. She said whatever I thought was good was fine. But it wasn't in an adventurous, surprise-me way. It was in a giving-no-thought-to-it kind of way."

I smothered a smile. Will couldn't fathom people who weren't interested in food. Not that he was a foodie. But passiveness toward food was beyond him.

"Anyway, I ordered, and she didn't touch it. I asked her what was wrong, and she said she didn't like fish. But she suggested sushi! And when I asked her why, she said it was because everyone says they like sushi on their profile, so she figured it was a safe bet. I don't understand the thinking. At all."

"So that's three down. You're ninety-six closer to your goal."

"Well, you're fired," he said, and I stumbled. He reached out a hand to steady me, and his hand sent delicious shocks up and down my arm.

"You can't fire me," I said. "Your project will never work."

"It's not working now. I'm going to pick some women this time. I can't possibly get it more wrong than you did."

"Yes, you can. That's why you're not married yet."

He made an annoyed rumble in his throat. "If I trip you in the next ten seconds, I swear it was a total accident."

"Give it a few more tries before you give up," I said. I needed more time to make him see *me*. We ran in silence then. It was the good kind, the kind that always fell between us, the easy kind.

When we rounded the lake toward home, he slowed down about a block from our complex. "Keep going if you want. I need more lead time to get my breath back."

I slowed with him. "I'm done too. You did well today, kiddo."

"Kiddo? I've got a million years on you."

"You mean three? And only three? Everyone knows that if you're twenty-one and older, age differences only matter in five-year increments. So we're practically the same age."

"What are you making up now?" he asked, genuine curiosity peeking through his labored words.

"I'm not making anything up. It's a true thing. Think about it. There's a massive difference between an eighteen-year-old and a twenty-one-year-old. But there isn't that much of a difference between a twenty-five-year-old and a twenty-two-year-old."

He thought about it for a minute, or maybe he was trying to get his breathing under control. "I feel like if I played that out, I'd poke it full of more holes than your colander, but I don't have the energy, so I guess I'm going to agree with you. But speaking of colanders . . ."

I grinned. "You want me to make pasta for dinner?"

"You're so sweet to invite me. I'd hate to disappoint you by turning you down, so, yes, you can make me some pasta."

I slugged him, and he rubbed his arm. "You can march yourself over and help. That's my condition."

"Be there in fifteen." He rubbed his arm again. I waved him off and skimmed up the stairs ahead of him, but I thought about the punch. We'd always had a sibling way of interacting with each other. Affectionate pokes and jabs and noogies. No one noogies someone they're interested in kissing. Not unless they're in middle school.

The next phase of my plan unfolded in front of me in an instant: I had to change our vocabulary of touch to something besides the language of old friends.

* * *

"So this is my question," Will said after he'd downed half his pasta. "Why am I taking Internet-dating advice from someone who's had zero success with Internet dating? You're still fired."

"You're taking advice from me because I have a lifetime of experience of being a woman. I know what they want. The Internet-dating thing doesn't matter." He looked unconvinced, and I sighed. "Who said I haven't had any success in Internet dating, anyway? You don't know everything about me, Will."

He leaned over and tapped my bare ring finger. "I could know nothing about you and still know Internet dating hasn't worked out for you."

"That's assuming my goal was marriage. I've had two entire relationships with guys I met online. So now I have double credibility: my gender and my track record."

He grunted. "I never saw these guys."

"Doesn't mean it didn't happen," I said. His expression caught me. If I didn't know him so well, I might not have noticed the tiny twitch in his cheek that meant he was irritated. But what had irritated him? Was it the mention of my other relationships?

I tested him. "They were good relationships and perfect for what I wanted at the moment."

He did it again, a tiny twitch when I said "relationships." A half-formed idea, conceived of the marathons of teen movies I'd watched through high school, burst out of my mouth before I could hold it back. "Look, I'll join you. I'll set up a profile on this site, and you'll see. I know what I'm talking about."

"You're going to do online dating?"

He sounded curious, not annoyed. The bubble of hope in my stomach burst, hollowing it out despite all the pasta I'd eaten. I didn't know who was stupider at the moment—him for his cluelessness or me for my crush. My twelve-year-long, pathetic, ridiculous crush.

I pushed the pasta around, suddenly not hungry, even though we'd made it with my favorite fresh-pesto recipe. The garlic left an ammonia taste in my mouth, and I shoved the bowl away.

"This should be funny," he said.

And that did it. "It's funny that someone would want to date me? No. What's funny is me. I'm hilarious. Did you know that? It's why guys want to date me. A lot of them."

He laughed, and I resisted the urge to dump my remaining pasta over his head. I didn't know why he was laughing, but all the possibilities made me mad. "You can't fire me as your technical advisor because I quit. Let's see who ends up with better dates now."

"It's not a competition," he said. His cheek twitched.

"You better believe it is. And it starts now."

I shoved away from the table to fetch my Macbook out of my bedroom.

"What are you doing?" he asked when I flopped on the sofa instead of coming back to the table.

"Schooling you, son," I said in a voice of icy calm without looking up. I was torching my own plan to set Will up with women he couldn't stand and practically shoving him into looking for women he'd dig, no question. But I didn't care. The only thing that mattered was to shatter his sisterly image of me.

"Geez, Hanny. I was just messing with you. I'm sure you can get all the dates you want."

"No, you aren't. But you'll see."

"Seriously, you don't need to prove anything." All the laughter in his voice was gone, and that finally made me look up. "I'm sure a lot of guys would go out with you, but besides me, every last dude on the Internet is trolling for hookups, and their motives are shady."

I clacked on my keyboard and ignored him again.

"Don't. Dave is going to kill me."

"Right. Dereliction of surrogate-big-brother duties."

"Exactly."

I typed faster.

"Hannah, you—"

"You're distracting me. Make yourself useful and clear the table or something," I said, not looking up from the screen.

He was quiet for a second before reappearing with a glass of water for me.

"I'm fine," I said, waving it away.

"Drink it, or you'll get a headache." He hovered until I accepted it, then he disappeared into the kitchen.

I paused in my typing to drink, trying to figure out how I wanted to present myself in the profile. What kind of guy would make Will realize that he was the only person on the planet besides Dave who looked at me in a brotherly way? I smiled and typed even faster, filling out my registration before I hopped up and headed down the hall.

"What are you doing?" Will called over the running water he'd turned on to do the dishes.

"My makeup."

"Right now?"

"Yeah. I need a good profile pic. We went over this. It's got to be just right." I shut my bedroom door behind me, plugged in my curling iron, and pulled out my makeup bag. I didn't wear a ton of makeup, usually, but I loved playing with it. In college, my roommates and I had spent hours watching makeup and hair tutorials on YouTube, playing with different looks and glamming each other up.

I was good at it, and I'd mastered the fine art of applying a dozen products while looking as if I'd put on nothing more than a pretty lip gloss. My eyes were bigger, my cheekbones sharper, my lips fuller, my skin more dewy. I put it all back in the bag and gave it a pat. Magic. Three more minutes and some big loose curls in front, and I was ready for my close-up.

I walked back out to the living room. Will had taken over the remote and was surfing for a game. He glanced up and froze, his arm extended with the remote at the end dangling as if his grip had gone as slack as his jaw had.

"I need you to take a picture on my phone," I said, reaching past him to root around the sofa cushion on the other side of him. That was where my phone always ended up if it wasn't on the coffee table.

"What did you do?" he asked, sniffing my hair. "Did you put perfume on? Why would you put perfume on for a picture?"

"No, I didn't put perfume on," I snapped back as my fingers closed around my phone and I straightened.

"But you smell good."

"Don't know what to tell you. That's pure Eau de Hannah. Maybe you're smelling my shower gel."

"Must be it," he said, leaning away until I straightened with my phone.

I handed it to him. "Shoot me."

"Don't you have to do some thoughtful pose too?"

"Nope. I'm going for confident sophistication. It's going to take a sincere smile and direct eye contact."

"A sincere smile that you're totally calculating?"

"You really want to talk to me about taking a calculating approach to online dating?"

He gave me a "whatever" face and held up the phone. I smiled but not too big and imagined myself shaking hands with my boss's boss. I did this whole routine before one of those meetings to get myself in a headspace where I projected the "I got this" vibe. The camera clicked, and Will handed over the phone.

"Do I look confident but warm and approachable?"

Will stared at me for three whole seconds, then turned back to the TV, unmuting it without a word. I checked the picture. "Dude, I'm a one-take wonder."

"Yeah. Who spent ten minutes doing her hair for that one take. Very spontaneous, Han."

"I spent three minutes doing my hair. The other seven was my face." I struck a *Vogue* pose. "Worth it though, right? I'm coming for you, Gisele."

He didn't even look. "Who? You clean up all right." But he was already deep into a baseball game.

"Gisele Bündchen?"

He didn't look up.

"Tom Brady's wife?"

"Oh yeah."

But the Rangers weren't letting him go. I gave up and sat beside him, opening my laptop to fill out my own HeyThere profile. I did the initial stuff on autopilot—gender, age, physical description. Next came the "About Me" section. "What are your three best qualities?" I read aloud.

Will didn't say anything.

"Will!"

"Yeah."

"What's my best quality?"

"Uh, cookies."

"That's not a quality."

"Making good cookies is a top quality, actually."

"It doesn't scream sophisticated. Name something else." My stomach tightened. I wasn't at all sure I wanted to know what Will really thought of me. Or worse, how little he thought about me.

The game broke for a commercial. He looked at me and blinked. "Dependable. Nice. To other people, anyway. Generous. Smart. Funny. Bossy. You could put you're a good leader for that."

I liked being thought of as smart and funny, but lumped with all the other attributes he listed, they sounded exactly like qualities on a list Dave would make about me. I unclenched my fists and smashed out my frustration in some lightning-quick keystrokes. *Spontaneous.* It hinted at an adventurous side without screaming of RealChillPill's wildness. *Intelligent.* It irritated me when people didn't want to own that about themselves. Why was it bragging to acknowledge that you were smart but okay to say you were spontaneous? It was kind of ridiculous.

I paused to consider what to list third. What did I like about myself the most? I was determined. I liked that. And I liked to take care of my friends. I drummed the keys for another minute before I typed *nurturing.*

I moved on to hobbies. *Running.* That was always good to list because it suggested I took care of myself. *Cooking.* Because the way to the heart, blah blah blah. But mainly because it was true. *Reading.* That might scare any nonbookworms away, but that was a good thing.

Will shifted on the sofa next to me, and our cushions dipped toward each other, our arms brushing. Goose bumps popped up on mine, but he only settled back again and turned up the sound.

I was a fixture to him. An ottoman. A throw pillow. That truth curled up in my stomach and folded itself into a hateful knot. Guys found me attractive. They wanted to take me out. I wasn't a dating machine, but I didn't have to sit home on Saturday nights unless I wanted to. He was infuriating. The dumbest genius I knew. At least about love. And me. And what he needed. Again: me.

My fingers flew over the keys again, the right words flowing. I watched them fall neatly into place the way code usually did when I had to correct bad programming from developers on my team. It was strange to do this with English instead of computer language, but the zone was the same, the path to shocking Will's long-held ideas out of him as clear as finding the bug in a stack trace.

I had always been Will's girl next door. But I wasn't everybody's girl next door, and he was about to see me through *their* eyes. I hoped.

I uploaded the picture and smiled bigger than I had for the shot. Will had snapped me at just the right moment. Now let him see who dated the Profile Me, who was nobody's girl next door.

Although . . . I loved the irony of the name. In two clicks of the mouse, I became HeyThere.com's very own DallasGirlNextDoor.

Chapter 7 ♥

Bam, bam, bam.

Will threw open my front door before I'd processed his super-loud knocks, and I jumped. "Dang it, Will. You can't come barging in here."

"I knocked."

"You're supposed to wait for people to answer the door. What if you caught me in a compromising position?"

"Like what? Do you have a drug habit I don't know about?"

"Ha. Yeah. Either that, or sometimes I walk around in my—never mind. Just stop barging in."

"In your what?" Will asked. The intensely curious look he got when he was figuring out how to reverse engineer a household electronic was written all over his face.

"Strawberry Shortcake slippers," I said. "What do you think?"

"Uh . . ."

"I said never mind."

"If you don't want people walking in, lock the door."

"Thanks, big brother," I said, catching him by the sleeve and tugging him toward the door.

He spun away and made for the sofa. "I'm not leaving. I need to talk to you."

"Hurry up. I've got plans."

"Your HeyThere profile came up in the network crawl I programmed."

Of course it did. Obviously the computer knows what you need better than you do. Get smarter, Will. "Congratulations. You can debug it to ignore me. I'll show you how. It involves lots of the use of the word *algorithm*. I know how much you love that."

"I wrote the algorithm for the search in the first place. I know how to make it exclude you."

I ignored the way that made my stomach pang.

"That's not what I'm here about. You need to change your profile."

"Why? Did I make a typo? I hate typos."

"Not a typo. Just misinformation. I don't think you realize how your profile comes off."

"What's wrong with it? Does it make me look needy? Stuck up? Ugh. I even showed it to Sophie, and she said it looked great."

"It's not that. It doesn't sound like you. You should fix it."

Irritation crept in. "What do you want me to fix?"

"It makes you look like a corporate wife in training. You need to put more information about yourself. And maybe some more photos that aren't so glamour shot or whatever."

The irritation grew to annoyance. "That was a no-filter picture that *you* took after I spent about ten minutes on my hair and makeup. That's exactly how long I spend getting ready for work. The picture is fine. What do you want me to do? Post a picture of myself when I come back from a run? Or maybe when I roll out of bed? You're supposed to put up a *good* shot of yourself. Now go home. I've got plans."

"But we haven't talked about your profile. Wait. What plans? Are you doing something with Sophie?"

"No. I have a date that I got using the fatally flawed profile you're complaining about."

"What kind of date?" He ran his eyes over me, noticing details for the first time. I was still wearing my tailored black trousers from work, but I'd switched my button-down for a filmy floral top layered over a cute cami and swapped out my ankle boots for strappy sandals. "Why are you so dressed up?"

"D-a-t-e." I spelled it slowly.

"Who is it with? Is he coming here?" He glanced around my apartment like I was hiding a contraband man behind one of my throw cushions. "That's not safe."

"We're meeting at a restaurant for dinner. Stop being dumb."

"It's dumb to paint yourself as something you're not," he snapped, and my head jerked back.

We teased. That was what we did. Even telling him to stop being dumb was an exasperated order. But snapping was not teasing. I stared at him, unsure of what to do next.

"Sorry," he said on a big sigh. He walked over and set his hands on my shoulders, brushing them with his thumbs, a soft stroke, like he was trying to calm a tense cat. He wasn't far off. I was wound up and more than tempted to hiss at him. "I'm worried. You're on that site looking enigmatic, like you've got good secrets. And guys will see you as a challenge. You're going to draw the hunters, the ones who want to make you a trophy."

"You think I'm an open book because you've known me my whole life. Trust me, Will. I've got secrets you couldn't dream I'm keeping."

His hands stilled, and a long pause followed before his arms dropped to his side and he stepped back. "I made you mad. Sorry. Of course you're a catch. It stresses me out to think about how hard these guys are going to work to catch you."

The stress in his voice smoothed my ruffled fur. I smiled at him. "You're being super dramatic. I feel like I'm starring in my own Lifetime movie and this is the scene that foreshadows all the bad things to come."

"I'm not being dramatic. I just know guys like you know girls, and I'm telling you, you're going to draw the wrong kind of guy."

"Putting the idea out there that I'm smart, together, and a touch sassy is going to draw the wrong kind of guy? Will, please.

Predators do *not* go for confident women with strong personalities, and that's all my profile shows."

"I don't mean you're going to draw predators. I know you're not twelve."

Do you? Really? Somehow I don't think so.

"You're going to get these slick guys who are big deals in the courtroom or the boardroom or whatever. And they'll chew you up and spit you out."

"Remember when you used to think I was smart?"

"This isn't about smart. Your brain is ridiculous. You're the smartest person I know." The fact that he didn't limit that to "girl" softened me in spite of myself for a second. Then he kept talking. "But smart is different from experienced, and it's also different from common sense."

My eyebrows shot up. I let them say, "Are you *kidding* me with this?" because if I'd used words for that, I would have yelled them. "Do you think I've been hanging out on my couch every weekend since you and Dave left for college? I know all this. I'm not naive or gullible or whatever insult you're going for next."

"But, Hanny—"

"Hanny, Hanny, my well-shaped fanny." I patted it for emphasis. "I started working on this years ago. You know what happened? When I started running farther every week, and I started thinking about what I ate and how it made me feel, and when I started lifting heavier weights, and I started realizing I could do hard things, the pounds started falling off. And boys asked me out. But they were kind of jerks.

"So I ignored boys, and I ran harder and lifted more and learned to cook and take care of myself, and thought about what I really needed. And you know what? I also started feeling good about myself. Amazing, even. And then guys started asking me out. Not boys. Men. Who were not jerks. Who liked me. *Me.* And not because I'm thinner now. It's because I'm funny and smart and strong. And pretty!"

I grabbed a pillow from the sofa and swung it at his head, aiming to smack some sense into it like I'd tried to a million times. He knew my moves too well, and his hand shot out to close around my wrist, stopping me midswing. Before I could yank loose and go after him again, he tugged me hard enough to tip forward, and as fast as lightning, I was pinned to his chest again. "I know how pretty you are," he said, and the warmth of his breath near my ear sent an involuntary shiver through me. "I'm really sorry I'm making you mad. I don't mean to. I want to look out for you. Sometimes it's confusing how to do that." He held me for another second, maybe waiting to make sure I wasn't going to lash out at him again. When I stayed still, he released me, slowly, still on guard.

I turned and cupped his cheek with my hand, brushing my thumb over the top of his cheekbone. A muscle twitched beneath my palm and sent tingles up my arm. "Let me wipe away those worried tears," I said, and he smiled, reaching up to pull my hand down. "I can take care of myself. But so help me, if I have to redo my hair right now, you're never using my remote control again. Go away, and let me get ready."

"When's the date?"

"Soon."

"How soon?"

I rolled my eyes at him. "None of your business, *Dave*." I injected my brother's name with all the annoyance I used to feel when he hovered. Will was being ten times worse.

"If you're as smart as you say you are, you know you better let someone know when to expect you back if you're going to meet a stranger for the first time. So tell me, or I'm going to text you every fifteen minutes to check on you."

"I'll turn my phone off."

"And I'll tell Dave."

"Oh my gosh. You are the *worst*."

He pulled out his phone. "You don't answer the first text, I call him."

Great. Another two-steps-forward, one-step-back conversation. "Fine. I'm meeting him at the Sun Grill at seven for dinner."

"What's the Sun Grill?"

"That new place by the gym. It's getting really good—never mind." I got behind him and pushed him toward the door. "You can Yelp it. I need to get ready."

"You're already ready. And that's still over an hour away."

"Yeah, but I have more HeyThere messages to open."

"You really need to change—"

"Shut up," I said, pushing him over the doorstep and closing it on him. I shot the bolt for good measure.

"Hey!"

Ignoring his protest from the other side of the door, I snatched up my phone and called Sophie. "This plan is not working. At all. And somehow I'm going out with some guy tonight that isn't my type."

"He might be," she answered. "You won't know until you meet him."

"Anyone who isn't Will isn't my type. Remember I have a stupid brain? What's that weird thing that werewolf did with Bella's kid in *Twilight*? Imprinted? I think I've been surrounded by a cloud of Will's pheromones for too many years. I've imprinted on him, but he hasn't imprinted on me, and, therefore, I'm going to die alone."

"Why don't I take you down to the animal shelter this weekend, and I'll treat you to your first cat."

"You're not funny."

"Neither is your whining. Think it through, Hannah. Plan A didn't work: have a silent crush on Will for half your life. Plan B is going to need more than a week."

"I want to believe that. But I know him too well, and I know our dynamic too well. His filter is set up to see me as a sister, period."

"Which is why you should shove him up against a wall and kiss him. He'd get the message."

Part of me wanted to do that the way a linebacker wants to take down a quarterback, but I imagined Will's reaction when I let him go. "It would make things totally weird. He needs to figure out on his own that we should be together. That's the whole point of making him see that anyone else is wrong for him. And so far he sees that, but he's still not looking at me any differently."

"So you threw a fit and set yourself up on a couple of dates because you were in a snit."

I moaned. "When have I ever made any intelligent decisions when it comes to Will?"

"Right. Good point."

I could only groan again, but Sophie wasn't one for wallowing. "So Plan C. Which is really more of an expanded Plan B. Keep Will going on these dates, but make him see you the way other guys see you. Once he gets over the shock of realizing you're a genuine grown-up lady, maybe he'll start thinking about himself in relationship to your feminine glory."

"Feminine glory?" I repeated.

"Sorry. We started a unit on the Romantic poets today. Had some Lord Byron in my system. But you get what I'm saying. Minus college, you've always been neighbors, so seeing you in your own apartment paid for by your own bona-fide career isn't really making the point. Think about getting him to see all the other sides of you too, to see you the way the guys who looked you up on HeyThere are going to see you."

"That's exactly what I've been doing."

"No, you've let him know you're going on a date. You have to figure out how to let him see you in action."

I straightened. "Maybe you're a genius."

"The *maybe* is cute. And, hey, if any of your HeyThere dates are decent, send them my way in case I ever surface from my grading stacks long enough to enjoy a meal with another human being."

We hung up, and I stared at the ceiling for a half hour, running different scenarios through my head. The nagging feeling that I was manipulating Will hadn't gone away, and this felt like more of the same. But there was no working around the fact that Will wouldn't see this on his own.

It's not like I could make him choose me. But at least if I made him see me as a choice, and if he still walked away from me, I'd know he did it with all the facts.

Chapter 8 ♥

I SPOTTED MY DATE, JARED, as soon as I stepped into the Sun Grill. He looked exactly like his picture, which gave him bonus points. Most people were smart enough to figure out the game was over if they met their date looking significantly different from the picture they'd posted, but according to my online-dating veteran friends, it still happened.

Jared was a square-jawed, all-American type, with sandy blond hair and intelligent eyes. They crinkled up at the corners when he saw me. "Hannah?" he asked.

I stuck out my hand for a shake, and he gave an appreciative smile at the firm grip. Dave had taught me that. It was amazing how far a strong handshake could get you. But since it wasn't a business dinner, I leaned in and planted an air kiss near Jared's cheek. It would make me seem warm and approachable but communicate that I had boundaries. I was kind of funny about hugging people. There were not a lot of people whose whole selves I felt like having smooshed against my whole self.

"It's great to meet you," Jared said. "Have you eaten here before?"

"No, but I'm excited to try it. I see a couple of waiters walking past with things I feel like I need to have right this second, so if the food tastes as good as it looks, I might not be able to stand it."

He laughed and turned to the hostess. "It sounds like we're ready for our table."

"Great. Give me a moment to make sure it's set up, and we'll get you seated." She signaled to a server behind her and waved us to the side. "Go ahead and wait right here, and we'll take good care of you."

The door opened behind us, and Will walked in with a strange brunette. Strange to me anyway. I blinked, but it was still him smiling at me. "Hey, Hannah."

"Uh, hi? What are you doing here?"

"You made it sound so good, I decided I should try it too."

Mother of pearl, was he *kidding* me? I didn't need him to "see me in action" with zero mental prep.

"This is my date, Raina. Raina, this is Hannah and . . . ?"

"Jared?" the waitress called before I could answer. "We're ready for you."

"We have a reservation," Will said. "I'll see if they can seat us at the same table."

Before I could object—and how was I supposed to do that in a mannerly way?—he was at the desk, smiling at the hostess, whose head bobbed three times in quick succession. My stomach bounced along with it, dropping further toward my knees each time. *Please, no.* I darted a quick glance at Jared, who looked confused but game, and Raina, who was measuring me with assessing eyes, like she was trying to figure out if I was behind this change of plans or not. I couldn't fault her for that, but I offered her a friendly smile. Yes, she was dating the guy I wanted. But right that second, I didn't. He was all hers, and good thing too, because if I had him to myself, I'd probably choke him.

Will rejoined us. "Great news. They'll seat us together."

I made a play to save myself from an evening of watching Will charm this Raina girl. "You don't have to do that. I'm sure you were looking forward to a quiet evening of talking. Go ahead and get your own table. It won't hurt my feelings."

"We don't mind," he said. "Besides, with four people, someone should always be able to keep the conversation going, right?"

The hostess cleared her throat, and four heads turned her direction. She stood with an armful of menus and a polite smile. "Ready?"

Jared nodded, and giving up, I followed him. He shifted to let me ahead of him and then placed his hand on the small of my back to guide me through the tables. It was a good move for two reasons. First, it suggested someone had raised him as a gentleman. And second, it was a cue that he liked what he saw so far since he was making physical contact.

Sophie had laughed at me when I'd pored over dating "how to" articles—how to decode signals your date was sending, how to carry on a good conversation, how to send your own signals. But I hadn't had enough experiences in high school to figure stuff like that out, and once boys had started taking notice in college, I'd felt like I did every time I landed on the Spanish station while channel surfing: I understood the general idea of what was happening, but the specifics totally escaped me, since, like an idiot, I'd taken French in high school. On dates, I knew the basics of what should happen, but when and how to ask a well-timed question was like AP Spanish the first few times I'd gone out.

Sophie had come home one night to find me sniffling that one of my dates hadn't called for a second date, but when she made me replay the dinner and movie we'd shared, she stopped me and said, "Wait, so he kept hogging the armrest in the theater, and you kept your hands in your lap?" Then she explained that I should have shared the armrest with him to signal that I wanted him to touch me. She'd hugged me and smiled. "He thought you were telling him you weren't interested. That's why he's not calling."

So I'd become a student of dating, even though it meant getting my tips from *Teen Vogue* and *Seventeen* since *Cosmo* readers were past those basics. Like, way past.

The studying had paid off. I knew that Jared's hand near the small of my back was a good thing if I wanted it to be.

The hostess stopped at two small tables right next to each other, and Jared drew my chair out for me. I smiled at him. Not pulling a chair out at dinner wasn't a dealbreaker, but doing it was a good sign. Chair puller-outers tended to be all around more considerate with other things too. But when Will pulled out his date's chair, then took the seat by me, I scowled.

"Do you not like the separate tables?" Jared asked. "I can ask her to seat us somewhere else."

"No! This is fine. I thought I felt a draft for a second, but it was my imagination." The only chill had been in the look I'd shot Will. He hadn't noticed. It was dumb to get mad. If he hadn't pulled out his date's chair, I probably would have picked on him for it later.

This was going to be an exhausting night. And we hadn't even started the small talk.

Everyone hid behind their menus for a few minutes and only discussed the choices. "I can't decide between the squab or the lobster," Jared said.

I caught Will's quirked eyebrows from the corner of my eye. I read it like a billboard. *What kind of pretentious tool orders squab?* But Captain Pizza and Nachos wasn't exactly a foodie, so I pretended I didn't notice.

Instead, I leaned toward Jared so I didn't have to raise my voice over the murmur of the neighboring diners. "I'm stuck between the lobster and the citrus chicken."

Jared closed his menu. "Why don't you get the chicken, I'll get the lobster, and then you can try mine?"

Will broke in, his voice amused. "Hannah knows what she wants. She'll do fine ordering for herself."

What? Did he just try to put Jared in his place? I closed my menu too. "I do know what I want. Your plan sounds perfect, Jared."

Will shrugged. I couldn't leave it alone. "Raina, we haven't heard from you. What do you think?" *Take that, Will. Which of these two women is on a date with a domineering male? Not me.*

Raina startled like I'd poked her. "Just choose whatever you think sounds good, and we can share it. I'm not super picky."

"Cool," Will said. "I think we should go with the blackened chicken pasta and the salmon."

"You can't get the chicken," I told Will.

He skimmed the menu again and frowned. "You're right. I'll do the skirt steak. That still okay with you?" he asked Raina.

"That sounds great, but why not the chicken pasta?" she asked. "I'm not one of those girls who's scared of carbs."

I gave her grudging points for that. "He can't eat mushrooms," I said, determined not to sound smug or, worse, possessive.

"Allergy?" Raina asked, reaching out to cover one of his hands on the table like she was comforting him for having tuberculosis and not a food sensitivity.

"More like an aversion," he said. "It's a texture thing."

"I totally get it. But I love skirt steak, so that's a great choice."

Somehow the way she said it made the subtext sound like, "Thanks for hanging the moon, Will."

I glanced at my watch. Had it only been ten minutes? The rest of the evening yawned even wider. Boo hisssssss.

"How do you know each other?" Jared asked, and I smiled at him. "Will is my brother's best friend," I said at the same time Will said, "I've known Hannah her whole life."

Jared nodded, and his face relaxed. "That makes sense. For a minute there, I thought maybe you two were exes, and I was sweating being in the middle of an awkward situation."

"Definitely not," I said, shooting Will a "shut up" look. "Tell me about your work. You said you're an attorney?"

Will's eyes immediately glazed over. He complained that the biggest jerks at his racquetball club were always the lawyers.

"Yeah, I am," Jared said with a laugh. "Sorry."

"Which firm?" Raina asked. "My brother is an attorney."

"I own my own practice, but I do immigration law, so I make enough to keep the lights on but not enough to pay for anyone else to have their name on the door."

"Wow. That's really admirable," I said, truly impressed. I'd assumed he was one of hundreds of hotshot Dallas guys who were gunning for top billing at the lucrative firms connected to the different oil companies headquartered in town.

"It's not financially smart though." Jared shrugged. "It feels right for right now."

Raina cleared her throat. "What kind of engineer are you, Will?"

Will's gaze had sharpened when Jared had said immigration law. His measuring gaze slid from Jared to me before returning to Raina. "I'm a rocket scientist." It came out a little braggy. *Tone it down, Will.* Or maybe Raina would find it off-putting. *Keep it up, Will.*

"Awesome. I love aeronautics," Raina said, leaning forward, her eyes bright. "Tell me what you do."

I hated her.

"Right now I'm working on a project with jet-engine mounts," Will said, fixing his attention on his date.

She could have it. I wasn't going to compete. Jared was too nice for that, and there wasn't much I hated more than watching an episode of *The Bachelor* and the women all becoming the worst clichés in fighting for the same man. It was much better when twenty-five men fought for one woman. But this table was evenly matched, and there was no reason for anyone to be fighting for anyone's attention, and if anything, I owed Jared mine.

I also owed Will a chewing out, which he would get later when I pounded on his door to yell at him for crashing my date. I wasn't sure yet exactly what I would say, but it would contain the words, "I'm a big girl now. Quit babysitting me."

I kept my eyes on Jared and executed dating tips numbers three and five on the list I'd compiled after an awkward date when I was twenty-one. *Smile like you mean it, and listen with interest.* "Tell me about your work, Jared. Is it hard?"

Jared's return smile showed the first sign of strain I'd seen on him, and a touch of tension stiffened the set of his shoulders. "It's so hard, but I can't quit," he said. "There aren't enough lawyers advocating for immigrants. There's no pay in it. The attorneys in the legal aid offices are burnt out and overloaded, and the ones working for hire are predators, charging a big upfront fee, and then they don't deliver results. They don't even try."

The waitress stopped by for our orders, and when she left again, I propped my chin on my hand and fixed my eyes on Jared. "Is it too exhausting to talk about?"

"It drains me, but I love it."

"Then I'd love to hear more."

He hesitated, but when I smiled, he nodded and detailed one of his cases. I listened, respect and guilt warring for the upper hand with my emotions. I related to people who loved their jobs and took pride in their work. Jared clearly did that. But at the same time, the stress of the work he did was bleeding into our dinner like the first cut into a rare steak, and it was clear that there would be more to come. And that there would always be more to come in his line of work.

I was not the woman he deserved sitting across from him, trying to listen to him but letting my mind wander to the man sitting next to me instead, trying not to flinch every time Will cracked a joke that made his date laugh. Jared needed a woman who could open her whole heart to him and help him carry the burdens he was shouldering alone. That woman was not me.

He at least deserved my fully present self tonight. I brushed my napkin to the floor to give myself an excuse to reach down and pick it up. I repositioned myself when I straightened to angle away from Will so that looking at him would require me to turn my head and force me to think about how often my attention was wandering his way.

"That's heartbreaking," I said as Jared wound down describing his case of trying to reunite a deported mother with her children still here in Texas.

He groaned. "I'm so sorry. I have a bad habit of taking work home with me, but it's inexcusable to drag it out on dates."

The waitress arrived with our meals, and I ooh-ed at my beautiful chicken while Raina aah-ed over her salmon. That made me wished I hadn't ooh-ed because I didn't want to do anything the same as Raina. And then that made me feel about fourteen. No, twelve.

Jared dropped his arms to his side and gave himself a vigorous shake, like a swimmer about to mount the starting blocks. "I'm shaking off work. Tell me about you."

"What do you want to know?" I asked.

"Besides the things in your profile, what do you do for fun?"

"She runs and watches Rangers games," Will said. "That's pretty much all you have to know."

I refrained from elbowing him, only because I knew I couldn't resist doing it hard and possibly causing a scene. "I have old-lady hobbies, mostly," I told Jared, ignoring Will.

"What does that mean? Do you play canasta at the senior center on Thursdays or something?"

I laughed. "That might be more interesting than what I actually do. I keep a container garden because I don't have a yard. Then I sit around sketching out the garden I'm going to have one day when I have a real yard. And sometimes . . ." I clapped my hands to my face, realizing what I was about to admit.

"What?" Jared asked.

"What?" Will demanded at the exact same moment.

I wouldn't have answered Will. His tone was incredulous, like he couldn't believe I had a hobby he didn't know about. But Jared's expression was so sincerely interested that I put my hands over my eyes and answered in spite of myself. "I order seed catalogs, and I read them for hours, memorizing planting schedules, imagining how they'll grow."

"Hey," Jared said, his voice soft and warm. I peeked at him through my fingers and dropped my hands when I saw his smile. "I think that's awesome."

"I think that doesn't make sense," Will said. "Why order seed catalogs? You can get all that information online. And if you're ordering the seed catalogs, they have the planting seasons printed on them, so you don't need to look them up. You've got some system inefficiencies in your process."

I took a deep breath and finally spared him a glance. "Do not make me stab you with a fork. Talk to your date, Will."

He stared at me for another long moment, his brow furrowed, before he shrugged and turned back to Raina, whose eyes betrayed the first signs of tension. I smiled a "He's your problem" smile at her and let it morph into something genuine when I refocused on Jared. "Anyway, old-lady hobbies."

"Any kind of hobby sounds amazing to me right now," he said. "I don't have time. For that. For almost anything. I'm not even sure I'd ever get out on dates if it didn't coincide with meals I had to eat."

That made me laugh out loud. It was so lacking in game that I couldn't help it. His cheekbones darkened. "I just played that back in my head and realized how it sounded. You're not a convenience or a . . . system efficiency." He darted a glance at Will, but I didn't follow it to see what my watchdog thought of the dig. "I meant that I don't come up for air sometimes, and only the fact that biology forces me to eat reminds me that I probably need to speak to nonclient humans too."

Suddenly Will's voice was in my ear, low and threatening. "His biology is going to have nothing to do with your biology."

I pretended I didn't hear him or notice Raina's drill-bit stare, but I did lean away from Will and farther toward Jared. "I understood what you meant," I assured him. "I'm glad to be a distraction." His flush deepened, and I grinned. "I mean it. I take it as a compliment that I'm enough to pull you away from work you obviously love."

Will coughed next to me, and I began a list in my head of all the ways I was going to exact my revenge on him over the week. First, hide his laundry detergent. Second, leave the following public message on his dating profile: "Hey! I didn't know how else to reach you since you're not returning my calls, but I have good news! The DNA test came back, and you're NOT the father!" Third . . . third would be worse. Whatever it was.

I decided to think happy thoughts, and my dinner made me happy. I took my last bite and sighed, half in enjoyment, half wistfully that it was all gone. "I don't get excited about chicken too often, but this is to die for. Thanks for suggesting this place."

"Thanks for being willing to try it out with me."

We had reached what one how-to-date article called "the fork in the road." He would either wind up for a pitch or leave the mound and forfeit the game.

He picked up his napkin and dabbed at his mouth before setting it down. "I'm sure the desserts here are great too, but if you don't mind a walk, I know where to find the best cheesecake in the city."

"Hannah loves cheesecake. That sounds good. We'll go with you," Will said.

"Does it?" I asked. Will hated cheesecake. "What about you, Raina? Does cheesecake sound good to you?"

Her plastic smile said that tagging along with us didn't sound good at all. But she said, "Sounds great."

"You sure?" I pressed. "You guys are totally committed to cheesecake?"

Will's eyes narrowed, suspecting something was up, but Raina jumped in before he could answer. "Absolutely. What girl doesn't love cheesecake? I might even love it more than you."

I leaned back and smiled at them. "You're probably right. I don't feel that strongly about cheesecake tonight, but you guys enjoy it. I'll take you up on the walk though," I told Jared, who perked up when he realized I wasn't quitting for the night. Yet. I wasn't going to string Jared along, but I wasn't cutting him loose with Will in earshot either. Besides, it would serve Will right to wonder what I was up to while he watched Raina eat her cheesecake.

"Great," Jared said, signaling the server for our check. "Nothing better than an Indian summer for—"

"Baseball," Will said.

"A walk on the town with a beautiful woman," Jared finished, ignoring Will, who suddenly had a cough again.

"Do you follow baseball at all?" Will asked, a challenge in his voice.

Jared might not have understood the challenge—Will couldn't fathom me ever being serious about a guy without a diehard dedication to the sport we loved—but he answered anyway. "I go to Rangers games sometimes," Jared said. "I've been too busy since starting my practice to keep my season tickets, but yeah, I still like it. I like soccer better though."

"Floppers," Will said.

"Yeah, because that doesn't happen in other sports ever. Just ask Manu Ginóbili."

That made me laugh out loud, and I wished I didn't have to end our walk by telling him we weren't going to hang out again. I did, however, wonder if there was a way I could get his number for Sophie.

The waitress set our checks on the table, and I reached for ours, but Jared snatched it up first. "Maybe I'm a chauvinist, but there is some of my mother's training in me that I just can't let go. Let me get it, as a thank you for some awesome dinner conversation."

I smiled and relaxed in my chair as he tucked his card into the check holder. Raina hadn't even reached for the bill, and Will was able to pay for their dinner without a peep of protest from her. Jared asked Will about a trade the Rangers had made earlier in the season to strengthen their batting lineup, and that conversation lasted until the waitress returned with the receipts and they each scrawled out their signatures on the slips. Or maybe only Will scrawled. For a guy who dealt professionally in precision and clarity, he had atrocious handwriting, like the ink could never keep up with his brain.

"Guess this is where we split up," Jared told Will, not sounding at all sorry about it. He jotted something on a cocktail napkin and handed it to Will. "That's the cheesecake place. Have a good night," he said as he hurried around to my side of the table to help me slip my cardigan on. Oh, man, I needed this guy for Sophie, big time. What a complete, total, absolute peach who deserved a peach like my best friend.

We headed out to the sidewalk, and Jared pointed south. "That way?"

"Sounds great."

As we waited for the light at the corner to change, I glanced back to the restaurant in time to see Will and Raina walking in the opposite direction. They weren't holding hands or even walking particularly close, but my heart lurched watching them step in sync. I wondered if Will had looked back for me at all, and the lurch became a squeeze when I realized that he probably had, since that, after all, was what good big brothers did.

Chapter 9 ♥

WILL'S DOOR SHOT OPEN AS I passed it, and I barely bit back a shriek. My hand flew to my chest while I took a deep breath and then shot him a death stare before walking to my apartment. I'd stayed out a whole hour after Jared and I had split up, not wanting to walk past Will's parking spot in the garage and torture myself if its emptiness mocked me by announcing he was still with Raina. He'd thrown open his door too fast for me to even process, much less enjoy the knowledge that he was home. How irritating.

He followed behind me. "Where have you been?"

"Go home, Will."

"I've been home for an hour."

"Congratulations," I said. I slid the key in my lock without looking back.

"You didn't answer my text."

"Yes, I did." I opened the door and set my purse on my end table.

"Telling me to stop texting you is not an answer."

I shut the door on him. He opened it again.

"If you used your deductive reasoning skills, you could have pieced together that I was alive and well and too annoyed to talk to you." I gave him a shove hard enough to move him out of my doorway and shut the door again, throwing the dead bolt this time.

He jiggled the handle. "I'm going to YouTube how to get around a dead bolt," he said through the door.

"You've got problems, Will."

"Yeah, you. You're a giant pain in the neck. Dave would never let you get away with crap like this."

I shot the dead bolt back and threw the door open to glare at him. "You know why Dave pawned me off on you? Because he figured out that I'm way too much work to babysit. That's what happens when you try to interfere with a grown woman's life. So he thought to himself, 'Who do I know that's dumb enough to take this on?'" I reached up and knocked three times on his forehead. "Ding, ding, ding. You're the winner. I absolve you. Dave conned you into doing an impossible job. You can give up in good conscience."

I tried to close the door again, but he stuck his foot in the way and muscled past me. I gave up and went to the kitchen for a glass of water.

"You're in a bad mood. Your date didn't end well?" He didn't sound at all sympathetic.

Yes and no. The perfect end to a date for me would be a shivery kiss and that feeling of floating back home. Instead, I'd had to find a way to tell Jared that I thought he was awesome, but I had a feeling we weren't going to be a good fit.

He'd understood immediately. "Will." He didn't even phrase it as a question, so I hadn't insulted him by denying it. I had, however, increased the awkward quotient exponentially by asking him if I could set him up with a friend. He'd said he'd think about it, but I'd shown him a picture of Sophie on my phone, and I'd left with his number to pass on. And he was smiling when we parted ways in the parking lot, so I was calling the whole thing a win.

"It was a good date." Minus the entire part of the evening where Will had been an absolute disaster.

"So where'd you go after?"

"Walking. Talking. None of your business."

His eyebrows shot up as he considered that, and he wandered in to flop on my sofa. "You surprised me. You were on point. You should give lessons to some of the girls I've gone out with."

Prickles of pleasure at the compliment danced up the back of my neck.

He wasn't done. "But I still think you're a little naive—"

I walked out of the kitchen before he could finish the sentence and shut my bedroom door on the rest of his words.

"—about what guys are after. Oh, come on!" he hollered as the door clicked shut. "That's as immature as it gets. Do you have your fingers in your ears too so you don't have to hear anything you don't like?"

I threw myself on the bed and dialed Sophie.

"Hey," she said. "Date report. How did it go?"

"Good news, bad news. My date's name was Jared, and he was great."

"Cool. What's the bad news?"

"I'm not done with the good news yet. Hang on." I listened for Will in the living room, but I heard nothing, so I wandered out. No Will. Good. "So the rest of the good news is that Jared is not the guy for me, but I'm pretty sure he's your future husband."

"Ooooh, tell me more."

"In a second. The bad news is that stupid Will was on my whole stupid date."

"You're kidding."

"He crashed it like a Miley Cyrus wrecking ball."

"Miley Cyrus writes trite metaphors."

"This one was accurate." I snuggled into my favorite couch corner and told her all about the stupidest date of my life. "And then he had the nerve to pounce on me when I was coming home and demand a report."

"Oh, Will," Sophie sighed. "What a dummy. What a duuu-uuuuuuuummy," she sang for emphasis. "So what did you do?"

"I tried shoving him out the door, but that didn't work. He still needed to lecture me, so I locked myself in my room until he called me immature and finally went away."

"Huh. So basically you acted like his sister, and he treated you like his sister."

"Don't be on his side! This was exactly the kind of night where he should have seen me as an equal. I was in a sophisticated outfit, sharing dinner and sparkling conversation with a handsome man, and the second I get home, he's waiting up for me like Dave so he can lecture me."

"We need to get back to the part about my future husband pretty soon, but while I'm 100 percent on your side, you also just admitted that as soon as he started in on you brother-style, you responded back sister-style. I'm going to fix this for you, but you have to see that pattern first. You can't morph when you're with other people, even when you're in his presence, and revert back to old dynamics when you're alone together."

"But—"

"Say I'm right, Hannah."

"He—"

"Say I'm right, Hannah. This is tough love."

"Fine. You're right. But you're going to have to explain what I'm supposed to do when he acts like that."

"It's simple, but it's hard. Can you imagine what would happen if I acted like my students every day? They'd treat me like one of them, and most of them would probably think that was pretty fun, but we wouldn't get anything done. So no matter how much their shenanigans make me want to jump in or how often I feel like getting caught up in Sicilian land wars when one of them feels like pulling me into a power struggle, I rise above."

"Did you just use a Princess Bride quote *and* a Maya Angelou quote on me? In one sentence?"

"Yes. I'm masterful. But take it as a mantra. Repeat that to yourself when you're with Will: I will rise above this. If he does something that treats you like a sister, think about how you would act if it was some random guy you were dating. You would never put up with one tenth of Will's crap from a date. You would put him in his place or walk out. And that's what you have to do with Will. Retrain him while giving him plenty of opportunities to see the adult you."

I slid to the floor and stuck my feet up on the couch. It was one of my favorite thinking positions. "It sounds like we're training a puppy. I'm not trying to change Will. I'm trying to change his perception of me."

"This isn't like puppy training at all," Sophie argued. "This is like last year when you wanted that promotion and you knew Parham"—and she paused so we could each make a fake spitting sound like we did every time we named my boss—"wasn't going to give you a shot."

Parham had thought I was too fresh from college, too young to handle it. He hadn't said it in so many words, but his actions had. So I had wormed my way into being an interim project manager when we were short staffed and killed it, and my promotion became a no-brainer. And the second promotion had come six months after that. My next move up the ladder would make me Parham's professional peer.

"It's all about making Will see that he's blind too. And if you can't let go of the puppy-training analogy, then, yeah, it's also about looking amazing around him and rubbing his nose in it every time."

I laughed. "You're the best."

"True. Now tell me who I'm marrying."

I told her all about Jared and got her blessing to give him her number. We ended our call, and I was wrapping up an e-mail to Jared, telling him more about Sophie, when a call from Dave came in on Skype.

"Good morning," I said, answering it. He often called when he woke up because that was right before I was going to sleep. Usually he answered with a "Good night" and a grin to acknowledge the time difference, but today he only grumbled, "Hey," and scowled.

"What's up?" I asked.

"You went on a blind date tonight?"

"I did," I answered, losing my own smile. It was going to be one of *those* calls, where Dave wasn't content with siccing Will on me and had to butt in for himself.

"From the Internet? That's not safe, Hannah. Come on."

I sat back and crossed my arms. "Will told you, huh? Did you give him the same lecture you're about to give me? Because he went on a blind Internet date too."

"It's not the same thing. He can handle himself." He winced. "I meant—"

"You meant exactly what you said. Your double standard is stupid, and you better change the subject right now, or I'm going to bed."

"He's a big guy, Hannah. No one's going to take advantage of him. So unless your date was smaller than you, I still have a point."

"No, you don't. I understand that I need to use common sense when I go out with strangers, which is why I told Sophie where I was going and who I was with and met my date at a busy restaurant. I didn't need Will hovering, and since I obviously made it home in one piece, I definitely don't need you hovering now."

"It's my job."

"No. Your job is taking care of your wife and your career and your life. Not managing mine. I love you, but I swear you're worse now than when you lived down the hall."

Jessica's head popped onto the screen. "It's because he feels like he's got less control now. Forgive him. I'm working on him. Hi, Hannah!" she said with a quick wave before she straightened and went back to whatever she was doing.

"Listen to your wife," I said. "I've got this. I'm safe, healthy, and happy. Now call Will off, and let me do my thing."

"No way," he said. "If anything, he's too lax with you." I heard a loud snort from Jessica. Dave ignored her. "The only reason I even accepted this job is because he promised he would keep an eye on you, but you're wandering off with Internet strangers. So don't worry, you're not even my first lecture this morning. I got on his case too."

I groaned. "Say you didn't."

"He definitely did," Jessica called. "Went on and on about how he's given Will the sacred trust of being the surrogate brother, and letting you wander off with strangers is not in keeping with that trust. And on. And on."

"Dave. Stop. I mean it. What reason have I ever given you to think I can't take care of myself?"

He pressed his mouth tight and glared at me.

"Look at you." I leaned closer to the screen to study his body language. "You're a stressed-out mess. There's no reason for it. I'm fine. I've been fine."

"You're fine until you're not, Hannah. That's how it goes. There's enough random, bad things that can go wrong without messing with known risks like Internet blind dates."

I took a deep breath, determined to hold on to my temper because I could sense the anxiety in his voice. The only reason I hadn't completely lost it with Dave over the years was because I knew he wasn't trying to control me personally—he had an extreme need to control the situation when it came to people he loved. And he loved me like crazy. Which was why I let him get away with driving me crazy. He'd been like this since the accident when our parents had disappeared from our lives in a matter of seconds.

"Dave."

"Hannah."

"I have not once in my whole life been in any danger. That's not luck. That's me exercising common sense. I'm fine. I'll stay fine. And I promise I'll always check with Sophie, meet people in safe places, and use good judgment. Please, spend your energy on something where you can make a difference. Because you taught me well. I'm going to be okay."

The tiny lines he'd developed around his eyes tightened. Will didn't have those yet because he wasn't a worrier like Dave was. Then the lines relaxed again, and he sighed. "I can't call Will off. He's the only way I'll have real peace of mind. I don't know how I would have survived your teenage years if I hadn't had him for backup."

A pang in my stomach made it hard for me to keep my expression neutral. Part of me wanted to complain that it was Will playing backup that was making it so hard to break through to him now. But the reality was that it wouldn't have mattered. I'd never been the kind of girl Will had gone for back then, and *that* was the whole problem now.

Chapter 10 ♥

THE NEXT DAY, AFTER WORK, I whipped up my version of the Sun City grilled chicken and walked down to Will's with two plates in hand. I tapped the door with my foot until he opened it and blinked at me. "You're talking to me now?"

"Yeah. You didn't tell me how your date went. Seemed like you hit it off. Was the cheesecake good?"

He grunted and took the plates from me to set on his coffee table. I went to the kitchen and dug up clean silverware and two blue drinks before I joined him.

"I don't know how the cheesecake was. We didn't make it that far. When you're running an efficiency model on your dating life, it's pretty easy to cut your losses."

I winced. "Seems kind of cold."

"It's better than spending a couple of extra hours and wasting their time, isn't it? I mean, I could hang around to be polite, but in the end, I'm not doing my date any favors if I'm not feeling it." He frowned. "Right?"

Right? The single-word question represented a tiny seismic shift between us. He was asking my opinion. About dating protocol. "Right," I agreed. I wasn't about to tell him to spend any *more* time with these women. *Right? Right? Right?* I rolled around his question in my head, enjoying the feel of him asking me for advice. Kind of. It was a small but distinct step in the right direction. Maybe this was what happened when I kept showing up at his house in my big-girl clothes instead of sweats and a Rangers T-shirt to hang out.

I smoothed down the blush-pink silk of my tailored work blouse, a perfect balance of feminine and professional.

Will noticed. "Where's your Rangers shirt? Game three starts in twenty minutes."

I stifled a sigh. He'd noticed my pretty work shirt for the wrong reasons, but he'd noticed. "I didn't feel like changing. So Raina's out. Who's up next?"

"I don't know. I have to rethink the approach. Batting zero means you change the lineup."

My chicken stuck in my throat, and I coughed to clear it. "We have a good strategy in place. You have to give it time, find your rhythm."

He shook his head. "I've got a large enough sampling size to know it's time to do this differently."

Stay calm, I ordered myself. "What are you thinking? Switching websites?"

"No. Switching up my profile. The one we put up doesn't feel all the way like me. I think I need to own up to being a science-loving baseball junkie who does extreme sports in my free time. None of that's in there now. I think putting it out there will draw more girls who think I'm fun instead of super serious. And I'm changing that profile picture. That broody shot is someone whose butt I would kick just because."

Crud. His inbox would be bursting with messages if he did that. And it would be women who liked the masculinity of his hobbies and respected his giant rocket-scientist brain. And Will being Will would pick the most gorgeous, petite, darling ones. And he would eventually choose one and marry it. Her. He would marry her. And he would be bored inside of three years. What kind of friend would let him walk into that?

I had to save him. For his sake, obviously.

Man. No one could lie to me as well as I could.

But I waded in anyway. "You're probably right that it's time to switch up your approach, but your way is going to get you a bunch of women like the ones you always date. So don't do it your way."

"You've got a better idea?"

"Always," I said.

He grinned and reached over to tousle my hair, but I leaned back and caught his wrist, setting his hand down on the sofa between us. "I'm having a good hair day. Let's keep it going."

He glanced at my hair and shrugged. "Okay."

I ran the mental analytics on new approaches to Will's online dating. "I think," I said slowly as a new idea bubbled up, "you do need to change your profile, but you need to become a woman."

He choked on his Gatorade. "What?"

"I mean it. You need to enter an experimental phase so you can figure out how to tweak your own profile for maximum results. I read that men contact women on dating sites at a far greater rate than women contact men." I hadn't read that, but it sounded like something that could be true. It was true for me, so that was enough proof for the case I was laying out. "If you become the initiator, you're going to have to do even more to set yourself apart from the other Dallas guys on HeyThere."

"And this involves a sex-change operation?"

"Yes. Brilliant, right?"

He set his plate down, and I knew what was coming next. Before he could haul me his way for a punitive noogie, I held up a "stop" hand and let his intentions slam right into it. "If you touch this very expensive shirt with your grubby boy fingers, you're dead to me." *Also, I'm not your little sister or your wrestling monkey.*

He froze and held his hands up in surrender. "It's pretty." His voice was grudging, but butterflies flapped up to my chest from my stomach, brainless little insects that they were. He'd noticed that my shirt was pretty. That was several steps past noticing I wasn't wearing a Rangers shirt. "What's your real idea?"

"I think you need to invent a profile for the ideal woman you want. Just build her. You can make her whatever you want, but it has to legit be the kind of woman you should marry, not the kind you always date. And then you post it and see what kind of guys are contacting her. Then study their profiles to see how to adjust yours to stand out."

"It seems kind of messed up to set a honey trap for unsuspecting dudes to come check out a profile for a girl who doesn't exist. It's not cool to waste people's time like that. And it's kind of manipulative."

A sharp pang twinged in my chest at the word. That was exactly what I was doing—going as far out of my way as I could to waste Will's time. I should drop the whole thing and help him do a straightforward profile of the Will I knew, but when I opened my mouth, I pushed ahead with my plan. "It's not manipulation. You're not going to respond to any of these guys. You're not going to lead them into some kind of false relationship. You're collecting data that will ultimately allow you to figure out how to present the best version of yourself so that you can really, truly find the person meant for you. It's science, tweaking the variables, not a head game."

I recognized the lines appearing around his eyes, and my stomach sank. Those were his stubborn lines, the ones that showed up when he was about to dig in. "Think about it, Will. How is this any different from observing people in a bar for a few nights, analyzing the way they interact, and then hitting the bar yourself with your best face forward? Most people show up determined to be only the awesomest parts of themselves. Is that manipulation? No. Dating is a social contract. We expect our dates to show us one aspect of themselves initially and then to reveal their whole identity over time. Nobody feels manipulated by that.

"The only difference here is that you're approaching it more thoughtfully, gathering more information, sitting in the bar, watching before you present the aspect of you that you think gives girls the best idea about who you are."

Will sat back, the stubborn lines smoothing out, and gave me a slight smile. "Tell me again why you didn't go to law school?"

"I hate bad guys, and contracts bore me. What's left to do in law? I've got a brain for code, and I know how to wrangle squirrelly programmers. Give me five years and I'll be the youngest director at my company by a decade. I'm doing exactly what I'm built for. Being a good debater is a bonus skill set I trot out for times like now, when I need to convince you to do the thing that's going to help you the most in the end."

"Are you helping me because you think if you get me married off I'll be out of your hair? Because you should give that idea up right now. I'm in your life permanently." He laced his fingers behind his head and leaned back, shooting me a smug smile.

My insides melted while I let myself imagine for a fleeting moment that he meant those words the way I wanted him to mean them.

"Big Brother is always watching," he said. And the melting became an uncomfortable acid wash in my abdomen.

"Hand me your laptop, and we'll start this new profile," I said. "Let's give it a few days to see if you're collecting useful data. If it's not giving you any insights into your own dating strategy, we delete the profile. This isn't a big deal, but it could be a good tool."

He considered it for another long minute before he pushed himself up from the sofa and retrieved his laptop from his bedroom, handing it over without further argument.

"Tell me what you want," I said. "Think hard about the girls you date and why those relationships never last for you, and then pick the opposite of all those qualities. Let's build your true perfect match. And if you say Adrienne Lima, I'm not helping you anymore. Take it seriously."

"But I'm serious as a heart attack when I say I would absolutely date a Victoria's Secret model."

I shut the laptop.

"Kidding, kidding."

I reopened it. "I'll start you off. You need a girl who's as book smart as she is street smart. You'll get bored if she can't keep up with your technical conversations."

"True," he said. "I need someone who is driven. She needs a career, something she loves doing so she gets it when I'm deep into something for work. I need her to not do Pilates."

I paused in my typing, and he glanced over at me. "Most of the girls I date are really into Pilates for whatever reason. So if we're into opposites, I should be looking for someone who isn't gym sculpted. But fit is not negotiable. She has to be able to keep up with my sports stuff."

"So someone who runs for the love of it, not someone who goes to the gym for the look of it." Like me, dummy. Totally fit because it felt better than being undisciplined, with zero interest in whatever mixed dance-martial arts-cardio-ballet craze was sweeping like a virus through Dallas gyms at any given moment.

"Basically, yeah. I guess she needs to have a passion outside of work too. My mom told me once that you have to have big things in common because it bonds you but that you need just as many big things not in common because it helps you remember who you are outside of a marriage twenty years in. She says that's why she and my dad never run out of things to talk about. They have enough separate activities that there's always something for them to be learning about each other. That's kind of cool."

"So does it matter what this driving passion is?" I asked. "Because Letterbox girl was pretty passionate about mailboxes."

"Yeah. That date was your fault, so don't sound so superior. And a collection of mailbox pictures isn't okay. I'm thinking more like someone who's into pottery or photography."

"So something creative," I said like I was pondering it. "Like making beautiful food." Like me. I did that. Food was my canvas.

"Exactly."

I clicked away. "What else?"

"Thinking in opposites, I guess she'd be someone with strong opinions about more than where we should get dinner or which movie to see. I mean, that's good too, actually. I like someone who knows what she wants. But I like someone who can argue about foreign policy or patent reform or . . ." He trailed off, trying to think of something else.

"Why *Doctor Who* is the most overrated cultural phenomenon of our time?"

"It's not," he said, his forehead slamming into predictable furrows. "It's a show that makes important observations about human nature."

"It's mildly entertaining serial television that doesn't work hard enough to justify the way it plays with the space-time continuum while it pretends to be superior genre entertainment to better shows like *Fringe*, which is tragically underrated."

"Your argument is invalid. *Fringe* fails to resonate at the level where you have fandoms built around it, like *Doctor Who* does. And it fails for the reason that it's not as good. Its themes aren't universal enough. It depends too much on the creep factor."

He was working himself up, and I smiled at him. "So someone who can have arguments like that. That's what you're saying you need." Someone like me.

"Nice. I fell for that. But, yes. Someone like that."

"Keep going. We need a little more to round this fake girl out. What music does she need to listen to?"

"Anything, as long as she's cool with variety. Shelley only listened to top forty. We were in my car once when a Beatles song came on, and she was like, 'This is pretty good. Is it new?' And I think that's when I knew we weren't going to work."

"Yeah, because stealing laundry isn't that big a deal."

"Stop being bitter."

"She has my favorite bra. I'll be bitter as long as I want to."

He rolled his eyes. "Buy a new one. *I'll* buy you a new one." My eyes flew up, and he reddened a tiny bit. "Never mind. You buy your own bras. I just meant you're being kind of dramatic."

"Right. Anyway. No top forty," I prompted him, navigating us back toward solid ground. For a second there, we'd been adrift in a place I didn't recognize. "Fake Girl now listens to a variety of music that suggests some hipster tendencies."

"But she can't be a hipster. I dated a couple of those. They're exhausting. You can't go eat somewhere where it's convenient. You have to go to these nests of slightly musty plaid-wearers built inside ironic buildings like former plumbing stores in industrial parks."

"I had no idea. No hipsters. I'll make her like me." Why couldn't he see that he'd been describing me to a T with his whole list? That I was the perfect antidote to these women who'd bore him within weeks, one after the next?

"What do you mean, make her like you?"

I shrugged. "I'm not into trends or movements. I like what I like, and I do it. Won't that be a good way to explain what you're looking for?"

"Yeah, actually."

"Okay. Turn the game on. I'll pull this profile together and have your perfect woman ready for you in a few minutes."

"Great," he said in a voice that said the opposite. "Can't wait until I find out what I've been looking for all along."

That made two of us.

I completed the profile before the announcers had even finished breaking down the lineups. "Got it. We need a picture."

"That's a problem. I'm not stealing a picture of some real girl off the Internet for this."

"We can use a picture of me."

"Good idea. Put up that one you made me take of you."

"Uh, no? Chances are any guys who are looking for this girl would also have turned me up in their search." Fake Girl was Real Me. "It's going to look weird if two different profiles have the same photo. We'll take another one of me, but I'll do my makeup different. Should I go for a drama queen look, red lipstick, all that? Or more of a Miss January look?"

"No pinup looks. And why Miss January? If I were a pinup girl, I'd be a good month, like June."

"If you were a pinup girl, you'd have to do way more waxing. And also, the summer girls are always blond. Brunettes get the winter months."

His eyebrow rose. "Spend a lot of time looking at calendars?"

"I guess the question here is, do you? Is that the look we're going for? Shiny, pouty lips? Bedroom eyes?"

He looked appalled. "You don't need a look. Just do a picture of your regular self. That's how you look best anyway."

I went a little melty again. "What's my regular self, Will? I play with my look all the time depending on what I'm doing."

"I know, but you look best when . . . you know," he said, giving up on words to wave his arm in the direction of my head.

"Shocking as this is, this"—I flapped my arm in imitation of him—"does not help me. Be specific."

"I don't know," he said, mild frustration coloring his words. "Just look like you."

"You got it." I slid his laptop off my lap and stood.

"Where are you going? It's almost time for Luke Bryan to throw out the first pitch."

I sat right back down. "I'll hang around for Luke Bryan."

Will's brow furrowed. "I thought you didn't like country music."

"I don't have to like it to appreciate Luke Bryan. I don't know if I want him to wear jeans or borrow some of those tight baseball pants to do this."

He scowled. "You were about to go do something, possibly something weird with your face?"

"Yes, Will. Making myself look like me is doing something weird with my face."

"Don't get mad at me. This whole conversation is weird. *You* are the one who took it to some meta level where looking like you somehow involves you leaving and coming back transformed. Why am I in trouble? I just want to watch baseball."

"I'll be back in a few minutes. If Luke Bryan is pitching in jeans, you'll be rewinding so I can watch that. A few times."

He grumbled, and I walked out, heading to my apartment like I had some plan. I had zero plan, but I did have a chance to make him really look at me again. He was going to be curious to see what I came up with. He'd study me, think through how my makeover would match up with the ideal girl he thought he'd invented, who was, in a convoluted plot twist, me. It was like being in a Christopher Nolan movie. If he did romantic comedies.

I had to somehow make the ideal woman Will had described align with me in his mind in a way he'd never considered before.

It was impossible.

I needed Sophie.

Chapter 11 ♥

"Subtle eye, deep berry lipstick, no gloss, which gives you a sophisticated sexy lip. It'll call attention to your mouth without him even realizing it, where a gloss will make him realize he's noticing your mouth, and that will kick his brain into analytical gear. You don't want him to think about this all clinical style. You want him to just experience you for as many seconds as you can squeeze together before he starts thinking."

She knew exactly what to do, and it was pulling me back from the brink of failure, the feeling that I was being handed a golden opportunity that I was going to blow.

"What else?" I said. "Hair? Clothes."

"No blush, just a highlighter over your cheekbones. Subtle jewelry. Diamond studs and the pearl pendant I got you for your birthday. Hair? Hair, hair, hair," she muttered, and I could hear her brain clicking through the options. "Curl it."

"Can't. I did that in my real profile picture, and I told him this one has to be different."

"Okay, low ponytail, but let it fall forward over your shoulder, and let some of it wisp out in front to make him think about reaching out and pushing it back behind your ear."

"Outfit? I'm in my pink silk work shirt right now."

"Ooooh," she squealed. "I love that shirt."

"Right? I need something this good. Swiss polka dots?"

"No. Refined but unapproachable. I know! Do that drapey turquoise shirt you have. It'll be great with the deep berry and so pretty with your eyes."

"Thank you," I breathed in something close to a prayer. "Gotta go become his dream woman."

"You don't need to become anything," she said, her voice sharp. She softened it to add, "You've always been her. Have fun. Get into some trouble."

"Haha," I said, ending the call.

I whipped through the changes, finishing off the look with my favorite jeans and my sparkly sandals. I grinned at my reflection when I smoothed on the deep berry. Sophie was good.

Come down here when it's a commercial, I texted him.

Why?

To take the dumb picture. I needed him to walk in prepared to see me as something different, thinking about me and that profile, not grunting at me when I walked back into his apartment because he was deep in the game. This would require his undivided attention.

Just take the picture here.

I have better light.

Fine.

Three minutes later, the sound of his hand on my doorknob gave me enough warning to arrange myself against my breakfast bar, leaned back with my legs crossed at the ankles, waiting for him while I texted Sophie. *I feel like I'm at bat with the bases loaded.*

Swing, baby, swing! She texted back as my front door swung open. I was smiling when I looked up at Will, who paused and stared at me.

Everything froze as he stood there, his eyes traveling over my face, stopping at my lips for a full second, moving down to the ponytail draped like Sophie had ordered, taking in the turquoise shirt and traveling back up to meet my eyes. He didn't say anything.

"This should do it," I said, my voice quiet. Speaking at normal volume would have felt like dropping a pebble into a still pool.

He swallowed and shut the door behind him. "Almost." He walked over to stand in front of me, and I straightened, setting the phone behind me. He tucked the loose wisps behind my ear, and heat scorched the path his finger took as it grazed my cheek. Could he feel that?

A small frown stole across his lips. "This isn't it, exactly." He reached behind me and tugged on the ponytail tie, working it out, careful not to pull too hard. It felt so good that it almost hurt, an ache each time he sifted the dark strands over his fingers.

I felt every one of his extra six inches of height as we stood this close together. I studied him through my eyelashes. Was the exact placement of my hair a variable for him to control in this profile experiment? Or was he feeling the heat that I did, the electricity that his touch generated, an energy so strong it lifted the small hairs at the nape of my neck?

His fingers kept combing my hair out, but it wasn't tangled, and when I let out a shaky breath, he met my eyes. His pupils flared for a millisecond before his stress lines appeared and his fingers moved to his own hair as he stepped away, scrubbing through it the way they did when he was thinking hard. He backed up farther, and his eyes took on the brightness that meant he'd gone into hyperfocus. Just like that, I'd gone from Hannah, the girl whose hair he'd touched like he couldn't stop himself, to a factor in an equation.

But the heat lingered. Because for a few seconds, he'd *seen* me. And it had scared him. And that was powerful.

* * *

"Let's go run."

I stared at Will standing on my doorstep in running clothes again. It was a new chapter of weirdness. After the loaded moment in my apartment the night before, he'd snapped my picture with my phone, disappeared back to his place, and only talked to me about the game for the rest of the night when I showed up a few minutes later.

I'd decided to do my own thing for the day, and I wasn't sure what I thought about having Will standing there, waiting to go run together. I'd sort of wanted to do a couple of extra miles for the stress relief and thinking time. But those intentions evaporated like fog in sunshine when Will smiled. I loved those smiles. I hoarded them. So I smiled back and nodded. "Okay. Give me ten minutes."

And in less than that, I was back at his door in the purple tank and running shorts. "I was thinking I would do some extra mileage today. You cool with that?" I asked.

"How many?"

"Two more."

"Fine. But in order to not die, I'm not going to be able to talk."

It was the best of both worlds falling into my lap: quiet time to think about Will, but Will still there in the flesh. The tan, toned, warm, fiiiiiine flesh. "Let's do it," I said and started a slow jog to the lake path. We passed the next forty-five minutes in silence.

Will and I spent a lot of quiet time together, me working a Sudoku on his sofa while he watched a hockey game, him unsnarling an equation at my table while I cooked up something in the kitchen a few feet away. Those moments existed full and complete, like they didn't need a single word added to them to make them feel right or comfortable. They were perfect as they were, and the run was no different. Even when every single thought I had was about how to get through to him, there was no one I wanted beside me, working hard and gritting it out, besides Will.

When we got back to our building, he bent over with his hands on his knees and took deep breaths.

"That was awesome," I said. "You're getting faster."

"Yeah?" He looked up at me, not quite oxygenated enough to straighten yet, but he managed a small smile.

"Yeah. That was a nine-minute pace. That's not bad over five miles."

"So what would be outstanding?"

"Seven minutes or less would make you competitive in most of the local 5K races."

He groaned and dropped his head further. "I can't do that. Nine wiped me out."

"If I can, you can." I gave his hunched shoulder a gentle squeeze.

He took a couple more breaths, the rhythm settling down. "You're saying you run a seven-minute pace?"

"Kinda."

He looked up again. "You do it faster, don't you?"

I smiled. "Yeah."

"Then why do you let me slow you down?"

"Because it's good for you to speed up. So I don't mind working at that level. I still get a good run in."

"But you can't get better doing that."

"You can," I said, chucking him on the same shoulder. "And that's worth it now and then."

"Not all the time?"

"Definitely not. Sometimes I need to run without anyone holding me back. But I don't mind you being my charity case every once and a while."

He straightened and narrowed his eyes. "That's it. We're going to play racquetball, and we'll see who's doing favors for who."

"Sure."

"You'll go?"

I took a long swig of water. "Bring it on, Will. It's a date."

He flinched and cleared his throat. "Speaking of dates, are you ready to see what Twilight Sparkle turned up for me?"

That was the screen name I'd picked over Will's objections for the profile we'd done together. He said it sounded like a stripper name, but it was the name of my favorite My Little Pony, and I liked that it was a nod to my dark hair.

My stomach clenched for two seconds until I remembered that the responders would all be *guys*. We were seeing what kind of guy his ideal woman would attract, not sorting through women hot for Will. And since Twilight Sparkle was 100 percent me, I was interested in the results too. "Sounds good. Nothing like a social experiment to finish out the day."

"Go shower the stink off of you and come over when you're done."

I gave myself a good sniff. "I smell like hard work and effort. What kind of monster makes fun of that?"

He leaned over and pretended to sniff me, and his face wrinkled up. "You still smell like peaches. How is that fair? I smell like the YMCA locker room."

"Truth." I danced out of the way when he took a swipe at me, bounding up the stairs ahead of him, laughing when he dragged himself up behind me. I was on the landing before he'd reached the fourth step. "I'll come over later. Try not to pass out while I'm gone. You'll just embarrass both of us." I only laughed harder when he answered me with a whimper.

He was on his couch, hair shower wet, two open Gatorades waiting for us on his coffee table when I let myself in a while later, my laptop under my arm. I tried not to be too obvious about breathing in the lingering trace of his shower gel in the air like it was my new drug.

"Why are you always so dressed up lately?" he asked.

I glanced down. "I'm wearing a T-shirt and cutoffs, Will. Maybe that's fancy in Hicksville, but I'm pretty sure around here it still counts as being plain old dressed."

"But it's a fancy T-shirt."

It totally was. It was lacy and flattering, as were my denim shorts, which I'd picked because my legs looked awesome in them, but I wasn't going to admit to that. "You have a weird definition of dressing up."

"But—"

"Oh, hush. Drop it, and let's talk about who wants to date me. I was so busy at work today I didn't even check the e-mail those notifications go to."

"*You* did not get any responses. Twilight Sparkle did."

"Semantics." I cracked open my computer and pulled up my inbox. "Oooh, eight. Eight men want to date me," I sang out.

"You better do a quality check before you get too cocky about it," he said. He scooted over so he could see the screen, and his weight made me slide a couple of inches toward him until we were pressed at the shoulders and knees while he leaned over to tap through the messages. "You are hot." *Tap.* "Hey, beautiful." *Tap.* "I'd love to see more." He yanked the laptop to his own lap. "He wants to see more? Who is this guy? What picture did you put up? Didn't you put up the one I took?"

"Yes, dummy."

"Why would anyone think that's the kind of picture where someone is dying to show him more? He's saying it like you posted a bikini shot." He clicked the link to take us to the profile page, and the turquoise-shirt picture came up. He groaned. "This isn't the picture I took."

"Yeah, it is. This is the only one that was on my phone. What's wrong with it? It's fine. I think it looks good," I said, hating that I could hear the faintest note of hurt in my own voice.

"It's suggestive."

"What? Give me that back." I looked closely, but I couldn't see a hint of cleavage or shoulder or belly or anything. "You're crazy. I don't even own skimpy clothes."

"It's your expression."

I looked at it again. I looked like I had a secret, a really good one. He'd snapped the shot while I'd been soaking in the tiny vibrations that had shivered between us when I'd sensed that for those few short seconds, he hadn't had a single brotherly feeling toward me. He'd clicked the camera, shoved it at me, and hurried out.

"It's my normal smile." It so wasn't. It was a cat-with-the-canary smile. "It's fine. I'm not redoing my makeup to take another picture for your dumb experiment."

"This is your dumb experiment. And you look . . ." Words failed him as he stared at the picture.

"I look like what?"

"Like you . . . never mind. Let's talk about these messages. They're lame." *Tap.* "You are hot." *Tap.* "You are beautiful." *Tap.*

"You already said those."

"No, two more guys said the same thing. Real original. Oh, and here's a third 'You're hot.' Dude. These guys have no game." *Tap.* "I'd love to meet you." He snorted. "Now there's a guy who's magic with words. *Tap.* "I can't wait to take you out to breakfast after—aargh." He closed the laptop.

"Someone typed 'aargh'?"

"You don't need to know how that sentence ended. Good news though. Eight messages, and I know exactly how to approach any women I see online who look interesting. Just don't be these guys," he said, thumping my computer.

"Stop. I keep telling you this is a numbers game. You need a bigger sample size before you can decide how you want to make your approach." And I needed a few days of breathing room before he went on another date. "Let's let my views get up to at least twenty-five so we can look for patterns before you revise your profile and go hunting."

"I'm not trying to bag a deer," he said, leftover irritation sanding his tone.

"But maybe if you're lucky, you'll land yourself a pretty little fawn or a Bambi."

His mouth quirked up in spite of himself. "You're the worst."

"The guy who wants to take me to breakfast doesn't think so."

"That guy's the worst. You're the second worst."

"On that note," I said, reclaiming my laptop and standing, "we've learned everything we're going to until I get more messages."

"Where are you going?"

"Game four isn't until tomorrow. I'm going back to my bat cave for some peace and quiet."

"But you barely got here."

"Yeah. I better get a head start on those twenty yards if I want to get home at a decent time."

"Shut up, Jimmy Fallon. I meant that we should probably strategize some more."

"It's okay," I said. "I think I want a mellow night."

He was quiet for a minute. "That's too bad." His tone was casual. Suspiciously casual. The kind of tone I used to use with Dave to tell him I was going to Sophie's when really we were going to a party.

"Why is that too bad?"

"I was about to make Tetris nachos."

And I was about 90 percent sure he'd decided that on the spot. He was trying to get me to stay. Why? He didn't need me for anything else tonight. My heart rate accelerated. I had to test him. "That sounds really good. But I kind of had my heart set on a *Friends* marathon."

He shrugged. "Just stream it on my TV. It's on Netflix, right?"

I narrowed my eyes at him. "You hate *Friends*. Why are you going to watch four hours of it?"

"I want nachos. I can't make a small batch of nachos. And they don't keep, so I'm not going to make a batch and waste half. So basically if I want nachos, you have to stay."

I tried not to smile. *Will is looking for reasons to keep me around!* I walked back to the sofa and sank down. "Go ahead."

"What?" he asked when I elbowed him in the ribs.

"You better get started on the nachos."

"Right."

I grabbed the remote from his hand and began the search for *Friends*. He sat for another minute until I gave him a pointed look, and then he headed for the kitchen. I was halfway through "The One with the Monkey" when Will walked through to the balcony. I heard the usual grumbling when he tried to wrestle the grill out of the corner and couldn't resist the urge to mess with him again. "Hey," I said, leaning against the open patio door. "I feel really bad. Take it easy on yourself. Don't do nachos. I'm just going to go home."

"What? No. It's fine. The grill's a pain, but I've got it handled. Go watch TV."

I smothered a smile and went back to the sofa. This was pretty fun. I knew I had the Twilight Sparkle experiment to thank for this. If I hadn't talked him into giving it a couple of days to collect data, he'd probably be out on another date tonight. Or at the very least searching HeyThere to find his next one. Instead, he was making me my favorite food in the whole wide world. I could get used to this.

Except I really couldn't, not unless I could think of another reason to keep him out of the dating pool and not distracted by other women soon. How long did I have left on this diversion anyway? I checked my e-mails, hoping no new messages had come in from the dating site. The faster we got to twenty-five, the sooner I had to think of a new distraction.

Two new e-mails were waiting for me. Dang. Was I the only woman in America who was actually bummed when men responded to her profile?

I opened them and laughed out loud. "Hey, Will," I called. "Some guy calling himself Johnny99 got really original and told me I had the body of a hottie. Should I give him a pass for at least rhyming?"

He slammed a cupboard shut. "Dave and I have been telling you for years that guys are idiots and you should stay away. There's your proof."

I opened the next e-mail, ready to laugh again, but it was a handful of sentences instead of a handful of words. *Hi, Twilight Sparkle. That's my youngest niece's favorite Pony, and she's a pretty cool kid, so you must be pretty cool to pick that handle. I don't think I could ever send a note to a Pinkie Pie. Also, I don't really know who Pinkie Pie is. It's the only other name I remember hearing her say. But in my defense, I could pick Twilight Sparkle out of a Pony lineup. Anyway, hello. I'm Jay. And I liked your profile."*

Nicely done, Jay. Pony lineup. Ha. I laughed out loud.

"Another loser? Read it to me," Will called from the kitchen, where he was mixing up a rub for the meat.

"It's nothing. This is my favorite part of the episode. Make the nachos, and stop distracting me, boy."

"You're the one laughing to yourself on the sofa, and I'm the distracting one?"

"Shhh," I said, waving to the TV without looking at him. I didn't glance at the TV either. I was glued to my computer screen. This Jay guy was funny. And his thumbnail picture was cute. I clicked to enlarge it. Not cute. Hot. And he had picked my profile. The real me. And had made the effort to start a conversation. The drive-by "You're hot" messages were the virtual equivalent of yelling at women on the sidewalk while hanging out of your buddy's truck window. But this Jay was trying to make a connection, not a pass. If I was looking for something besides crumbs of Will's attention, it would have thrilled me.

Ah, heck. It made me feel good even with Will standing in the next room. Maybe even *because* he was in the next room. I wanted to shove it at him and say, "Funny, good-looking guys want to take me out." But I didn't want him getting any ideas for himself from Jay's message about how to approach women.

Still, efforts like Jay's should be rewarded. I opened his profile to repay the favor of responding to more than a headshot. His screen name was FenwayJay. He was loyal to all Boston teams. Our love was doomed, then, but I liked that even though he seemed to have been transplanted to Dallas from the East Coast, he wasn't letting any of the outsized Texas personalities that surrounded him cow him into hiding his love for the devil spawn Red Sox. His interests section cracked me up again. "I like long walks on beaches and dancing in the rain, if you do. Ditto cozy fires and warm cocoa. Otherwise, I'm more of a Gatorade and golf kind of guy. I'll watch romantic comedies if it will make you happy. But if I ask you what movie you want to watch and you say you don't care, that I should pick, prepare to spend the next two hours in 3D glasses."

Down to earth. It sounded like a boring quality for someone to have, but it was incredible how rarely I found it. I clicked his message back open and hit reply. "I'm not going to lie. I'm on this site under duress, and I'm not really looking to date right now. But I couldn't let your love for the Red Sox go. Every swear word I learned by the time I was eight was from hearing my dad curse the Rex Sox. Clearly we're not meant to be. Besides the Red Sox and Celtics and Patriots thing—dear heaven, the Patriots thing—there's also the small problem that even if you liked walking in the rain, I wouldn't. Which is too bad, because there's not much I like better than 3D movies." I pressed send and went back to watching as Chandler broke up with Janice again on TV.

"What are you typing in there?" Will called. "You Hemingway all of a sudden? No, he wrote short books. What are you up to, Melville?"

"It was nothing. Answering an e-mail. Make me nachos, house boy."

He answered by tearing off a sheet of aluminum foil and letting it crackle so much I had to turn the TV volume up.

A minute later, another message popped up from Jay. "Anyone who isn't a Patriot is a traitor. Is that even allowed on HeyThere?"

I snorted and typed back. "Nothing against present company, but it's beginning to look like *anything* is allowed on HeyThere."

His reply was instant. "It hurts how true that is."

Suddenly my laptop disappeared, shooting over my head as Will whisked it away. "Give that back!" I said, lunging for it, but he spun out of reach.

"I want to know what's so funny."

"*Friends*, duh."

"Really?" he drawled, inclining his head at the TV screen, which now showed the season-one icon and a prompt for me to press play on the next episode. "You think the Netflix load screen is hilarious?"

He skimmed the open dialogue box and looked up at me, his eyebrows drawn together, his smile fading. "What's this?"

"Nothing. Just a message from one of the guys on the website."

"More than one message. And from you too. Is this the breakfast guy?" His expression darkened.

I stood and faced him, my fists clenched at my side, but I wasn't going to act like his sister. I coached myself, imagining Sophie's scolding voice in my head. "Yeah, it's the breakfast guy, because I don't have the sense of a gnat."

Will's face stayed clouded over as he read the e-mails in more detail. His eyes flew up. "What do you mean you're not looking to date right now? Why'd you go out with that snorefest the other night?"

I didn't have a handy explanation for that beyond the truth. *I'm hung up on you, and there's no point in wasting anyone else's time.* And for an intense few seconds, the urge to say that out loud forced the words to the tip of my tongue, and I could almost taste them. But then bile surged up the back of my throat at the memory of Will laughing off my teenage confession of love, and I walked past him to the bathroom, calling out, "It's a strategy!" before I closed the door and took a minute to splash cold water on my heated cheeks and think of how to back myself out of the corner his snooping had painted me into.

Will was in the same spot when I walked back out. "What strategy?"

"I say I'm not really up for dating because it builds in an emergency exit. So if I let him flirt me into meeting him, he feels like he's extra special because he was able to change my mind. And if I don't, I have a built-in excuse for saying I'm sticking to my no-dating policy, and he can chalk it up to that instead of taking the rejection personally."

Will's mood didn't seem to be improving. "And either way, you come out smelling like roses."

I sniffed a strand of my hair. "You said peaches."

He shook his head. "How did I not realize that you're so . . ."

"Smart?"

"Calculating."

It was too close to the bone, too much of an echo of the doubts I'd had about my strategy for winning Will over. "It's not. It's smart, a way to keep us both safe from an awkward situation."

"This doesn't seem like it would be awkward," he said, scanning the screen again. "Seems like you hit it off great. So are you planning to let him 'flirt you into meeting' him or not?"

His question changed the answer I would have given him three seconds before. Or not so much his question but his tone. His voice was rough, spiky emotion running through it. It wasn't annoyance, which, combined with condescending indulgence, was the way he'd talked to me since I was a kid. It was a tightness I recognized because it mirrored the fierce possessiveness I felt every time I walked into his place to find some girl who wasn't me sitting on his sofa and watching a game.

My chest warmed, and my heart beat harder, louder, bigger. Will was jealous that I was flirting with this Jay guy, because he'd recognized as easily as I did that this Jay guy was cool. And there was a meanness in Will's tone, the same cattiness that I couldn't filter out of my own voice when I felt threatened by his more beautiful dates.

It was sick that I was getting so much satisfaction from watching him stumble through the same ugly emotions I'd dealt with for years, but it was even sicker that I didn't feel an ounce of guilt. It was awesome. I walked around the couch and scooped his laptop up, settling it against my hip. "Give me back my computer, or I'm getting into your HeyThere account and sending a message to Letterbox that you've found a mailbox you want to show her."

He snorted but closed my laptop and dropped it with a soft thud on the couch. "Whatever."

I fought a grin. A grin of victory. He was getting the tiniest taste of the medicine I'd been swallowing for years. He went back to the kitchen, and all I wanted to do was fly down the hall to my place and call Sophie to tell her what had just happened. But it would look junior high–ish because it was a maneuver he'd seen me do at least a hundred times back then. And I kinda wanted to stick around to see what else I could read in his body language and deliciously telling scowls. Those scowls were practically novels to someone with my experience in reading him.

I went back to the bathroom and slid my phone out of my pocket. Even typing fast, it took a few minutes to tell her the condensed version, but I sent off the text and followed it up with, *THE PLAN IS WORKING!!!*

She shot back, *YESSSSSSSSS!!! Pick blue bridesmaid dresses!*

When I walked back into the living room, Will had taken over my spot on the couch, and it was him typing like a madman. Was he checking his own messages? Finding a date for himself? Copying Jay's approach with the pretty women on HeyThere?

I padded up behind him and snatched the computer from his lap like he'd done to me. "What's this?" I drawled in a perfect imitation of him from minutes before. "Jealous that Jay was able to pull your dream girl with a single message?"

"He pulled a made-up profile. It doesn't make him a baller."

His dismissive tone slid right under my skin and itched. "It's not a made-up profile. Twilight Sparkle is pure me. There's not one thing made up in there, not a single word that isn't true. Why is that so freaking hard for you to understand?"

He looked like he was about to argue, and I waited, but ultimately nothing came out of his mouth. There was nothing to say. I was right. "I know it felt like a thought experiment to you, but you described the ideal woman, and there's no doubt that if you stick my face on the facts, somehow you ended up describing me."

The muscle at the corner of his mouth jumped, but I kept my voice quiet and even. "I'm sorry if that weirds you out, but that's your problem. Jay, on the other hand, doesn't seem at all weirded out by it. Get over it." I gave him my best evil grin and set the laptop on the counter, finally taking a good look at what he'd been up to.

"It's only going make you mad," he muttered, heading out to the patio to check on the carne asada. I was glad because that way he couldn't see the way the IM in front of me wiped any smile, evil or otherwise, right off my face. He'd been talking to my brother, jumping into it like those two always did.

WILL: Your sister is losing it, man.

DAVE: What's she up to now?

WILL: She's messaging random dudes online and going on dates with them.

DAVE: How random? Like weird hookup sites?

WILL: No, it's the same dating site as the last one, but I think she's planning on going out with another guy.

DAVE: So don't let her.

WILL: Have you met your sister?

DAVE: Just explain why it's not smart. She'll listen to you.

WILL: She hasn't yet.

DAVE: She's on a stubborn streak?

WILL: You know how she gets.

DAVE: Yeah. She's not going to listen to you. So you have to make her check in.

As I watched, Dave popped up with *???*, waiting for Will to answer. I felt the touch of Will's gaze and looked up to find him watching me. I wanted to cry. My plan wasn't working at all. This wasn't the conversation of someone coming to his senses about how I was his true love. This was the same old, same old.

But I couldn't cry because Will was looking at me, and if I cried, he'd know. He'd know everything. And while right this second I didn't know how to process the news that my relationship with Will was exactly what it had always been, I did know I couldn't let him know how much it hurt that I was only the girl next door. Or three doors down the hall.

Chapter 12 ♥

I HAD YEARS OF FAKING it, and even though it hurt like fire to shoot him a careless grin, I did. "I'm not your sister. And even as Dave's sister, he's still not the boss of me. Why do you think he's telling you what to tell me instead of doing it himself? I don't listen to him either, because I'm a grown woman, and you guys are clueless." I closed his laptop and carried it back to him on the couch. "Resign yourself to the fact that I'm going to do what I'm going to do." I held his laptop out to him and picked mine up instead.

He frowned at me. "Okay, but I'm sitting right here and watching over your shoulder to make sure you don't give this guy the wrong idea."

"Because you didn't hear a *word I just said*? Does it help when I yell it? You'll mind your own business, or I'm leaving. And the problem with that is you can't eat all those nachos by yourself, and you're going to waste them."

"You're holding me hostage via nacho."

"Of course not. I'm blackmailing you."

The oven timer beeped to announce the nachos were done.

"Be a shame to waste those," I said, icy and threatening.

"You are cold."

"Thirty more seconds and you exit the prime cheese melt window and tip over to burnt."

He shot off the couch for the kitchen. "I shouldn't share these after that."

"I'm not even scared of you. No one loves those nachos more than I do, and you live for my nacho praise."

"And yet you would walk away from them because you can't stand a little caring concern."

"I can't stand nosiness, and, yeah, I hate it more than I love nachos." What I really hated was being here and trying to keep up the jokes when my heart was barely holding together, disappointment wrapping a tight band around my chest and making it hard for it to beat, much less for me to breathe through the hurt. I'd thought we were getting somewhere. I'd thought I'd felt a change in the way he looked at me, a difference in the energy between us. I thought he'd felt the same tiny electric shocks I did when he touched me.

I choked back a bitter laugh. There was no new paradigm. He was taking my dating more seriously, but he was only thinking about how to put more limits on me, not looking at me in a new way and fumbling through what that meant to him.

"Fine. I'll drop it." He muttered, "For now," under his breath, but I pretended not to hear it and sat back down to my laptop. Jay's message waited for me, and it was the only reason I didn't let the tight dam of tears behind my eyes break and release all the frustration to pour out.

Technically, Jay was better looking than Will. He was the kind of guy Will wouldn't think in a million years that I could date. And I hadn't even gone looking for Jay. He'd come looking for me.

Well, time for another newsflash for Will. He wasn't the only hot commodity on the second floor of building H.

I typed a message to Jay, picking up our conversation. "I've come to the conclusion that I'm the only normal human on this website."

He typed back immediately. "Not possible. That's me."

"One of us is going to have to prove it."

"Can I IM you? This is serious. We've got a problem to solve, and I think the severity requires instant messages."

It made me smile, and I needed to smile. I sent Jay my info, and he pinged me within seconds.

JAY: How are we going to settle this? Feats of strength?

ME: Chili cook off?

JAY: Bake sale! Highest profit wins.

ME: Sack race?

JAY: Scrabble?

ME: Arm wrestling.

JAY: All of the above. Which is going to take a while. We should take these one at a time. Let's start with a bake sale. But instead of a bake sale, maybe we could meet at a bakery. And then buy stuff there. Then try it. Then give them money for it. Then maybe sit around and talk.

ME: Sir, did you just ask me out?

JAY: Yeah. I don't see how else we're going to prove that I'm the only normal one on this dating site.

ME: But I told you I'm not really up for dating right now . . . and yet, I'm considering this. Are you . . . are you a wizard?

JAY: I really want to make a corny joke about casting a spell on you, but I think it undermines my "normal" argument. Which I'm trying to prove by winning the "come out with me some time" argument. (How am I doing?)

"*Hannah*!"

I jumped at Will's shout. "What? What's wrong?" I asked, scrambling up from the couch.

"I asked you three times what's so funny, and you haven't heard me once."

I pressed my hand to my pounding heart and glared at him. "I'm not talking to you again until I get my nachos." I plopped down in my seat to rescue Jay before he felt like I'd left him hanging.

ME: You're effective.

JAY: It was the promise of baked goods, right?

ME: Yes. So I guess that means we need to find a place with chocolate chip cookies as big as my head so I can work my way through one while you argue for your normalcy.

JAY: Right. But you're not going to make your case?

ME: No. I exude normalcy. It's interesting that you feel like you have to convince me.

JAY: Oh man. I walked into that.

ME: Yep.

JAY: This is going to be fun. Let me look up "chocolate chip cookies as big as my head," and then we can pick a place. Hang on.

Take that, Will. It felt so good to have a guy flirt with me after the utter wipeout of realizing it would never cross Will's mind to do it that I whooped and threw my hands up in victory as Will set the nachos down on the coffee table.

"Now what?" he asked.

"I've got Tetris nachos and a date with a hot guy. I'm so stoked I'm debating getting up to do a happy dance."

He grimaced. "What can I pay you not to do that?"

"Ha. These are enough," I said, scooping up a tortilla chip holding more meat and cheese than seemed structurally possible. I took a bite and moaned. "This might be all I ever need for perfect happiness." For a few seconds, as I savored the delicious mouthful, it occurred to me that Will's nachos were almost an acceptable consolation prize if I couldn't have Will himself.

He flashed a grin at me, and that was all it took to remind me how much more I loved him than the chips. But I'd lived with my lovesickness for him too long to let it get in the way of my appetite. My sleep, my mood, my daydreams, sure. But not my eating.

He disappeared down his hallway when I turned up the volume on *Friends*, but he was back moments later with the block of cocobolo I'd bought him for his birthday months ago, a beautiful piece of striped wood from Central America. I loved his carvings, and I'd been dying to see what he would do with the wood, but he hadn't touched it until now.

He pulled a *Wired* magazine from under the coffee table and leaned over it, shaving off thin curls of the block, his face relaxed. Later in the whittling project, he'd have more furrows in his forehead as he concentrated on the technical execution, but this part, roughing out the shape, was mindless for him. I think it did for him what running did for me.

Sometimes I liked to know what he planned to make. Sometimes I liked to be surprised, watching the twists each piece took. Since most of his work was abstract, no matter what words he used to describe it, my imagination still never matched his final result.

I turned back to *Friends* and enjoyed it for all of ten minutes before he set down the wood and picked up his laptop, his forehead scrunched and fingers flying.

"What are you doing?" I asked when the mouse clicking and the keys clacking went on for about five nonstop minutes.

"I had an idea when I was working on the wood. I don't need a bigger sample size from the Fake Girl experiment."

"Don't call her that anymore. She's me."

"Whatever. You know what I mean."

Yeah. *I just wish* you *knew what* I *meant.*

"I'm going to set up profiles on different sites that are me, no 'curating' the details. None of this is going to work if I don't describe myself accurately and they end up all surprised and appalled by the fact that I'm a sports nut or whatever."

My stomach clenched at the idea of him putting his true self out there, in all its irresistibleness. Given all the other great things about him, not one girl was going to have a problem with his sports-watching. "I don't think that's a good idea," I said. Because it wasn't, for me. "Women are tired of guys who do nothing but play video games or watch football. And baseball is worse because there are more games."

He looked at me like I was touched in the head. "Of course I'm going to put down other stuff I'm into."

"But even mixed in with other things, putting that stuff down is going to be like a red flag if it's showing up in your main interests at all. Let me help you with a new profile."

"Nope. Your help got me a fistful of lame dates. I'm going from nothing"—he held up a closed fist to indicate zero—"to this." And he did a victory fist pump.

"But I really—"

"Nope."

"But you should—"

"Nope."

"I think that—"

He shoved another loaded chip into my mouth. "Quiet. Watch *Friends*. Although I don't know how you can stand it. That Ross guy is the only tolerable character on the show."

"He's the worst. He's so boring."

"Really? The guy with the real job in the sciences is boring?"

"Ugh. The way . . . he talks . . . is so . . ." I said, in an imitation of Ross Gellar's speech patterns.

"Whatever. He's funny too. And he's good to Rachel. How come she finds him so sexy if he's such a loser?"

My eyebrow rose. "You know an awful lot about this show for someone who can't figure out why I'd be watching it."

"Shut up," he said, his fingers busy at his keyboard again.

"You really should let me help—"

"*No.* Watch TV." And he shoved another chip in my mouth, ending the argument.

I ate it. But as I listened to him work on his laptop, it occurred to me that I felt totally miserable for someone who was eating her favorite food and watching her favorite show in the entire world.

* * *

I used my copy of his key to let myself into his apartment early Tuesday morning.

"Will!" I hollered. His bedroom door opened, and he padded out in gray pinstripe slacks, but barefoot and shirtless as he ran a towel over his wet hair.

The view was better than Tetris nachos.

"What are you doing here?" he asked, his voice muffled under the towel.

"I need your opinion on an outfit," I said.

He popped his head out. "You what?"

"I'm meeting Jay today at lunch, and I can't figure out what to wear."

He gave me a long stare, his glance running from my curled hair, over the pink dress I'd picked, down to my tan wedges. "You look nice. But isn't this what Sophie is for?"

"She picked a different outfit for me last night, but I changed my mind about it this morning. She went for fun, which is good for a date, but I need something that would be appropriate for the office too. And also not boring for a date. So what do you think?" I did a slow turn, holding my breath until I could see his face again. It was my favorite dress, and not even kind of appropriate for the office. It covered everything that needed to be covered for work, but the dress screamed party, not project manager.

"I know it's hard, but try looking at me like I'm a real girl. Imagine if you were meeting me for the first time, what would you think?" And *that*, of course, was the whole sneaky point of coming over before he left for work this morning. Another desperate plan to get him to think about me the way Jay might.

"I don't think any ladies would be wearing something like that in my office."

"I'll figure out how to make it work for the office. A jacket, maybe. But what do you think for a lunch date? Does it say I'm fun?" *And that I have amazing legs that I earned the hard way? And a great summer tan that's still sticking around?*

"It says . . ." He cleared his throat. "Sure. It says fun."

"So if you saw me in a bakery cafe in the business district with a bunch of people, men and women in suits, I'd stand out in a good way? I'd look like someone you'd want to get to know?"

He paused for a long moment, and his eyes darkened before he glanced away and toweled his hair some more. "I'd say Jay will think that, yes."

That was as good as it was going to get, but it was pretty good. There was maybe some progress. "I should go," I said. "I'm heading in early so I can take a longer lunch in case it goes well. Wish me luck."

"Text me when you're done so I know not to send out a SWAT team or something."

"Sure." I let myself out and grinned all the way to my door.

"Rome wasn't built in a day," Sophie had reminded me the night before when I called to tell her that my plan wasn't working after all. "You definitely have his attention. Now you need to change the lens he's looking through. Eventually he won't be able to go back to seeing you as a sister or even a friend."

And maybe it was better for it to happen gradually. It might be sensory overload to have the full force of Will's attention all at once. As I slipped back into my apartment to change into what I was really going to wear, something cute but more subdued and light-years more office-appropriate, a shiver danced down my back. Yeah, intense Will was nothing to mess with. The slow build was definitely the smart play.

Chapter 13 ♥

"How was lunch?" Sophie asked.

"Kinda great," I said. "He's pretty fun."

"So are you going out again?"

"I don't know. Doesn't seem fair."

"Because of Will?"

"I think I just heard you roll your eyes at me."

"You deserved it. Kinda great lunch with a fun guy and you're going to pass on this one too?"

"Yeah. I'm not really available. Not emotionally, anyway."

"But you are in every other way. You're available to have fun. So you should. How is it unfair for you to have fun with this guy if he's also having fun?"

"I don't know. Everything is really confusing right now. At least ten times a day I feel bad for manipulating Will with all this stupid scheming. I'm not sure I need another guilt trip for Jay, leading him on when I know it can't go anywhere."

"So don't. Tell him up front that you're only looking for something casual. As for manipulating Will, I guess you're going to have to sort through that on your own, but I stand by my previous argument. You can't make him do anything he ultimately doesn't want to do."

"Yeah, but showing up in an outfit and pretending I'm going to wear it out to get his attention is different than just being around and doing our thing. It's . . . dishonest, maybe? And very junior high now that I'm hearing myself say it out loud."

"So commit to being real. And if you feel like it's scrambling your brains, take some distance. Give yourself space from him for a couple of days and see if you're breathing easier, if it gives you any clarity."

"Part of me wants to do that. And part of me is worried about this clock he's put himself on to get married. It's like having the *Jeopardy!* theme song on a constant loop in my head, all urgent and naggy."

"You think a couple of days will make that much of a difference? Anyway, not that you should see this as a manipulation thing, but maybe it's good to give him a couple of days to miss you. You're always together lately. Go out with Jay, do a craft by yourself, rent some movies, do anything but hang out with Will and see if it gives you perspective, a chance to rethink your approach, make sure it's what you want to do if you keep questioning it so much."

"Jay did ask me about dinner tomorrow night."

"Check you out! If he's asking you out for the next night and not even trying to play it cool, then he must feel like lunch went spectacularly well. Wait. He's not clingy, is he?"

"No. Just up front. Which is more than I can say about myself lately."

"You know I'm on record in support of you laying it all out for Will. But you're not going to do that, are you?"

"I can't. And you're right. I need a couple of days to rethink all this, see how it feels."

"Do you also need a date with Jay?"

"Yeah." She whooped, and I shut her down with a stern warning. "I'm making it very clear to him that it's a strictly fun thing."

"Which is exactly what you need. And I need to grade some midterm exams before I drown in them. If you ever don't hear from me for more than two days, I've been suffocated under a pile of tests."

"Speaking of that. You're a workaholic. You need to breathe. Did Jared call?"

A long silence met me.

"Sophie? That means yes and you don't want to talk about it."

"You're right."

"Really? Dang. He seemed like such a good fit for you."

More silence.

"Uh-huh. What else aren't you telling me?"

She cleared her throat but didn't say anything.

"Sophie! You talked, and it was really good! And you don't want to tell me because I'll nag you even more about laying off of work! Yay!"

"If you know everything I'm going to say, why am I even on this phone call?"

But it wasn't enough to deter me because I could hear her trying not to laugh. "Details! Now."

"I don't have a lot. We talked for an hour. I haven't had a long phone conversation with a guy in forever. It's always texts about when or where we're meeting. And it was pretty fun."

"So when are you going out?"

"I don't know! Neither of has time this week, but I have a feeling we'll talk again soon."

"I want a turquoise bridesmaid dress."

"Shut up," she said, and we hung up laughing.

I dithered for a few more minutes, but finally I sent Jay a message. "Dinner tomorrow sounds good."

When Will texted me to come over and watch game six of the World Series with him the next night, I wasn't sure if I was sorry or glad that I couldn't do it. But a big part of me was glad I didn't need to sit beside him for three hours acutely tuned into every breath he took, like that creepy old '80s song. Being away from him let *me* breathe more freely.

And I was even less sorry once Jay and I sat down to dinner. It was a fun night. He was easy to hang out with. He'd picked a steakhouse for dinner, and the TVs in the corners showed the game, although the sound was off. He entertained me by providing the commentary, only it had nothing to do with the actual game. He narrated made-up thoughts the players might be having about whether they were developing some serious hat hair and if they should have worn their man-Spanx under their uniforms.

It helped that he was cuter than I'd remembered. His hair was a warm dark blond and long enough to curl but not to raise eyebrows in a professional setting. The tips of his bangs brushed the top of his eyebrows, which framed dark-brown eyes. They reflected his intelligence and crinkled when he smiled. They crinkled a lot, and when his mouth got into the act, his teeth were white and almost straight except for a slightly crooked canine, which made his smile mischievous.

At the end of the night, I was kinda sad our date was ending. But not sad enough to invite him over. Definitely sad enough to say yes to another date so I wouldn't have to be sad anymore about dinner ending.

Wednesday night I told Will when he called that I couldn't hang out with him because I was hanging out with Sophie. He sounded miffed, but that was probably because he'd wanted me to keep him company while he did laundry, something we did together often. I went over and helped her with her grading, organizing and alphabetizing the huge stacks so she could put them into her computer faster, all the while doing a dramatic reenactment of my date with Jay.

"He sounds hilarious," she said. "Can he be my future husband too when you're done with him?"

"Definitely."

"I really like this system," she mused, pulling another stack of papers toward her.

"Alphabetizing? It's revolutionary."

"Ha. No, I meant the thing where you go out with dudes first, and then I can decide which ones I want to take a crack at. It's a totally efficient filtering process."

I snorted. "For you!"

"Right. That's what matters here, isn't it?"

I smacked her and kept on alphabetizing.

But Thursday when Will texted, I didn't have it in me to reply, mainly because a migraine had climbed into my skull and started excavating it, concentrating especially hard on hollowing out the area behind my right eye. The spots had appeared when I was halfway home from work, and the nausea had hit as I'd unlocked the door. I'd made it to my guest bathroom and thrown up twice, then crawled out into the dim hallway and lain there, my phone chiming every five minutes in the pocket of the jacket I couldn't even move to take off. I didn't want to pick my head up again or I'd puke.

That was the only thing that kept me from banging my hard head against the floor over and over again. *Stupid, stupid, stupid.* I only got migraines when I was dehydrated. I always remembered to drink plenty of fluids when I was running, but the past two days had been really busy with nonrunning stuff, and sometimes it didn't occur to me that I still had to hydrate.

Normally it wouldn't be a big deal because Will always made me drink a whole bottle of blue stuff when I was at his place for this very reason. And now, I wanted to die because I hadn't remembered to flip the faucet on and save myself from this misery.

My phone chimed again. Third text from Will. That meant it had been fifteen minutes from the first one. He did it sometimes to be funny until I answered him, but there was no way I was shifting to get the phone and igniting my brain with lightning. A few minutes later I heard him outside my apartment.

"Hannah? Why is your door open? Hannah, are you okay?" he said, already inside. "Hannah?" His voice was urgent, and I could hear him moving from the living room. "Hannah!" he yelled when he saw me, and I winced in pain at the volume. He dropped down beside me, his hands moving over me, shaky but determined, his voice tense and low. "Talk to me. What's wrong?"

I swallowed. "Migraine," I whispered, and a tear slipped out, even though my eyes were closed.

He bit back a curse and immediately took his hands off me, knowing that jostling me would make it worse. "It's okay, Hanny. I've got you. Just tell me why you're on the floor. Did you fall? Did you bump your head?"

"Nausea," I whispered.

"Okay," he said, his voice calmer. "Hang in there. I'll fix this."

He rose and stepped over me into the bathroom, rummaging through my medicine cabinet until he turned up an over-the-counter migraine medicine. "I'm going to go get one of my Gatorade bottles with a sport cap so you can get some water to wash these down without sitting up. I'll be right back." I heard him flipping the blinds in the living room to keep any light from leaking into the hall. Then I heard his retreating footsteps, and not even two minutes later, he was back at my side.

"Drink this," he said.

I couldn't. I couldn't even tell him no. A tiny protest came out of my throat, and even that hurt, a new cymbal crash behind my eye.

"Hanny, sweetheart, I know this hurts, and I know the pain sucks, but we have to make this go away. You need water and some painkillers. Just drink enough to swallow these pills, and when they kick in enough that you can pick your head up without vomiting, we'll get the rest of the water down." Cool plastic touched my lips, and his voice stayed low and soft, coaxing. "Come on, sweet girl. Just sip. Please."

I took a few swallows.

"Good. Now we'll do a couple of pills." He held one up to my lips, and I tightened it, instinctively rejecting the chalky taste I hated. He stroked his thumb softly at the corner of my mouth, like I was a baby he was tickling into a smile. "I know this is hard. But you have to. You need to feel better. Come on. It'll be down before you know it."

I opened up, and he popped the pill in, following it with the water bottle, and when that stayed down, he coaxed me into doing it again. His voice was so soft beneath the static noise migraines always made inside my head, but I swam through the sound to focus on his words, making the medicine go down and willing it to stay there.

When he'd convinced me to take the second pill, he settled back against the wall, his legs stretched in front of him somewhere past my head. I closed my eyes. "You can go," I said, knowing he wouldn't. He'd been through this with me a few times before, and I could never make him leave. And I never wanted him to. But there was something about hearing him say he wasn't going anywhere that helped even before the medicine kicked in.

"I'll stay here. I've got stuff to check on my phone. Let me know when the nausea is better."

It cost too much to say anything. I drifted, trying to separate myself from the noise and the grinding pain. When I woke, I had no idea how much time had passed, but the hall was completely dark, not even the weak light from the living room windows coming in. It had been close to sunset already when I got home, so it could have been one hour or six that I'd been lying there, but I could sense Will in the exact same spot, a warm, solid presence next to me. The second I shifted to push myself up, he was on his knees, his hands around my shoulders to steady me.

"Hey, champ," he said in that same quiet voice. "You doing all right?"

"Better," I croaked. "Not good."

"You better enough to go change, maybe?"

I nodded and winced. The meds muted the pain, but I could always feel it lying under the veneer of the magic the pills tried to do, waiting to surge back if I let it, if I moved my head the wrong way or even coughed.

"Okay. Get some water down. Drink as much as you can, and then go find some pajamas? Anything but that jacket. I've been sitting here for an hour trying to figure out if I could cut you out of it like the EMTs do so you'd be more comfortable."

I tried to smile. I think I flickered, but he seemed to understand. When I sat up enough to rest my back against the wall, he handed me the water bottle and watched until I'd gotten half of it down. "How's your stomach?"

"Okay." The water made my voice easier to use. "I think I can get up, get changed."

He climbed to his feet and leaned down to offer me his hands. I dropped my head back against the wall and eyed them before shutting him out with my eyelids again. No. Never mind. Too much energy. He leaned over, picked up my hand, and set it on his bicep, wrapping his hand around my upper arm and holding his other hand out for me to repeat the process. "Let me do the work, Hanny." He braced himself and straightened, letting me counterbalance as he helped me to my feet, not letting go until I stood. When I had it, he let go. "I'd help you change but, uh, that's maybe . . ."

I waved him off, too numb to be entertained by his embarrassment. "I got it. If I'm not out in ten minutes, I probably died, and it's definitely better that way."

"Don't even joke," he said, his voice tight. "It was scary to find you in the hall like that."

I squeezed his arm as an apology and shuffled the few feet left to my bedroom. It took five times longer than it should have, but I managed to shed my work suit on the floor and climb into the sweats and T-shirt sitting on the top of my laundry basket. I rested on the side of the bed for a minute, a slight wave of nausea creeping back up on me.

Will knocked on the door. "You okay?"

I pushed myself up, stupidly proud that I could pull that off. "I'll survive," I said, opening the door. He slid his hand under my elbow, giving me a gentle tug to pull me out.

"Come to the living room. I texted Dave, and he said I have to make sure you stay on top of your water intake, that you'll just go to sleep if I leave. You need to rest on the sofa until you're at least kind of hydrated again."

I didn't bother arguing. He was right. My head was clearing enough to remind me that the meds would be pointless if I didn't get down all the water I needed. He helped me out to the couch and eased me into my favorite corner before tucking another water bottle into my hand. "Drink this. And while you get that down, I'm going to figure out what you can eat."

"I don't want food."

"You threw up. You need food."

"Please don't."

He crouched in front of me and smoothed my hair out of my face, tucking a strand away that had been sticking to my cheek. "Please do. Please."

I sighed a giving-in sigh, and he breathed out a matching sigh of relief when I lifted the bottle to drink. He was in the kitchen within seconds, opening the fridge and digging through it. A minute later, he padded back over, and I realized he'd shucked his shoes. I smiled my first smile in hours. "You hate shoes."

He glanced down at his bare feet. "Yeah. I found a carton of strawberries. Will you eat some mixed into steel-cut oats? I think that will be okay for your stomach, right?"

I nodded and regretted it as a bolt of pain lanced through my eye again. "I'll eat it," I said, resting my head against the couch arm before I was stupid enough to rattle my brain again.

He slid his hand beneath my head, and as gently as he might have scooped up a week-old kitten, he lifted my head until it was straight again. "You can't do that until you drink all of your water."

"So mean."

He leaned down and pressed a kiss to my hairline. That burned too, but it was like fire, not the electrical pain that had dropped me to the floor hours before. "Sorry. Gotta be cruel to be kind. Drink. Then rest."

I drank, wondering if it would cool the tingling spot where his lips had touched me. It didn't. I didn't want it to. I closed my eyes and took sips while he puttered in the kitchen. I could tell he was moving slowly and trying hard not to make more noise.

I concentrated on my forehead tingle, so glad to feel something good there instead of the dark presence of the migraine.

When Will put a bowl of warm oats in my lap, he peeled the water bottle out of my fingers and tucked them around a spoon. "Eat. I'd feed you, but I think that would create new problems."

He sat on the other side of the sofa while I scooped up a spoonful of cereal. It was good. I ate half of it, 100 percent more than I thought I would, and set it aside. "Thanks for taking care of me."

"You're welcome."

"What time is it, anyway?"

"Eight thirty."

"You've been here three hours."

He shrugged. "No big deal. I didn't have anything to do."

"You can go. I'll be okay now. Isn't there a game on?"

"I recorded it. I'll watch it later."

"You can't skip game seven of the World Series for me." It was unheard of. Will would miss his own funeral and reanimate to come back to life if it meant watching the Rangers in a game seven for the championship.

"I didn't skip it. I'll watch it later."

Guilt twisted up my insides. "But you could have, I don't know, at least turned the game on over here."

"Didn't want the noise to bother you."

"You could have watched it with the volume off."

Will gave me a long stare, then reached over for my bowl, moving slowly but deliberately to set it on my coffee table. He scooted down the sofa, careful not to jostle me. He slid his arm around my shoulders, and again, handling me like a tiny kitten, he nestled my head down next to his neck. "You did good, and you get to rest again."

I settled against him. I was too tired to resist even if I'd wanted to. But no part of me wanted to.

Once he felt my body relax, he brushed his hand over my hair. "You scared me to death, Hanny. I wasn't moving until I knew you were okay. I'm glad you feel better, but I can tell you're still not right. So humor me and let me stay here until you are so I don't have to stress at my place."

I sighed and felt bad when my breath raised goose bumps on his skin beneath my cheek. He couldn't be comfortable, but I was too weak to give him up, and that wasn't the kind of weakness that hot oats or rest would cure. But the migraine shadow had eroded any chance I had of showing some willpower. "Okay. But at least turn on the game here. If you don't mind watching with the sound off, you can watch the second half live."

"You sure?"

"I'm sure," I murmured, already drifting again, fading into the scent that was Will, that unbottleable himness that I couldn't get enough of.

He leaned forward to get the remote, and when he had the game on, he carefully maneuvered me down until my head rested on a couch pillow in his lap, and he slid his fingers into my hair, gripping handfuls of it and pulling with a steady pressure before he let go. "Let me know if this hurts," he said, his voice low. "I read up while you were sleeping, and this is supposed to stimulate blood flow if you alternate it with massaging wherever the headache is. I'll stop when it bothers you, so say when."

Any other day and his touch would have made my skin come alive, sending currents along every nerve in my whole body, connecting it all to his fingertips on my scalp. But this time, it released some other magical substance, the mellow cousin of the endorphins he'd sent rioting through me so many times before, and I dissolved even further, no longer braced against the pain that lurked. It receded with every pull and release of my hair in Will's hands.

Before long, I could crack my eyes open to watch the game. It was the sixth inning, and we were down by one, but our best hitter was at bat. This was where Will would tense and stare at the TV like it was the only visible thing in the whole universe, yelling if the swings weren't connecting the way he thought they should, yelling louder if he didn't like the umpire's calls. But even when the Rangers' hitter sent the ball soaring over the far stadium wall, Will didn't say a word. He didn't even move, just kept combing his fingers through my hair, not changing his rhythm even as one of the Rangers on base rounded home followed almost immediately by the hitter.

"Will?"

"Mmmm?"

"We scored two runs."

"You should keep your eyes closed."

"You should celebrate."

He let go of my scalp with one hand, the single greatest sacrifice I'd ever made in my life, and pumped his fist. "Yes!" he said, barely more than a whisper.

"That's it?" I mumbled, too tired to goad him harder. "You can do your home-run dance if you want to. I'm fine. I know it doesn't feel real unless you do the dance."

"I'm fine right here," he said, his hands back to working their magic. "Now stop talking. You're ruining the game."

I could only smile. In the midst of a brutal migraine, I was somehow having the best night of my life, lying on a sofa, watching the TV with no sound, and being taken care of by Will.

"You got a few texts while you were out. I slid your phone out of your pocket so it wouldn't wake you up."

I blinked in acknowledgment, too afraid to nod, words feeling like too much energy.

"One of the texts was Jay. He was wondering where you are."

I winced. "We were supposed to watch the game together tonight. I better tell him what's up."

"Don't worry about it. I texted him back and said you were too sick for it."

Something about that was off somehow, and the sense of a problem that needed solving niggled at me, but it couldn't work its way through the fog in my brain, so I let it go. It would come to me later.

* * *

Normally when I woke up the day after a migraine, moving through the morning felt like picking my way through spiderwebs, filaments of the headache sticking to me, weird aftereffects like sound halos and the hint of something bad each time I turned my head. But Friday wasn't like that.

The Rangers had won the World Series. Will had excused himself for a minute the night before, and I'd heard his muffled whoops of joy through my bathroom door before he'd come out again and scooped me up from the couch to carry me down the hallway and tuck me into my bed with stern orders to stay there. He'd made sure my cell phone was beside me but on silent so no texts would bother me, but he made me promise to call him if I needed anything. Then he let himself out, and I'd fallen into the deep dreamless sleep that migraines and pain pills always sent me into.

But there was no migraine hangover this morning. Only pure, crystalline joy. He'd texted to check on me as soon as I'd turned the volume up on my phone. I promised him I was fine. More than fine. I was fantastic, even. Floating, possibly.

Even the exchange I found in my texts between him and Jay didn't throw me. Jay had texted wondering where I was.

WILL: She can't come out tonight

JAY: Who is this?

WILL: I'm her friend. She's not feeling good. She'll text you later.

JAY: Is she okay?

WILL: If she were okay, she'd be going out.

Since Will was answering from my phone, Jay would have no idea if it was a girl or guy texting him back, which was good. Except that he probably thought it was one of my friends trying to blow him off for me. Especially since Will had been terse to the point of rude. Not awesome. I'd have to straighten it out with Jay later, once I'd gotten to work and settled into my routine.

But I wasn't the least bit irritated with Will about it. Because he'd cared. So much. And taken good care of me, to boot. And I couldn't wait to poke my head in and tell him so. He was on his couch with a bowl of cereal.

"Hey," I said, smiling. A nervous energy jittered through me. We'd moved to different territory last night, but I only knew the landscape we had left, not the one we'd entered.

"Hey." His answering smile was as soft as his hands had been on my head the night before, not his usual distracted smile when I came by. "How are you feeling?"

"Much better than usual after a migraine. You're a good nurse."

"I'm glad. Scare me like that again and you're grounded forever."

I didn't love the big-brotherly joke, but it's not like habits were going to break overnight. "I have to go to work, but I wanted to prove that I'm healthy again. Bye."

"Wait. I'm glad you stopped by. I need you to help me pick out a shirt."

"For what?"

"I have a date from one of the profiles I set up. She definitely seems like the coolest one so far. We were texting last night, and she made me laugh a couple of times. Out loud. I'm kinda stoked, but I don't know what to wear."

Everything inside me iced over like Elsa had blown through. I forced a smile and glanced at my watch. "Sorry, I have to leave now, or I'll be late. I'm sure you'll pick something fine. Catch you later," I said, closing the door on his protest.

When I got in my car, I gripped the steering wheel hard enough to turn my knuckles white.

Unbelievable. *Un-freaking-believable.*

Nothing had changed at all. How many times could I do this—give myself whiplash with my interpretations of his moods and send myself up and down on a roller coaster that was apparently entirely of my own making?

I'd been planning to text Jay an apology for the short texts from the night before then let him down gently about going on another date. I was so sure Will and I were taking some kind of next step. I'd been daydreaming from the second I'd woken up about what it was going to be like when we met up after work, how possibly awkward but awesome it would feel for us to figure out a new way to be around each other.

Such. An. Idiot.

Him.

Even more so, me.

I was willing to drop a handsome, funny, successful guy like Jay—an *interested* guy, one who wanted to be with me—because Will was nice to me when I had a headache.

A new headache, a stress one this time, started in my temples, and I dropped my head between my clenched hands on the steering wheel. Sophie had been right from the very first conversation: the only way to get Will to look at me differently was to let him know how I felt.

But even if I was willing to do that, the creeping anxiety I'd brushed away since I'd started this experiment billowed into full-blown fear. It would change everything for me to speak up. But not in the way I wanted. If Will was going to fall in love with me, it would have happened by now.

I sat up and called the department director to let him know I'd be taking my first sick day in almost two years. Then I put the car in gear and drove to the grocery store for supplies and to give Will a chance to leave for work before I went back home to figure out how to reconstruct my life. Again.

* * *

It took the first three miles of my run to stop crying. I spent another five being angry. I ran the last four miles home with my mind blank. Numb, even. Just the *slap, slap, slap* of my feet on the asphalt or concrete in front of me, counting the lines in the sidewalk or rearranging the letters of street signs I passed into stupid anagrams. Larkspur Avenue became purse rave and naval eke and a dozen other dumb unscrambles. But by the time I got back to my apartment, my head was clear.

I couldn't do this. I couldn't stand in Will's way if he was ready to be married. I had failed over three weeks of my best efforts to make him see me as his one true love. And I'd done him very wrong in trying to manipulate him into it. I'd only succeeded in failing utterly as his friend by keeping him off track from what he wanted.

Will wasn't my meant-to-be. It was hard to imagine that, but I had to accept it. I had to because there was no changing it. And I had no idea how I'd get myself to being okay with that, but for both of our sanity, I had to find a way to let it go.

So I pulled out the notebook, fresh pens, and two pounds of fruit and whole grain treats I'd picked up from the store—the latter to keep me from drowning myself in the fat/sugar/oil trifecta that had put so much weight on me after my parents died—and I went to work. On myself. On seeing things differently.

I wrote. And I wrote. And I wrote.

Will texted me a few times. I ignored him, finally turning the phone off after the third one. I wrote more, letting every hope and dream and wish come out. It was journaling the way my grief counselor had tried to make me do as a teenager. And it poured out. And over the next three hours, I saw the words shape themselves into a tidal wave of truth that I'd refused to look at, and it crashed down around me. Through the early afternoon, I was awash in a wave of self-recrimination and the evidence of the hundreds of ways I'd been sabotaging my own non-Will relationships for years, even when I'd thought I'd been done dreaming about him.

I took a break for a short nap, residual exhaustion from the migraine that I hadn't expected. And when I got up from that, my insides were tear soaked and empty, but I looked at the journal through clear eyes, a more honest vision than I'd ever used for looking at my life. And I started a new section, one where I wrote about what I would let into my life by accepting Will's true role in it, not the one I'd daydreamed about for years.

And I wasn't happy about any of it, not in the way that daydreams about my future with Will had made me happy, but I felt good about the choices I was making, especially the ones I was making to leave Will free to go the way he wanted to.

I didn't know what I was looking for now that my goal had changed so utterly. But I made a three-page list of all the ways in which I could give myself opportunities to figure it out.

And then I opened a second fresh, clean notebook and made a new plan for how to disentangle my life from Will's so I could breathe as much as I needed to. It would be hard because I'd gone so far out of my way to tangle my life up with his for so long.

By five thirty, every part of me was wrung out. My hand hurt, and the pad on my finger where the pen had rested while I wrote for hours was sore. But I'd done it. I'd pulled a Gwyneth Paltrow and figured out how to consciously uncouple from Will. Except I was the only half of that relationship who'd ever thought we were a couple, albeit in embryo. It didn't matter. I was done. I'd figured it out. And I'd do it. I'd do it because I was his friend, and true friends do hard things for each other.

I'd also do it for me because I'd earned the right to pick a path that would make me happy. Someday. Maybe.

I scooped up the first notebook and took it down to the pool, where I set it in one of the charcoal grills the complex installed for the residents, and I let the notebook full of the hopes and dreams and wishes of a young girl who should have figured it all out much sooner burn.

Chapter 14 ♥

When I walked past Will's door on the way back to my place from the pool, I reminded myself not to poke my head in for a fix of him. That couldn't be a part of the routine anymore.

But I hadn't accounted for him opening it as I passed and pausing for a startled moment like I'd given him a heart attack. "Geez!" he yelped, and I jumped.

"Whoa. Sorry. You know, for walking down the hall where I live."

He shot me a dirty look. "I didn't expect you to be right outside my door."

I waved at my door. "I have to be outside your door several times a day if I want to get to mine. And I do want to," I said. I started down the hall again, but he protested.

"Wait. You gotta help me pick my shirt for tonight."

"I really don't," I said. *Don't get in Will's way anymore* had made the list of how to be in my post-Will reality. *Help Will with dates* had not. "Good luck."

I slipped into my place and collapsed on my couch with a pillow over my face so I could scream into it. How could he have been so clueless for so many years? How had I let myself settle for that? Never again. One more frustrated bellow and I'd get up and do one of the first things on my "Figure Out What Makes Me Happy" list: call Jay. And tell him I was working on a broken heart, but if he was okay possibly being my rebound, I was down for more dinners and adventures and baseball arguments.

But I didn't even have time to let out the second scream before my front door opened.

Ugh. I should have thrown the bolt. I'd been too focused on getting away from Will to think about it.

"What is wrong with you?" he demanded. "Is this a PMS day?"

It enraged me on multiple levels. First, that guys always assumed that girls being angry at them must be a function of hormones and not a legitimate beef. Second, that it was such a sibling thing to say. And third, it was so condescending. Guys could spout their clueless sympathy about that stuff the day they started dealing with it. But fourth, PMS had nothing to do with anything.

"Why would you even say that?" I demanded, shoving myself up from the sofa and pushing my hair out of my eyes so I could glare at him.

His eyebrows quirked at me, then he pointed to the kitchen table and shrugged. "You've obviously been home all day. That wasn't there last night." As evidence went, it was kind of damning if you didn't know the facts. Several empty water bottles, empty nutrition bar wrappers, banana peels, discarded orange rinds, and crumpled bits of notebook paper littered the surface.

But I did know the facts of the day. And it made me crankier with him. "You don't know nearly as much as you think you do," I growled. "If this was a hormone thing, you'd see empty bottles of Coke and Snickers wrappers."

"But something went down," he said. "You all right?"

"No."

"What's wrong?"

What was wrong was that I had to execute the hardest part of my plan. I had to break off a relationship Will hadn't known he was in. I had to find a way to tell him the truth so I could buy the distance I needed from him. If I didn't give him a reason why we couldn't treat each other's apartments as an extension of each other's living space any more, then I would never get the emotional space I was going to need. Desperately. And so I'd have to tell him enough of the truth to scare him away, more than I'd ever wanted to expose about myself but still not so much that it wrong-footed us in a way that we could never get back to some kind of normal, even a new normal, between us.

I'd worked for a full hour on this part alone, writing out all the things to say, and I itched to pick up the notebook behind him and read him the carefully crafted script.

But that had only been for me to organize my brain, and reading it aloud would add a hard varnish of awkwardness to seal what was already going to be a painful conversation.

I cleared my throat and pressed my hands together like that would somehow channel the words to come out the right way. "I kind of had an epiphany fueled by health food and the realization that my personal life is a disaster."

He frowned. "Something go down with that Jay dude who wouldn't quit texting last night?"

"Yes and no." The words weren't going to come out. I could feel it. I could imagine them falling between us, the bombs I'd told Sophie they'd be, detonating any chance of even a normal friendship. My throat closed up. I couldn't do it.

But if I didn't, if I didn't somehow make this all right, there would always be something between us in our friendship anyway. It would come out of me at some point, and knowing me, it would be the worst possible time, when it would wreck the most things. So I had to do it. To save Will and Hannah as friends, this amputation of my ghost wishes had to happen *now.*

"Hannah?"

I closed my eyes for a second, running through my script, and then I started a controlled detonation. "Remember when I was seventeen and I told you I had a massive crush on you?"

I expected him to get the grin he got every time we talked about shared funny memories. He didn't. He went still. "Yeah."

"It seems like these things are cyclical. Something about you announcing you were looking to get married set off a panic inside of me, and I decided that it was you and I who are meant to be together." I held up my hand when his eyes widened and he opened his mouth to speak. I dropped my hand and looked down at my lap. "It's okay. I made an elaborate plan to make sure you couldn't find anyone you'd really like online, then I went out of my way to show you that I'm really the girl for you." I smiled. I wished it didn't tremble, but I was proud that my voice stayed even.

"It was dumb. I know. 'Meant to be' is a concept both people have to be aware of. It's pretty clear in hindsight that it can't all be in one head to be true. And I've had a couple of epiphanies over the last few days." I swallowed, wishing I hadn't worked my way through all my water bottles already. I didn't want to get any from the tap because it would bring me too close to Will, and I didn't need that right now.

"What were these epiphanies?" he asked, his voice low. And gentle. And I hated that. It was the voice people used to talk to a panicked child or a hurt animal, something they were trying to soothe, to talk down from the wild edge of hysteria.

"*Epiphanies* is probably too strong a word, I guess." No, it wasn't. The truth had sliced through me with breathtaking clarity, a laser of pain. But this conversation was about pushing through. So I'd play it cool. I smiled and waved my hand, my fingers drifting through the air to disperse the extra-dense molecules that seemed to have gathered around me to mess with my breathing. "I realized that I've gotten back into a rhythm with you since you moved in practically next door. It took me back to our growing-up time. And it took me back to wandering in and out of each other's houses and watching ball games and snitching food. That's comfortable for me. Like going home. But I think it also took me back to another part of that time, which was that stupid crush." I looked up to see him flinch at the word *crush*.

"It's okay. I told you I figured it out. I just fell into an old habit," I continued.

He didn't look reassured. His forehead was furrowed, and he wore the expression he always had when he was taking a rare moment to pick carefully through his words before speaking them. My heart lurched a little that he would do that for me, and the automatic analysis started. *He doesn't do that for just anyone. At some level, you're special to him, or he wouldn't be trying so hard to be diplomatic.*

But I shut that voice down. That voice had led me into wearing rose-colored glasses for so long that I'd forgotten how the real world looked. But that was where I had to plant my feet now: on solid ground, not dreamy cloud wishes of happily ever after. I searched for a way to make him understand that I was going to move on and we were going to go back to normal. "Going out with Jay the other night made it all gel for me."

His head jerked in surprise. "Why? What happened?"

"Nothing special. But maybe that's why it was special. We laughed. A lot. I don't usually laugh like that on dates. There were no awkward silences. It was a constant stream of things to talk about it. I came home happy. It was a good night. And then he . . . never mind."

"What?" His voice was hard.

"Nothing. It was just a good night." And if Will had inferred, as I hoped he would, that my evening with Jay had ended with some highly favorable kissing, good. It hadn't happened, but if Will thought it had, it might help convince him that I was going to move on and leave this crush far behind me.

I was going to try. Because at the moment, the only crushing that was happening was the vice around my insides as it tightened at Will's slow nod. He leaned against the counter and ran his hands down his thighs a few quick times, a nervous habit he had. But he settled down and put his hands in his pockets and nodded again, a decisive nod. "I'm sorry I didn't realize, Hanny. I thought we were such good friends that . . . I don't know. I'm sorry. I'm sorry I didn't know."

"I wish you didn't know now. Or not that. I'm glad I told you. I wanted to clear the air between us. I was afraid if I didn't tell you that I would start acting even weirder and ruin everything between us anyway. But I love our friendship, so I want everything to be clear, you know? And I know it's maybe going to be awkward for a little bit, but I think we'll be okay." I pulled up the smile I always used when I was teasing him. "My plan to put us back to normal is even better than my plan to get you to marry me."

He lost some color at the "marry me" part. "You . . . we . . . what?"

I rolled my eyes at him. "Quit being weird."

He choked. I ignored him.

"I'm on an honesty campaign now." *Not really. If I were, you'd know that my heart is trying to push in on itself, to fold up and go away, somewhere it can't hurt.* "So I'm going to offer Jay a chance to be my rebound guy. Tell him I'm coming in emotionally damaged and probably not emotionally available but that I promise to make him laugh and be good company. And I'll see if he goes for it. I think spending time with him might be the perfect antidote."

"To me? Because I'm some kind of illness?"

I shrugged like it was no big deal, even though his tone had been heavy. "Yeah. Now that I'm not in denial, this should all be easy to fix."

"To fix," he repeated.

"Yeah. I've been freaking out about how if you got married it would change everything. And then I changed everything by being weird. But I've been forcing myself to look at reality for the last few days, and I'm going to be okay. You and I are going to be okay. This'll be fine. But I had to put everything out there if we were going to move past it. So you can congratulate me on being a grown-up whenever you're ready. Oh, and P.S., the sheer maturity I'm demonstrating right this second should be all the proof you need that I'm an adult and you can quit hovering over me all the time. I can handle myself."

Will listened with no expression, his arms folded across his chest, but his eyes had the hard look they got when he'd drilled in on the core of a problem, the look he got right before he'd drawn up the diagram that finally worked for the Gatorade fortress in his spare room.

"Will?" I wanted him to say something, anything. Or maybe I didn't. I would have been less naked if I'd stood up and stripped my clothes off. But he stayed silent, his focus fading to a problem-solving blank gaze into a distant point only he could see. "Will!" I repeated, sharper than I'd intended.

His eyes jerked to mine, a quick flash inside them that made my stomach clench before he stared at me like normal, except for the tight line of his jaw. He hadn't been as far away as I'd thought. "You just told me you've been plotting to marry me for weeks. Which is . . . crazy. And now you're not. And while, in your mind, you're pushing us right back to the footing we were on before, you're going to have to give me time to work through it. I've had about three minutes to process all of this. I'm going to need longer."

"Sure, take some time. Or you can do what you did when I was seventeen, and you can laugh and forget about it, and we can move on."

He scrubbed his hands over his face, a quick, angry motion, like he was trying to scrub my confession off of his skin. "It's night and day. This isn't the same thing at all."

"It *is*. They're my feelings. I know whether it's the same or not."

"You know whether it's the same or not for you." For a second, my heart slammed against my rib cage and shot up into my throat before it plummeted at his next words. "To me, it's all confusing. Was what you said at seventeen built on anything? It didn't seem like it could be. It's a rite of passage, isn't it? To develop a crush on your older brother's best friend? I mean, I brushed it off, you know? And you seemed fine after that. It was done. But as you like to remind me constantly, you're not a kid.

So when you tell me something like this *now* . . . I don't know. Is this real? It seems like it has to come from a different place. Doesn't it? And I don't know what I'm supposed to make of it. But I know it's going to take me more than a handful of minutes to come up with something."

The wobbly hold I had on my mood slipped away completely. I had wrapped myself into knots over this for weeks, first agonizing over my stupid plan and then making this confession. But despite his misguided opinion to the contrary, there was nothing for him to sort through. They were my feelings. Mine. Not his problem to solve. Mine. And I was so tired of him doing this, of stepping in and trying to fix things for me. "I get that this puts you in an awkward position, and I'm sorry," I said, trying to keep the tension out of my voice. "But I'm telling you right now, I'm letting this go, and you're going to have to let it go too. I gave this to you as something for you to know, not something for you to fix. *I'm* fixing it."

He started to say something, but I rushed in ahead of him. "Give me a few days. I need space and a lot of distraction, and we'll be fine. Spend those few days figuring out how not to be weird about this, okay? Please?" His eyes darkened, and the corner of his mouth turned down, but I pressed him. "Please. I've grown up in every way except emotionally. Let me do that. I've told you the truth like a healthy adult should, and I'm confessing that I've never been able to shake the childhood crush I had on you. Somehow my vision of true love stalled out at seventeen. It's stupid. I know that. You're a habit of years. But I'll break the habit. And then you and I can be friends more like you and Dave are, on equal footing. But we'll have this whole great shared history. And I can be me inside of it, not the version of me that's trying to be the perfect girl for you. Just Hanny, same as always. But I need the time and space, okay?"

His arms had locked across his chest again, the same tension playing along the tight line of his jaw. He kept his eyes on the floor in front of him for a long moment, and I was thankful. It meant I could endure my stinging cheeks without a witness. The heat was fading by the time he looked up. "Total honesty from now on, Hannah. You should have told me forever ago that you still had that crush."

"No way. It is the stupidest thing in the world for a twenty-five-year-old to be as swoony as her high school self."

"But it could have wrecked us."

I curled my hands into the sofa cushions, grasping as much of the soft twill as I could, filling my hands with fabric so they were too busy to flail with the irritation surging inside of me. "We were cruising toward that whether I said anything or not. If we wreck now, it's because you let us. So don't. Give me some space to breathe. We'll reset. We'll be fine. I'll preoccupy myself with this handsome boy. You do your thing. Don't worry about me. And then when I know I can be cool around you, we'll do our Will and Hannah thing."

"Our Will and Hannah thing," he repeated, his voice void of any emotion. "How long do you think it's going to take to get there?"

I don't know. I wanted to scream the words. *I don't know because I'm barely holding myself together to act like this is some funny aberration and not like my insides are scaling away in an acid peel.* "It takes as long as it takes," I said. *Forever.* "Maybe a few days. Maybe a few weeks. Not forever. I'm not going to disappear."

He glanced my way, finally. "Okay. You're not allowed to anyway. Dave will kill me."

It was a twist of the knife in my gut, a reminder that regardless of the roller coaster my emotions had been riding for weeks, he'd stayed grounded in big-brother territory. I tried to keep my face neutral, to hide the hurt, but I must have given myself away because his eyes pinched at their corners, distress etching new lines there for a moment.

"Sorry," he said. "I just . . ."

"It's okay. We are what we are. It's fine, really!" My voice sounded loud and overbright. I summoned a big smile. "But this is why I need the space. It's all about the reset. Imagine I'm bowling pins, and all of me has been knocked down, but this isn't an automatic bowling alley. So instead of a nice, tidy reset, I have to wait for a really old dude to reset my pins one by one. Maybe it'll take a while, but the end result is the same."

"Sophie would totally flunk you for that analogy," he said, the first hint of a smile appearing. But even the shadow of his smile was enough to give me some of my breath back, to let me inhale around the pain in my gut. It was a glimmer of hope that maybe we could be okay, find a new footing where we were friends on both sides, not just on his.

"Probably. Don't tell her."

He nodded, and a silence fell between us. I didn't know what else to say. I sat with an easy smile on my face, but I wasn't sure how long I could keep it up. I didn't want to talk in my overbright staccato again, so I looked at him and then past him to my kitchen, down the hall, back toward my living room windows, even though the blinds were drawn. Everywhere but at him. He cleared his throat. "I'll go, I think. I have to . . . I've got stuff to do." He walked to the door and hesitated. "I don't know how to . . . I mean, what comes next?"

"Don't call us, we'll call you," I joked.

It was a long moment before he nodded. "Whatever you need, Hannah." He closed the door behind him.

I sank down, letting go of the sofa and grimacing at the unpleasant volcanoes my grip had created in the fabric. I smoothed them out, and it didn't help. *I did it*, I thought, pressing harder. *I said all the things I needed to. And I kept it together.* But when the fabric still tufted up in weird lumps, I punched it, trying to get it to settle. And I punched harder. And faster. And even though I had said and done everything exactly how I'd planned, even though the cushion upholstery was settling back to normal, I realized I was crying. And it was a long time before I stopped.

Chapter 15 ♥

JAY WENT FOR IT. I couldn't believe it, but he did. I e-mailed him and explained that I was as emotionally distant as I'd promised from the start, but I was interested for the first time in seeing if there was a cure for it, and would he like to go to dinner again?

YES.

Simple, all caps. It made me feel better.

We met for dinner, and it was weird. I kept worrying about saying or doing anything to give Jay the impression that I was open to love or something. So I laughed, but not too loud or long. And sometimes if I'd laughed too many times in a row, I would give him a polite smile when he said something funny instead. Which had to be confusing because sometimes I ended up doing the polite smile for his funniest comments.

He cracked fewer jokes as the evening went on. By the time he pulled into my apartment parking lot, I was ready to throw myself from his car before it even made a complete stop. Surely some massive scrapes and contusions would be better than the soul-crushing awkwardness. It couldn't be worse.

I flew up the stairs and stopped in front of Will's door, ready to open it and complain about how badly the night had gone. I'd turned the knob halfway before I realized that this was the habit

I had to break: Will. And he was indirectly the reason the night had gone so badly. I let go of the knob, hurrying down the hall and digging out my phone as I went. I should be calling Sophie, not Will.

I closed my front door behind me just as I heard Will's open, but I shut mine before he could even finish calling my name.

"Good news," I said when Sophie picked up. "The Jay date was a disaster, but I've had no Will contact today. So that's one day down, the rest of my life to go, and I should get through this fine."

"What happened with Jay? He sounded like he had potential."

"He did. I don't. I was a total psycho. I was like an android with a damaged emotion chip, laughing too loud at some stuff, not at all at the actually funny stuff. I even moved all glitchy, dropping silverware all night, dribbling my water when I drank at dinner. It was weird and horrible."

"Oh, sweetie. I'm sorry. What went wrong?"

"I told you. My wiring misfired. It was humiliating."

"I'm sure it's not as bad as you think it was."

"It was so much worse."

"Well . . ." Sophie drew out the word, and I knew she was trying to find the right thing to make me feel better. She believed that every situation in life had a magic set of words but that some were harder to find than others. "So here's the thing." That was what she always said when she'd found the words she needed. "You're saying this was all you, not him, right? That he was fine, you were the weirdo at the table?"

"Yeah. Pretty much." I was too demoralized to complain about her bluntness.

"So would you want to try again to get to know him better?"

"Yes. Except for the part where I'd ever have to look him in the eye again. Or let him see my stupid face again."

"I like your stupid face. Be nice to it. But also, this is where I give you some tough love. Ready?"

"Should I flex all my feelings in case you're going to punch me in them?"

"Definitely. Got my fist cocked and everything. Jay is not the love of your life. But he *is* the first guy who has been interesting enough for you to be nervous and screw up the date and, even better, feel embarrassed about it."

"Even better?" I repeated. "How is that even better?"

She laughed. "Trust me. You need to take another shot at this Jay guy, try hanging out with him some more. You can't quantity date in this situation. Everyone is going to fall short of Will. You're going to have to go for quality, and Jay is it, I think. At least for this round. So fix it."

"It's not that easy." I gave a maniacal laugh, and Sophie squeaked. "That's what I did when he made some dumb pun about being on a roll while he buttered his bread. But then he told me this truly hilarious story about this work trip that went wrong, and I overcompensated for being a dork by being a robot. He finished the story, and I went, 'Heh.' Like, a laugh-till-you-cry hilarious story, and I say 'heh.' *Heh*!" I hollered.

"Ouch!" Sophie hollered back. "That was bad. But didn't you say you've been totally straight with this guy from the start? So play that card again. Text or e-mail him or something right away. And tell him that due to your conflicted emotional issues or whatever, you've sort of forgotten how to be normal, you overthought it because you didn't know how to feel, you forgot to feel, and you want a do-over."

"I can't."

"You can. You need to. I know you. If you slink away, it's going to make you gun-shy about going out again for a while, especially if it's someone you find cool. That's not going to help you with Will. So think it through. What's the worst that can happen, really? Just e-mail him. Tell him what's up. And maybe he doesn't respond. So what?"

"But maybe he does, and he says something about how we're not a good fit."

"I still say so what. It's not like you have to look him in the face while he says it. And the flip side is that he might not have thought it was nearly as big a deal as you do. Or that even if he does, he's game for another shot."

"I kind of hate this."

"That's why you have to do it. You can't fall back into that rut of being like, 'Oh, I like Will, so what's the point?'" She said it in a falsetto, and I grimaced.

"I don't sound like that."

"I was going for the silly quality, not fidelity of sound." She paused for a moment, and I heard clicking.

"What are you doing?"

"Nothing. Fidelity of sound is a cool phrase. I wrote it down so I don't forget it in case I want to name my band that."

"The band you don't have?"

"It's just a thing people say. Anyway, this is not the point. The point is that I was making fun of you, and now you need to let that work and shame you into at least giving it a shot. E-mail Jay."

I laughed. I couldn't help it. "You have an answer for everything."

"Yeah."

"All right. How does this sound?" I opened my laptop and my e-mail and hit "Compose." "Dear Jay, I'm not always terribly awkward. I can provide sworn affidavits that say so. I think I was trying so hard not to be weird that I was weird. But it's entertaining to watch, right? So can I make it up to you with lunch this week? Or something where we're not sitting across from each other trying to figure out when eye contact is too much or not enough. How about . . ." I trailed off, trying to think of what to suggest. Running? No. That was what I did with Will. I'd spend all my time running with Jay thinking about how different it was from running with Will. Which would mean Will was more or less on the date with us. No more of that.

"That's good," Sophie said like I'd given a great analysis of *Beowulf*. "But how about what? What are you going to ask him to do?"

"How about bowling?" I said to Sophie as I typed it. Why not make the life metaphor I'd used with Will my reality? "I suck, and I promise you'll feel good about yourself."

"I like it," Sophie said. "It's kind of, sort of the flat-out perfect tone. Hey," she said, her voice suddenly bright. "Can I use that e-mail as an example when I teach my mood and tone unit next month?"

"No!"

"Fine. I think it's great even if you're not going to share it. You should send it."

"No?"

"Yes. Do it." I hesitated. She pressed harder. "Do it now before you talk yourself so far out of it that I can't talk you back into it."

She was right. I didn't have anything to lose. If I'd humiliated myself, this wasn't going to make it any worse. He would probably say no, thanks, but at least I might have rehabilitated myself by having a sense of humor about everything.

"Okay, I hit send."

"Good girl! Now I have some news for you."

A nervous undertone ran through the words, piquing my interest immediately. "Spill."

"You say that like you think it's going to be juicy."

"It will be. I can feel it. Stop stalling. Spill."

"I—"

I waited. "Yes. You what?"

"Have a date."

"What? With who? Yay!" Sophie was pretty, and she charmed people regularly, but she always claimed too much grading or exhaustion when the weekend rolled around as a reason she couldn't invest energy in dating.

"So your friend Jared texted me. And I texted back. And we've been talking, I guess. I mean, mainly by text. But he called me last night. And he asked if I'd like to meet, and I said yeah."

"Hooray!" I shouted. "When? Where? This weekend? What are you doing?"

"I don't know. Not this weekend. I've got too much—"

"Don't you dare say grading."

She stayed silent.

"Sophie," I groaned. "You will always have too much grading. I promise you that your students are not dying to get their final grades on their unit tests. I'd bet most of them would rather not know, am I right? Grading cannot be a thing."

"But my AP class—"

"Will only benefit from you having a life outside of you dreaming up what to torture them with next. Whoa. Incoming," I breathed as Jay's name showed up in my inbox. "E-mail from Jay." I clicked it open and skimmed it. *Bowling sounds good. But can we mix it up with some other humans so that the strain of my jokes falling flat doesn't kill me and I can hide behind conversation with them?* He wanted to double date. Perfect. "Tell Jared you'd love to go out with him sometime, and in fact, you want him to come bowling on Saturday."

"Not really how I pictured my first date with Jared. He seems too sophisticated to bowl."

"Then I'm wrong about him being your future husband. People who are too good for bowling are no-fun-having-cranky-pants."

"True. I'll ask him."

"Because you're the best friend ever."

"Also true. Now. We need to discuss last night's *Eye on the Runway*."

We chatted for another twenty minutes about our favorite reality TV vice, but the second we hung up, my house felt too quiet. I itched to text Will for . . . nothing, really. It was the same reason I'd texted him hundreds of times before. But it wasn't time yet. I hadn't elbowed out nearly enough space for myself.

Instead, I e-mailed Jay so we could start nailing down the bowling date. And when we'd said everything there was to say about when and where to bowl, the apartment felt kind of echo-y again. So I turned on the TV, cranked the volume up five clicks louder than usual, and squeezed a throw pillow to my chest to keep my hands tied up for two reruns of *Friends* until the urge to text Will had passed.

Not passed. Become manageable.

I was going to need some new hobbies.

* * *

It was emotionally harder and logistically easier than I'd ever thought it would be to avoid Will. I wanted to imagine him picking up his phone and putting it down as many times as I did. But if my mind wandered that way, I forced myself instead to imagine him out on a date with someone new. It was a string of petite blondes. With PhDs. And ambition. And good senses of humor. And lots of stamps in their passports. In other words, I pictured him going out with his real dream woman, and every time my mind tried to paint my face into that picture, I erased it and replaced it with someone who looked like she could be in a swimsuit catalog.

I made sure never to leave or come home when I thought he might be heading out too. I'd started a lot of my days in the past by walking down to the parking garage with Will. I had no idea that it would be a harder habit to break than, oh, say, heroin.

The second day of no Will contact was torture. The third day was torture. The fourth and fifth days were torture. The sixth day improved to miserable. It was Saturday, the bowling date with Sophie. Well, with Jay. And I would have backed out on it except I couldn't bail on Sophie. I met her at her apartment two hours before dinner so we could drive over to the bowling alley, where we were meeting Jared and Jay.

"Hey," Sophie said, opening up to let me in. "Don't change."

"You don't even know what else I brought," I said, hefting the bag with two more outfits I'd lugged over.

"Don't need to. You look super cute. I won't like anything else that well."

I glanced down at my coral striped knit shirt and skinny cuffed jeans. "Yeah?"

"Yeah. Hey. Is this going to be weird for you?"

"Probably. But that's why we're doubling. So you can kick me when I start making an idiot of myself. You'll be able to tell because Jay's smile will start looking painted on instead of real. His eyes might dart toward the exits."

"Not that, dummy. I meant hanging out with me and one of your recent dates."

"Right. That. I thought about it. But Jared and I didn't connect in that way, you know? So as long as you two connect, and I'm pretty sure you will, then there will be no reason for any of us to feel awkward. Except, you know, for me. Because I'm going to make an idiot of myself in front of Jay again."

She studied me, but I didn't have anything to hide. I could foresee zero problems with Jared. "All right. Then let's go pick out what I'm supposed to wear to meet my future husband."

Hanging out with her until dinner was the first tolerable two hours I'd had since my breakup with Will. No, not breakup. That was a word for people who'd been together in the first place.

By the time we got to the bowling alley, my smile had regained some of its muscle memory. Maybe I could get through this date with Jay without looking like an idiot.

I spotted both Jared and Jay in the entrance alcove seated on opposite benches. I introduced everyone, studying Sophie's reaction to Jared as casually as possible. Her cheeks pinked when they shook hands. Good sign. Jared gave her a big smile, and when Sophie looked away for a moment, he shot me a quick look and a lightning-fast "thank you" quirk of his eyebrows. I gave him a nod.

Jay watched the whole exchange with interest, and when Sophie turned back to Jared, I grinned at him. I'd filled him in via e-mail on my one-and-done date with Jared, and Jay's expression said he found the whole thing amusing. When he caught my eye, he wiggled his eyebrows in a wild exaggeration of the message Jared had sent with his, and I burst into laughter and walked over to give him a hug. "Thanks for going out with me again even though I was a total weirdo the last time."

He shrugged, a smile turning up his lips. "It seems like the benign kind of weird. And weird is interesting. So saying yes was kind of a no-brainer, especially when you suggested a double date stuffed with potential drama and loaded silences. How was I going to say no to that?"

"Yeah. Well, you've seen how it is with Jared and me," I said, raising my voice on his name. He and Sophie looked over. "Jared, although it was hard for me to move past it, I forgive you for dumping me. I promise to be a grown-up tonight."

He pretended to weigh out my statement. "All right, then. If you can be so big about me dumping you, I'll be gracious too and not rub your nose in it that I crushed your fragile sense of worth like an eggshell."

This time it was Sophie who erupted in laughter. She tucked her arm through Jared's. "You're going to do just fine. Now let me rent you some fancy shoes."

Jared shot up an eyebrow. "Sorry. I know it makes me a total sexist, but I'm not going to be able to let you do that. To be honest, I can't even let you pay for your own shoes. And I don't mean to brag, but I can spring for all the soda you want tonight."

I pointed at the big sign next to the shoe lane rental desk. FREE SODA UNTIL MIDNIGHT.

He shrugged. "See? I told you I could afford it."

Jay shook his head. "I have a feeling this night is going to work out."

I stuck a hand on my hip. "You should know my bowling score is going to make you feel really good about yourself. You should also know I'm losing on purpose."

Jay gave Sophie a "Really?" look. Sophie shook her head. "It's sad how low her score will be for as hard as she tries. But she's right that you'll feel good about your own game."

"That's what I'm here for," I muttered.

The rest of the night went down that way, an easy rapport among the four of us, jokes and Cokes flowing freely. By the time we all separated in the parking lot, I realized that while I hadn't forgotten Will for more than two minutes at any given moment, he was a dull ache and not a sharp pain. It was a start. I only needed to find and deliver the right self-talk, and eventually I could shove the ache into a box and hide it somewhere in a mental file cabinet. Locked. Abandoned. Forgotten as often as possible.

When Sophie and I were in the car, she started the ignition, put the car in gear, and was halfway out of the parking lot before I couldn't stand her silence anymore. "So? What did you think? He's great, right?"

"Yeah. You and Jay have a nice chemistry."

I smacked her arm. "That's not who I'm talking about, and you know it!"

"Yeah, I know."

"Jerk. You don't have to tell me anyway. I know. You guys so clicked. You have to name your first baby after me."

"Very funny."

"Whatever. Don't try to deny it. Total chemistry."

"No, I meant Hannah would be a funny name for a boy. Because we're definitely having a boy first."

I whooped. "Dibs on maid of honor!"

"But speaking of chemistry, it looked like it was there with Jay too. He's the perfect distraction for you."

"He's pretty all right."

"Pretty all right? Does that mean 'hot guy with a great sense of humor?' Because if so, he's totally all right. And he was digging on you. Hard."

We giggled all the way back to her place, repeating jokes Jared or Jay had made, analyzing their body language. Just their bodies, really. They'd each obviously worked hard on them. They deserved a little commentary. A lot. So much commentary.

When we got up to her place, I stooped to pick up my bag of stuff, but I paused and straightened empty-handed. I didn't want to go home tonight. I didn't want to walk past Will's door and fight the urge to step through it. I didn't want to pass it up either and wonder if he was even in there. Or if he was out on a date too. Or worse, if he was home but not alone. I wanted to stay in a different head space. And that meant a different physical space.

Actually, I probably needed to call the leasing office soon to find out when my apartment contract expired. It would be a little obvious to move out of the complex completely, but maybe I could move to a different building, ease the psychic scars I got every time I passed his place and tortured myself with wondering.

"Soph? Can I stay here tonight?"

She glanced over the fridge door she'd opened in search of a post-bowling snack. "Everything okay?"

"Yeah. I'm tired all of a sudden. And I realized I have a change of clothes, so it seems like a good solution."

"Mi sofa es su sofa, sister."

"Thanks."

I moved the decorative cushions over to the love seat and made myself a sleeping space.

"Hannah?" Sophie called, her voice soft. I looked up. "It'll get better. It will."

"Don't say Will."

She grinned.

I knelt on the cushion in front of me and propped my elbows on the back of her sofa, dropping my head down between them, the weight of Will inside of it suddenly too heavy. "You think I'll be okay?"

"I know so. You've got nothing but good things coming your way. It'll just take time."

"You're the best."

"Yeah."

I grabbed the last throw pillow and lobbed it at her without looking.

"You missed."

"It was a warning shot."

"I'm going to bed now. Right after I write in my diary about my crush on Jared. And when we get up in the morning, let's paint our nails and make paper fortune tellers. Spoiler alert: all of the fortunes I write in yours will end up with you marrying a hot guy named Jay."

"I know you're joking, but that really does take me back ten years to when I did all of those things about Will. When will I outgrow him?"

She climbed onto the couch beside me, propping her chin in her hands along the back of the couch too. "When you understand that you deserve to."

"Wow," I said, turning to stare at her. "That kind of shocks me. He's a good guy. You know that."

"I do know that," she said, her nod slow and thoughtful. "I do. But I also know that he's not good enough for you. If he were, not only would your plan to get him to see you have worked, but you also never would have needed it in the first place. But he's not able to recognize quality. I like him, but there's no denying that's a big character flaw. Chew on that, Hannah-girl. It deserves some thought. Now. Go to sleep. And remember, fortune tellers in the morning. We're sorting out your future."

I thought about what she said until I fell asleep, but the giggling and bowling had worn me out enough that I nodded off quickly. And despite her threats to solve all my problems with first-grade origami, the only thing we made in the morning was breakfast, veggie omelets that were the grown-up versions of the unhealthy cheese-and-bacon-filled omelets we'd had every Saturday morning as teenagers.

I gathered my stuff and headed home around eight, eager to change and take a long run to clear my head. Will's door opened, and I stopped, clutching my overnight bag against my chest.

"Whoa," Will said. "Hey."

I swallowed, willing my heartbeat to slow down.

"What are you . . . ?" He trailed off, his eyes fixed on my overnight bag, his face tight.

"I was at—" I broke off, realizing what he had inferred. His expression said he didn't think I'd been at Sophie's house. And it also said very clearly that he didn't like his conclusion. Well, forget him. How dare he assume? He knew me better than that. If he was going to imply something so ridiculous, then I didn't owe him anything. Where I went and who I was with were none of his business. "I was at a friend's."

He waited like I was going to tell him more. I lifted an eyebrow at him.

"Oh." He stood halfway through his doorway like he wasn't sure which direction he was supposed to go. After a long pause, he leaned against the doorframe. "So. How have you been?"

Subtext: Since you told me you loved me and I just blinked at you.

My cheeks heated, and I hated it. "Fine." I shrugged and hefted the overnight bag, drawing his attention to it and his bone-headed conclusions. "Great, actually," I said, forcing a small smile that was supposed to be knowing and mysterious all at once. I hoped it looked real.

"Good," he said, but his tone didn't match the word. "So as much as I hate running, I think I need to get out there again."

"Keep at it. It gets all right after a while."

"You think we could—"

I cut him off with a shake of my head. I was absolutely not ready.

"Right," he said quietly.

"I'm tired. I need to go," I said, crooking my head toward my apartment door. "See you around." But not for long. I really needed to talk to the leasing office. I put it on my mental to-do list.

He nodded, and I walked to my door without looking back, making sure my shoulders were straight and my chin was up. *I'm good, Will. I'm great.* It wasn't until I was inside that I collapsed and took inventory to see if I really was.

Maybe, I decided. I didn't want to cry. Or punch him. Or say just the right thing to charm him. It was a first step. Now I only needed a thousand more to get a fraction of the distance I still needed.

A knock on the door scared half my life out of me.

"Hannah?"

Will. Guess I wasn't getting any distance this morning. I pressed my hand against my heart and waited for the adrenaline to settle so I could hear. Instead of his footsteps walking away, he knocked again. "Hannah?"

I hesitated for a couple more seconds before I turned and opened the door. "Hey."

He shoved his hands in his pockets. "Hey." He rocked on his heels a couple of times. I didn't need my PhD in Will Hallerman Body Language to deduce that he was wildly uncomfortable. I fought the urge to say something to smooth it over, to make it better for him. I didn't want to punish him, but it wasn't my job to fix all the things for him anymore. Instead I waited.

"So it feels like a long time since we talked." He winced. "I don't mean *that* talk, specifically. I mean, in general, how we usually do. And it's strange to run into you in the hallway and not know what to say to you. A once-in-a-lifetime experience, I guess, but not the good kind."

My heart squeezed. I hated the strangeness too, but I didn't know how to be yet.

"I don't know how to act," he said, startling me with how closely his words mirrored my thoughts. "And I know that you probably need more time, but I guess I'm asking if you know how long."

I clenched my jaw. Was he seriously standing there telling me that my emotional difficulties were an inconvenience for him? Asking me when his comfortable Hannah would be back so his life could go back to normal?

His eyes widened when he saw my expression, and his hands flew up in a warding-off gesture. "That came out wrong." He plunged his fingers into his hair. "Take as much time as you need. I didn't mean I want you to hurry up. I want us to be friends again,

Hannah. I just hoped that you could give me an idea of how long so I can pace myself. I can wait as long as I need to for us to reset. But I guess I'm wondering if it's going to be this hard for a month or for a year."

It was my turn to lean against the doorframe so I could rest my too-heavy head against it. "I'd tell you if I knew. I don't. It takes as long as it takes."

He stared down at the ground and nodded. Again the urge to make him feel better bubbled up, and it frustrated me. I couldn't do that anymore. It would become someone else's job sooner than later. It had never been my job to do, anyway. I'd just claimed it.

I straightened. "I feel pretty stupid talking about this."

"Right." He glanced up but looked somewhere past my shoulder. "Right. Sorry." He paused for a second before he nodded and walked back down the hallway.

I stayed where I was and watched him go.

Chapter 16 ❤

WORK WAS TOO BUSY FOR a few days for me to see Jay again, but not too busy to keep me from wondering every other minute what Will was up to. Every time I reached for the phone to text him and see, I snatched my hand back. Wednesday morning, like a dieter who padlocks their fridge at night, I handed my phone to my administrative assistant and asked her to keep it in her desk until the end of the day. It helped. Thursday, I didn't even need her to hold it because I knew I wasn't going to pick it up unless it was to coordinate dinner plans with Jay for the night.

It felt good to climb the stairs to my apartment and be looking forward to something besides Will for once. I hadn't seen Jay since our bowling date, and he'd invited me to the Dallas art walk. It sounded kind of awesome, both the date and the conversations I predicted we'd have about the art. And since not one thing about him had activated my "predator" radar, he was picking me up from home. It was funny that in the age of online dating, picking someone up at their own house felt like a relationship step.

I couldn't decide if I hoped Will would see us together or not. I decided that it was not a great sign that I was even thinking about it. When Jay knocked on my door at seven, I managed to think about him marginally more than Will, a both massive and pathetic victory. "Hey," I said, opening the door and stepping out to lock it behind me. We weren't at "come in and judge the way I keep my house" yet.

"Hey," he said, reaching out to hug me. That was when I heard Will's door open. When I stepped back from returning Jay's hello, Will was standing frozen in front of his place.

I wished him away so I wouldn't be awkward with him watching me interact with Jay, but he didn't dissolve into atoms and disperse, so I hitched my purse over my shoulder, slid my arm through Jay's, and gave Will a smile as we passed him on the way to the stairs. He nodded, his eyes hooded, his forehead a mess of wrinkles.

"Have you ever done an art walk?" Jay asked as he opened the door of his Range Rover for me.

"No. I'm excited to check it out."

"Cool. So you won't have any idea if I'm blowing smoke when I comment on the artists' use of line and color?"

"No," I said, giving him the side eye.

He caught it and grinned. "This is going to be a fun night."

He was right. It was. It was a different kind of night. I was still nervous, worried I'd check out on him and my mind would wander back to Will, but I stayed focused, mainly because Jay took a lot of opportunities to touch me. A hand on my back to guide me through a door, grazing his finger against my arm to draw my attention to something, a soft bump of the shoulder if I teased him about something. It was nice. No, it was good.

And he kept making me laugh. Anytime a gallery employee would approach us, he would refuse to break character as he pondered the art he was facing. At one point, he was pondering the meaning of a collage depicting three grasshoppers sitting on the bank of a creek. I was pretty sure the meaning was clear in the title, "A Summer Day," but when an employee wandered over, maybe hoping to make a sale, Jay furrowed his brow and murmured, "It's a moving meditation on the nature of time, isn't it?" And I probably would have kept a straight face if the employee hadn't looked startled and said, "Yes, deeply moving."

As it was, I had to excuse myself and wait until Jay followed me out to the sidewalk a minute later to grin at me. "Are you up for ice cream?"

"I don't know. Is it deeply moving? Will I need to meditate on it?"

"Definitely. You have to approach the work of the masters, Baskin and Robbins, with a certain reverence and really give yourself up to the experience."

"I was going to tap out until you said Baskin Robbins. I'm in."

After dawdling over ice cream for another hour, we walked back to his car, and his hand brushed against mine. I could have turned my wrist, a tiny rotation, and we'd be holding hands. But I was funny about hand-holding. It felt more committed to me than kissing. But hand-holding wouldn't be too far off because I had no doubt that when Jay walked me to my door, he was going to lean in and wait for me to cross the last 10 percent. And I was going to.

Nerves tickled my stomach on the short drive back to my place. And when he walked me to my door and waited for me to dig my keys from my purse, I fumbled them when I caught a smile playing around his lips. "Stop," I said when he scooped them up before I could.

"Stop what?" he asked, still grinning.

"Stop making me nervous."

"Okay. How do I do that?"

I blew out an exasperated sigh and reached up to catch hold of his collar. Forget the lean. I brought him the whole way down to meet me, pressing a kiss against his lips before I stepped back. "There. Problem solved. Now I'm not nervous." I shot him a sassy grin.

His return grin was lazy with a touch of mischief as he slid his hands around the lapel of the denim jacket I'd thrown on over my knit dress. He tugged, drawing me back to him slowly. "I kind of love that you're so tall," he said. He brushed another kiss against my lips and said quietly, "I dig it. A lot."

"It's nice being almost eye level with you," I said as he slid his arms around my waist. I hooked my hands around his neck. "Maybe I'll always wear heels."

"Whatever you want." He kissed me again and straightened. "Because this is pretty awesome."

"We won't know unless we compare," I said, letting go with one hand and balancing myself on his shoulder with the other while I slid off my shoes and threaded my fingers through the straps. "We should try it this way."

This time his eyes darkened, and he dipped his head to kiss me, taking his time. I swayed and curled my fingers around a handful of his shirt to stay upright. I disappeared into a haze, and when he finally lifted his head to mumble "Door," I blinked up at him, dazed and unfocused before patting the door I suddenly realized I was leaning against.

He gave a soft laugh. "No, I heard a door."

I hadn't heard anything, but my stomach clenched before I even glanced down the hallway and saw Will standing with his hand on his doorknob, keys and wallet in his hand like he was headed out somewhere. A split second of jealousy flashed through me as I wondered where he'd be going at almost ten at night, but a realization followed it and distracted me: I hadn't thought of Will once in the last few minutes. I'd been wrapped up in a pretty good kiss, and that was the only thing that had been on my mind. Since I'd never kissed Will, this was the one area where Jay or any other guy wouldn't—couldn't—fall short by comparison. For the first time in a long time, longer than I could remember, I'd had a whole fistful of Will-free minutes.

I looked away from him and smiled up at Jay, relieved that I'd found the first chink in the Will spell. I planned on hoarding a lot more of these minutes. If the gleam in Jay's eye was a hint, he'd be happy to help me.

I pressed my hand against his chest to give myself some room and straightened enough to kiss him on the cheek. "Bye," I said softly. "I had a really good night."

He stepped back and slid his hands into his pockets. "Me too. I'll call you."

I turned to open my door, away from Will in case he was still standing there. I didn't want to risk getting pulled into his orbit again, and I might if I made eye contact.

I shut the door behind me and pushed out the glimpse I'd seen of his face, still and expressionless, and sank back into the memory of kissing Jay. It had been so good to feel like I was finally breathing in a Will-free space. Ironic that it happened when my breaths had all been tangled up with Jay's.

I liked the entanglement. A lot.

* * *

Sophie wasn't as excited for me when she called me during her prep period the next day.

"'Supah fly kisses,' Han? Really? I feel like I need one of my sophomores to translate this text."

"If you got out of it that Jay kissed me last night, then your translation skills are just fine."

She squealed, then laughed. "Okay, maybe I'm the sophomore. But I don't care. He kissed you? Tell me."

"I guess it's more accurate to say I kissed him." I told her the story, getting to the funny part. "And then Jay hears a door, and I look up, and Will is standing there staring at us."

"No!"

"Yes! But it was fine." I said. "So apparently the universe is trying to help me out and sent me the anti-Will, which is Jay, who is possibly a cure. Awesome," I concluded, the words sing-songy in my giddiness.

Sophie was silent.

"Soph? You there?"

"Yeah, I'm here."

"Aren't you excited?"

"Yes."

It was the kind of yes that was wrapped in a giant "But . . ."

"Then why don't you sound more excited?"

"It's just . . . do you like Jay?"

"I just told you how awesome the night was."

"Yeah, but I guess I'm wondering how much of that is because Jay is truly awesome and you like him for him, and how much is . . ."

"Say what you want to say," I ordered.

"The middle of your workday is probably not the time to bring this up. Can I come over with ice cream when you're home from work?"

"No way. I'm going to obsess about this all day now. You can't tiptoe me up to the edge, then refuse to let me look over."

"I love you."

"Stop avoiding the conversation."

She sighed. "You have a great life. The world's greatest best friend, a cute place of your own, no debt except student loans. You're rocking everything. Your fitness, your profession."

I could hear the "but . . ." again. "Say it."

"Emotionally, you're still in high school. That's when you fell in love with Will, and you've never moved past that. Trust me, I see this all day, every day."

I didn't even know how to respond to that.

"Hannah? You there?"

"Yeah."

"I'm so sorry. I'm not saying you're immature or anything like that. But you *are* having a different conversation about your love life than most twenty-five-year-olds are having right now. Most of them are talking about moving on from their first live-in boyfriend, not deconstructing a first kiss."

The words were knives so sharp that she didn't even have to thrust them at me for the blades to slice deep. "You're killing me here," I said, only able to respond at all because her voice had been so full of love and not judgment. "What do you want me to do? Become someone I'm not, push this thing with Jay to a place I've never been willing to go so I can, what . . . grow up?" I bit the words out, stunned that Sophie of all people might be suggesting it.

"I know that's not you. Come on, Hannah. Just hear me out, okay? You're a relationship novice. It's okay."

"Oh, come on. You've been front row for all my relationships."

"Yeah. You've had a couple. But none where anything was truly on the line. None of those guys ever had a chance to hurt you because the deepest parts of you were wrapped up in Will. And you couldn't really hurt them because you never gave them enough of you for them to miss it when you were gone. I mean, maybe there were bruised egos on both sides, but you've never been hurt enough to call in sick to work for three days because you couldn't even function like a human. But you're in dangerous territory now. I'm worried about you, and I'm worried about Jay."

"Jay? Why are you worried about him?"

"Because you're opening up to him a little bit more. And I think you believe you're truly letting him in, but he's only going to get so far before you shut him out. And . . . I don't know. I like him for you. And I think if he's not into you yet, he's going to be very soon. And I just don't think that's fair to either of you. You're going to hurt him. For real, for once. And that's going to hurt you. And it's going to end up bouncing back in your face and making you even madder at Will. I don't see this ending well," she said, her voice pleading, like she wanted me to tell her it was okay that she was saying all of this.

"I don't get it. You've been wanting me to move on from Will for years. No, forever. And now you're telling me not to date Jay?"

"I'm not saying that at all. I'm saying you're barely moving out of your Will fog. I still don't think you see things clearly. And Jay's a nice guy who doesn't deserve to get caught in the crossfire."

"So dump him? That's how to avoid hurting him?"

"No. But maybe quit running away from Will and making everything you do a reaction against him. Go out with Jay because you want to go out with Jay. And if you do go out with him again, be totally upfront about what's going on with you. Let him walk in with eyes wide open."

"I already told him I'm a mess."

"But have you told him why?" A bell rang in the background. "I have to go. I have my worst class coming in. I'll love you no matter what kind of a mess you are. You're so good at reading the dynamics between other people. Step outside yourself, read the situation, and see what you would tell Jay and your clone, and figure out what you'd advise each of them to do. Would you tell Jay to run? And if the honest answer is yes but you wish you could tell him something different, think about what you would tell yourself to make it okay for him to stay." Voices shouted and catcalled each other behind her.

"That's the worst journal prompt ever."

"Gotta go," she said with a smile in her voice.

I set my phone down on my desk and stared up at my ceiling. How was I supposed to untangle the giant rubber-band ball of feelings she'd handed me to examine each strand? I mean, since I apparently had the emotional IQ of a Clearasil-coated teenager, I probably wasn't even capable of sorting it out.

I stared out of my office window at the uninspiring view of the top of the building next door. The industrial air-conditioning unit and patches of bird poop offered no answers.

What was I supposed to do now?

Chapter 17 ♥

QUIT RUNNING, I DECIDED. I picked up my pace. Not on the trails. But from Will. Sophie was right about that. Maybe about all of it. I was running from Will because I didn't think I was strong enough to be near him. How was that in any way moving past him? I'd read an article a while ago about how doctors were successfully curing some kids of peanut allergies by constantly exposing the kids to the peanuts in a controlled setting, a little at a time.

All of my free time had been about Will, especially since he'd taken over Dave's lease. I'd never questioned it because I'd been so happy to have him there. But now . . . it was like in college when I had roommates who would go sit next to their boyfriends on the couch for hours while the boyfriend played video games. I'd always thought it was lame since only one of those roommates in four years had liked video games herself. I'd asked a couple of them why they'd gone when they complained about all the *Halo Duty* or whatever it was. And they'd each shrugged and said something like, "I just like being with him."

I'd been trying to get Will to see and interact with me as an adult, but I'd been acting like those old roommates. I accelerated, trying to outrun the shame threatening to smother me. It was so pathetic. And I'd gone and exposed all of that to Will with my confession.

I ran harder.

There was no way to take it back. And I couldn't disappear into a string of physical relationships because that was what kept Will out of my head. So what was I supposed to do?

I blew past a girl I saw on the trail most days and barely registered her surprise at my pace. I ran until my legs ached and my lungs screamed and I had to slow down, the first time in years I'd pushed myself as hard as Will had to work to keep up with me.

Will.

It all came back to him in the same way the trail I was on always led back to my house. Was this full circle? Or a vicious cycle?

I slowed further, trying to let my breath and heart rate find a rhythm that didn't feel like a cardiac event.

Was I done with him?

Yes. I needed to be. But I'd never truly, in my heart, tried to figure out how to disentangle from someone who was always going to be in my life in some way, in the periphery. He'd always been there, so I'd always loved him.

And I could put distance between us, apartment buildings, entire states even, but he'd never go away completely. He'd be there in the background of my conversations with Dave, an even bigger shadow if I tried to tell Dave why we couldn't talk about Will anymore. And when Dave and Jessica had a baby or two or five, I couldn't be the reason those babies' christenings were awkward, the reason my brother had to coordinate his socializing so that Will and I didn't have to cross paths.

I slowed to a walk, my breath finally leveling out. I'd already put us at risk for that. The few times we'd seen each other since I'd blown everything up had been a high wire both of us had been terrified to step on.

I had to lower the stakes. I could figure this out. And somehow, in doing that, I had to solve the Jay problem too. This was going to take deep breathing and a long walk around the lake and then home. I gave myself one mile to come up with a plan.

Was the answer to break up with Jay? Not that we were together, exactly. But maybe I was supposed to stop it before it went further? My breath sped up again just thinking about removing a layer of protection between Will and me. Sophie was right, but I couldn't make myself give up Jay's force field. Or kisses. Those were good. But I wasn't a terrible enough person to keep him around purely because it made me feel better. So Sophie was also correct that the right thing to do would be to let Jay know why I was a mess. Maybe he would be willing to downshift and be cool with us still hanging out but keeping it light.

I composed the e-mail in my head for a quarter of a mile. But at the halfway point around the lake, I shifted to the bigger problem because there was no way my legs were going to make another full loop after I'd pushed them so hard on my run.

So. Will. Will wasn't going to go away. Not for the rest of our lives. So we had to figure out how to occupy the same space around Dave as the two people he loved most besides his wife. We'd made room when she'd come along. It had been weird at first when we'd realized Jessica was the real deal for him, but we'd made it work. Will and I could figure this out too if I could get myself right, figure out how to act.

Acting. That was the problem, and it had been for years. I'd spent years acting like a lovesick puppy. Then I'd spent years trying to hold on to my spot in Will's life by acting like the little sister. Then I'd spent a couple more years acting like I had outgrown him. Then I'd spent the last few weeks acting like the perfect woman I thought he needed, waiting for him to see. And then I'd acted like it was no big deal when he didn't.

The answer unfolded as simply as the wings stretching out on the egret lifting off from the lake bank beside me. I stopped and watched it go, watched it leave the ground behind.

It was time to drop the act.

Chapter 18 ♥

ME: CAN WE TALK?

I initiated the IM, wondering if Jay would suddenly become invisible online. He didn't though. The dots that showed he was typing blinked almost immediately.

JAY: Is there ever a time when those words don't make someone want to yell no and walk the other direction?

ME: No. You get bonus points for not pretending you didn't see this message.

JAY: Maybe only one point because I definitely considered it.

ME: Fair enough. It sounds dramatic, right? The "can we talk" line.

JAY: Yep.

ME: That's because it is. I'm going for the "little drama now so there's no drama later" thing.

JAY: That's a thing?

ME: Yes?

JAY: At least you're sure.

ME: :-P

I lifted my fingers from the keyboard and drummed them on the table, trying to figure out how to word what I wanted to say. *I'm a mess. Date me anyway.*

I shrugged. Why not? It's what I meant.

ME: I'm a mess. Date me anyway.

JAY: Okay. I don't know what I expected you to say, but I don't think it was that. Maybe "You're nice, but . . ."

ME: You are nice.

JAY: But?

ME: But nothing. You just are. And I want to go out again.

JAY: Agreed. So why are we having this talk?

ME: You might have glossed over the part where I said I'm a mess. You shouldn't. I am. A big one.

JAY: First, you already told me that. Second, I don't think you're the mess you think you are.

ME: I'm about to put my cards on the table. I think you're going to hate them.

JAY: Why? Is your hand like UNO draw 2, double reverse, skip, wild draw 4?

ME: LOL.

ME: Wait, not LOL. What's the acronym for high-pitched nervous laughter?

JAY: Just lay it out for me, okay? My brain is a little sore.

I hesitated, trying to find the right words to be honest with him but not send him screaming away. But that was the whole problem.

JAY: Hannah? Sorry. Maybe my tone got lost there. Read my last msg as not intending to be rude.

ME: It's okay! I'm the sorry one. I was trying to figure out how to say what I wanted to say and still get exactly what I want. But I can't make decisions for you or anyone or try to shape the way you feel. So here goes.

JAY: . . . okay . . .

ME: I wasn't kidding when I said I'm emotionally unavailable.

JAY: I heard you.

ME: But did you believe me?

JAY: Yessss . . . did I give you some kind of vibe to make you think I'm overly invested or something?

ME: No!

JAY: Good. I mean, that was a good kiss, but it was only a kiss. Not in a bad way. I just didn't take it as more than that.

I probably should have been more bothered that he was filing it under "only a kiss." But relief fluttered through my chest. It had been a fun kiss, one of the better kisses I'd gotten in a long time, but, yeah . . . it was just a kiss.

ME: That's too bad. I took it as a stellar way to end a date.

JAY: Ha. I took it as that too.

ME: I feel sort of stupid having a long conversation about a kiss like I'm fourteen or something. I guess I better confess that it was a really good kiss. Like, really good. But I have a gnarly, shredded-up heart, and it's going to take more than a kiss to make it better. And I have no idea how long I'm going to be all present with you before I get broody. Is that a word? *Broody*?

JAY: Let's go with it. Keep talking.

ME: My point being, when I get all broody, and I think that it's just a matter of time, I want you to be able to walk away like, "I don't need that drama," and be happy to see me go. I don't want to be a heart squasher.

JAY: I hear you. Let me try to explain. Give me a minute . . .

It took closer to five. After the first minute had ticked past, I picked up an apple and chomped on it, the chewing a good outlet for my nerves. It was gone by the time Jay chimed back in.

JAY: I appreciate that you're being upfront. You're saying that us hanging out is just for fun, right?

ME: Yeah.

JAY: And you're saying I shouldn't wade into deeper waters with you because you're the Bermuda Triangle and you will wreck all of my feelings.

ME: Well, yes. I guess?

JAY: Noted. I like fun. When you start acting crazy, I'll wave good-bye as I walk away. Feel better now?

ME: Yes. I think? I feel like I'm trying to be like, "I don't want any drama," but I'm being nothing but drama by even bringing this up.

JAY: I kind of wish we were sitting down to dinner so I could say this to your face and you would know my voice isn't mean, but yeah. It's a little dramatic. I'd be worried if I hadn't already hung out with you and seen for myself that you're low key. I'm fine with keeping it low key. If you're trying to say that the kiss didn't make you fall madly in love with me, uh . . . okay?

ME: I'm such an idiot for having a conversation about one dumb good-night kiss.

JAY: NOW IT'S DUMB?

ME: I DIDN'T MEAN IT LIKE THAT! I. Am. Mortified.

JAY: I'm messing with you. What is the way to say "Relax" to someone so it doesn't sound condescending?

ME: Don't worry. I got the msg. But I'm pretty sure after IM-ing you about this, I can never face you again.

JAY: That's a shame. You have a good face, as faces go. I was hoping for some more kisses that don't mean anything after more hanging out just for fun.

ME: You're trying to embarrass me.

JAY: Yes.

ME: It worked.

JAY: Yes!

ME: I guess if you want to hang out again after this ridiculous meltdown, I'm totally in. For the fun thing.

JAY: Too bad. I'm in for friends with benefits until either of us wants to move on to something else.

ME: I'm in until I figure out how to explain my issues to a therapist who will then order me to leave the guys of Greater Dallas alone until I pull myself together.

JAY: *Holds up imaginary glass for a toast* To fun times until the therapist gets involved!

ME: *Clinks glass* To fun times until you find a friend with better benefits.

JAY: You're pretty funny.

ME: Thanks. I steal all my jokes from sitcoms.

JAY: Ha. Can I ask a serious question before we move on?

ME: No.

JAY: I'm asking anyway. What exactly messed you up so much?

ME: True love.

JAY: True love is the worst.

ME: Especially when it turns out it wasn't really true love. Just unrequited love. Because a no-big-deal, end-of-a-date kiss is not the only thing I'm an emotional fourteen-year-old about.

JAY: I think you're kind of hard on yourself.

ME: Not hard enough. Should have been talking tougher to my mirror a long time ago.

JAY: All right. Well, the next time I feel like doing something fun, I'm probably still going to call you.

ME: I'm going to say yes.

JAY: Gotta go. Catch you later.

I signed off and stared at the screen for a long minute. Despite feeling stupid, I did have a clear conscience. I'd been up front. And I'd watch Jay carefully to make sure he was as laid back about everything as he seemed. That meant I could text Sophie to report. *I warned Jay he's dealing with a crazy person. He's cool with it. Now. Time to flip the script with Will again. Wish me luck.*

LUCK!!!

The next text went to Will. *Hey.*

He texted back as fast as Sophie had. *Hey.*

It's been a weird couple of weeks for me.

Weird over here too.

Everything good?

Depends. Are you good? Because if you are, then I am.

No. Everything is off-kilter.

Yeah.

So maybe we straighten it out.

How?

Instead of answering, I walked down the hall and knocked on his door. He yanked it open before I'd even knocked a third time.

"Hey," he said, his eyes searching my face. "I'm glad you're standing here, but I feel like I have no idea what the rules are and what I should or shouldn't say."

"That's what I'm here for."

He stepped aside to let me through, and I headed straight for his fridge and a bottle of Gatorade. I turned to face him, and his face relaxed the tiniest bit around his mouth.

"That's almost like old times," he said and grimaced. "I don't know if I should have said that. Maybe that's the last thing you want."

I climbed into his easy chair and drew my legs up to my chest. "I want us to figure out how to be real with each other."

He collapsed onto the sofa and dropped his head into his hands to stare at the floor. "I thought I knew how to do that." He looked up at me, confusion in his eyes. "You changed everything."

I nodded. "I get that it seems that way. But one of the things I figured out is that I haven't been real with you in years. But we're connected through Dave pretty much forever, and if we're going to get through this with any kind of grace, I've got to start being real. Beyond that, I have no idea what I want. I'll have to spend some time figuring that out."

"Is . . . do you . . . um." He stopped, and I hated the halting words. I hated that it was my fault. I wasn't sorry I had told him. But I was sorry for the way I had done it.

"Sucks, huh?" I asked. "That's on me, I think. I wish I could tell you I knew how to fix this. I don't. I just know that I want to. Maybe we have to try a bunch of things until we hit a groove. Good news is we have plan A out of the way. Avoiding each other and pretending like you don't exist seems like a stupid plan in hindsight. I guess that means we hang out again. But in a cards-on-the-table kind of way. So what do *you* want?"

"For us to be friends again. It stresses me out to even say that, like maybe it's the wrong thing. I mean, if I really liked a girl and she said . . ." He trailed off when I lifted my head to glare at him. "See? I can't get this right."

"You were doing pretty great until the last part." I straightened and rolled my half-empty Gatorade bottle between my hands. "'Cards-on-the-table' means it's good to know that you want to be friends. I want that too. But I also don't want to talk about my stupid feelings or my stupid confession."

"It wasn't stupid. Feelings aren't stupid, are they? They are what they are."

I shrugged. "Whatever. I'd be glad to never talk about it again. But I'm good with figuring out the friends thing."

"We could make a plan." Good ole Will. He was perking up at the idea, like he was going to draft a schematic for a rocket-engine part. I snorted, and he looked up at me, but I didn't explain. Why not do a schematic? It's not like my approach had worked. "Can we hang out again?"

"Yes. But less. Smaller doses is best for me."

He didn't look happy about that, but he nodded. "Cool. What else?"

"The faster we move on, the better. That means you need to get serious about finding your wife, dude. Once I know you're locked down, maybe it will force the pragmatic side of me to move on. And I guess that means I have to move on too. Rebound. Hard."

His forehead wrinkled like he wanted to say something, but he pressed his lips together.

"What? Spit it out. It's fine."

He shook his head.

I started to nudge him with a foot, a lazy poke like I would have done before, but I set my foot back down and cleared my throat, realizing I was going to have to add something else to the plan in a minute. "It's fine, Will. Say what you were going to say."

"You sure about the rebound thing? I mean, I'd expect an idiot guy like me to do something like that on purpose, but you're a decent human being."

"Um, thanks? Maybe? I can't tell if you complimented me or judged my choice on this."

"Both, I guess."

I smiled at him. "That's probably good. It's something a friend would do."

He smiled back. "Progress."

"Don't worry about it though. I'm rebounding with someone who's fully aware of what he's walking into."

His smile disappeared. "As your friend—"

I put a hand up. "Stop. If you're about to warn me against this, ask yourself this: If Dave were telling you this as his plan for himself, what would you do?"

He was quiet for a long moment. "Fist bump him," he admitted.

I held up my fist. He shook his head and bumped it.

"Let me do my thing, Will. I spent all these years trying to convince you I'm a big girl, but I really don't have anything to prove. I can handle myself. I'll be all right, and no guys will be harmed in the making of this new Hannah."

"Old Hannah is fine."

"Old Hannah has some growing up to do. That's what cowboy-ing up with you right now is about. You've been my most unhealthy habit since I was fifteen, Will. Last time I went through a bad-habit-breaking process, I lost fifty pounds." I pointed at him and smiled. "This time I gotta lose about one eighty."

"Ouch."

"Suck it up, buttercup. I am. And I'm the broken party here." But I smiled as I said it, and he shook his head and smiled back. "Here's another thing." I took a deep breath, and Will's eyebrows rose. "I need physical distance from you. No wrestling. And stuff." I wanted to die for a few seconds and be revived when my face was a normal color again. I wasn't going to spell out that Will's touch had an effect on me, and if he picked this moment to try going back to our old joking rapport and tease me about it, I really might die.

His cheeks flushed a tiny bit too. All he did was stare at the floor and nod. It almost made me feel worse, like he was trying to look away to give me some privacy because it was an embarrassing condition for me to have.

I pushed past it and gave him the next thing I'd thought of. "No barging into each other's apartments."

"Right. Boundaries, I guess, huh?"

"Yeah. Plus I don't want to explain to Jay why the guy down the hall feels like he can walk into my place whenever he wants."

"Jay. That's the guy you were . . ."

I nodded. "My super helpful rebound."

His cheeks went darker, and his eyebrows drew together, but all he said was, "Fair enough. I've had to explain you to my dates often enough."

"Yeah. Sorry. That was one of my idiot strategies. I'm done. I swear."

He leaned back and laced his fingers behind his head, staring at the blank TV instead of me. "To sum up, we're friends again."

"Not again," I said, not able to help the interruption. "We were always friends. We were always just friends. But now I accept it."

"So we're friends. I won't wrestle you like I'm Dave. I'll be careful about what I say in front of you about other girls. I'll stay out of your"—he paused to swallow—"out of your love life. But somehow we're still keeping all our cards on the table? Being totally honest about stuff?" He shook his head. "I'm not sorry you told me how you—"

I cleared my throat in warning, and he nodded his head and rephrased.

"I'm not sorry you told me what you did, but cards on the table—I hate that it changed."

"I get it. I'm sorry for making it so weird. But cards on the table is what will help us make that friendship comfortable for both of us. Eventually. I definitely don't want to hear the details of your wife hunting. But I want to know that you're getting closer to happily ever after. The closer you get, the more it will free me up to find mine. I'm sure of that."

He sighed. "Whatever you need, Hanny."

My heart tripped at the nickname. *Shake it off.* "Thanks."

"Cards on the table?"

"Yeah. Shoot."

"I feel like we've had some sort of breakup or something. Or not a breakup. I don't know. I have no idea how to explain this, but Dave and I have never had a fight, and I kind of wonder if this is how it would feel if we did."

"I'm not mad at you."

He shook his head. "That's not what I mean. I think I'm saying that I'll do this however you want, but it's not going to be the same, and it kind of sucks. Okay, I'm putting more cards on the table."

"We have a lot of cards."

"Triple deck, easily. Here's what I'm dealing out with this hand. Part of me is kind of mad at you for changing everything."

I took that in and weighed it. I appreciated the honesty, but it still didn't feel *good*, exactly. "Can we go back to the hand where you were sorry for being so oblivious and more of the bad guy in the scenario?"

"Take your lumps, Becker."

"That right there is proof we'll get to normal. I'll prove it." I stood up and pulled his laptop off his coffee table.

"What are you doing?"

"Putting the real you out there for women to find. That's all anyone worth anything will ever need to know to want to date you. Take it from an expert," I joked, and Will flushed again, but he smiled. "So I'm tweaking your profile, and I'll do it right."

"You don't have to do that." He reached over like he was going to take it from me, but I shooed him back to his cushion.

"I do have to. Remember? Get you on your way so I can get on mine?" He was silent, but I could tell he was biting the inside of his bottom lip. That was his "tough problem" tic. "What's up?" I asked.

"It doesn't feel right to let you redo my profile. The more I look back on it, the worse I feel that I ever let you write it at all. But I'm clueless, not a creep. Hand me back my laptop. This isn't your job."

"I was wrong to interfere with your goals. I need to make it right."

Will stared at the blank TV screen again, unfocused. He gave himself a shake. "Okay. Do it. Put what you see as the real me out there. Tell the world about all my obsessions and fixations."

"Hush. I got this." I tapped out his new profile message, totally sure of what needed to happen.

Dear world,

Allow me to introduce the best big brother a girl ever had, the guy in the picture to the left: Will. He let me take over his page for a minute because I said I could do a better of job of explaining him than he can. He'll tell you the facts about himself, but I'll tell you the whole truth.

Will is made of awesome. He's got a sense of adventure the size of Mt. Everest, which he'll climb someday, I'm sure. And he's got a sense of curiosity as deep as the Grand Canyon. So not only is he always up for an epic life experience, but he's totally there and present all the way through. He's asking questions about the people, learning about the place, understanding how the small part of the world he's standing in relates to the whole.

He's generous to a fault. Whether it's money for a panhandler or time for his friends, he gives without grudge or complaint. And he has no idea how amazing that is. It seems like the right thing to do, so he does it. It's that simple.

And that's another thing about Will. He's both simple and complicated. He has a brain like you wouldn't believe. He's literally a rocket scientist. He's worked on stuff that's out in space right now, collecting data and advancing science. He disappears sometimes in his thought experiments, but he always comes back to you.

You will have to watch a lot of sports. Or at least understand why he does. It's partly because of all the complicated things happening in his brain. Calculating the trajectory of a hit or the speed of a pitch is actually relaxing to him. Baseball is the top of the list. He'll tolerate football, but he perks up again for hockey. You'll have to roll with it all because . . .

He's not that guy that will disappear into sports and you'll never see him because there's always a game on somewhere. He's loyal to his hometown teams. That's it. Astros and Rockets fans will be incompatible. Sorry. But you get so much of Will between games. Hilarious conversations, spontaneous trips to an out-of-the-way restaurant because *"why not?" Conversations about the world, our place in it. Talks about your problems. He'll solve them if you let him, but he'll listen if that's what you tell him you need.*

He is fiercely protective. He gives the best hugs ever. His smile can turn a bad day around. His friendship is worth anything. Everything.

Good luck. He's special. I hope you are too. He deserves that.

I hit "post" and then held up my phone to snap a picture of him. I tried to take in the details as an impartial observer. He was in a black T-shirt, his hair mussed, and he needed to shave. In other words, he looked like a Calvin Klein model. I'd gone weak in the knees when he opened the door. I hadn't really steeled myself against it, even after being in his place for almost an hour.

But the analytical part of my brain recognized that this picture was the shot that would be fired around the Dallas dating world, the one that would kill any chance I had with him as it brought women out of the woodwork. It was exactly why I had to take it. Except for one small thing . . .

"What are you doing?" He eyed the phone in exasperation. "You already took a profile picture."

"Six Flags, 2002, the Shock Wave."

He looked startled, then grinned. I snapped the shot as he remembered the time we'd gone on the roller coaster four times in a row and Dave had vomited on the loop-de-loop during the last ride, sending puke spraying everywhere.

I checked the photo. It was so perfect it hurt. I clicked and swiped a few times and got it uploaded to his profile.

Yeah, game over. Some amazing women were about to discover him. The perfect one wouldn't be able to help it. I'd given her everything she needed to know to make her way to him.

I shut the laptop, as drained as the battery was. "You're set. I gotta go. Stuff to do." Like lie in the dark and find my breath again. Like make my heart go back to the right rhythm instead of this accelerated tap dance it was doing. Like calm my stomach down, make the hollow inside of it go away. I stood and leaned over to kiss him on the forehead. "Bye, Will."

Chapter 19 ♥

I HAD TURNED OFF MY phone when I got home, but when I woke up the next morning, a few texts popped up from Will. He'd sent the first an hour after I'd left.

I read the profile. I don't know what to say.

Twenty minutes later, when he'd followed up. *That was stupid. What I meant to say was thank you. No one's ever said anything so nice about me before. That sounds stupid. But I don't know what else to say. This whole text is stupid. When does this all stop being weird?*

I smiled and texted him back. *Never, because you're weird.*

His replay was instant. *There you are. And I changed my mind. You calling me names is normal. I like it better when you're saying how awesome I am.*

I rolled my eyes and tapped out a response. *I hate you.*

Is there an apology emoticon?

Ha. *Figures you wouldn't know where to find it.*

Ten seconds later, a "sorry" face popped up on my phone.

Did you have to Google that to find it?

Yes. But I still mean it. Just being real, the stuff you wrote humbled me.

Just being real, it was all true.

A long pause followed before he texted back. *All of it?*

Yeah. I said I'd put the real you out there, and I did. Did it work?

Another long pause. *Seems like it, yes. Not sure I'm up for it though.*

I wanted to pull my hair out at the words. *After everything that has gone down over the last three weeks, you had better be. I don't want to have turned myself into a head case only to find out that this dating seriously thing was a whim for you.*

Can I come down there?

NO. I'm running Will-free this morning. Make that free-Willing this morning. Haha. Get it?

No, because it's a bad joke, and I can't encourage stuff like that. I need to go.

Wait.

I waited, but when he didn't text back for a while, I climbed out of bed and stumbled toward the bathroom and my toothbrush. I was foaming at the mouth with Aquafresh when my phone beeped. I spat and scooped it up. Will again.

The idea of trying to be Mr. Perfect on a string of first dates right now makes me exhausted. I need a break.

"Aaargh!" I yelled to my sympathetic reflection. "Is he kidding me?" I tapped out an answer and wished each letter would hit his eyeball with the force of the annoyance I typed it with. *Srsly? NO. No way. If you want to stay friends, you need to date. For real. Women who seem cool. That I would like. That I would be okay hanging out with at one of Dave's barbecues. IT'S ONLY FAIR.*

I rinsed and spat, eying his reply on my screen.

The rules are CONFUSING.

Because I'm making them up as we go. Do what you want, but if you want to hang out with me, I need that buffer. Date a cool chick, W. Do it with my blessing.

And if I do this, we can hang out? That's how it works?

Maybe. Sometimes, probably.

Soon?

Eventually.

We need to get to a new normal. But all versions of normal include us hanging out again. Brace yourself.

I didn't answer him. He'd have to wait. I'd fallen in love with him over the course of years. It might take that long to fall out of love again.

The thought made my stomach hurt, and I did the only thing that had offered any hope of escape lately. I texted Jay. I needed something to look forward to. *Hang out soon?*

I'll wear my best basketball shorts.

Wha . . . ?

It was a rebounding joke.

OH, HA. Make it your running shorts. Then we'll see who's laughing when we hit the lake trail.

Game on. I'm going to make you sorry. Tomorrow morning?

It sounded like the perfect way to spend a Saturday, and I texted him a relieved yes. It was nice to think about a run with Jay instead of my next run-in with Will. And Jay was fine with it. Note to self: ask Sophie the word for a Christmas miracle in October.

* * *

Jay knocked at ten the next morning, and I opened the door to find him in a faded Captain America T-shirt and running shoes. The shirt fit him like it had been cut and sewn with his pecs in mind. I appreciated the view until he cleared his throat and I looked up to catch the corner of his mouth quirked up in a smile as he watched me.

I grinned, not at all embarrassed. "What's my superhero alter ego?"

He leaned against the doorframe and pretended to take the question seriously, scanning me from head to toe. His eyes lingered on my running shoes. "The Flash. You're going to smoke me today, aren't you?"

"Like a candy cigarette. Ready?"

Chapter 20 ♥

I STEPPED INTO THE HALL with Jay at the same time Will came up the stairs from the parking lot, dressed in shorts and a T-shirt too. A pretty redheaded woman in shorts that made her look so good I was instantly jealous and a baby-blue tank top I immediately wanted followed behind him. He paused when he saw us. I didn't want even one second of weirdness between us because Jay might put that together with my confession of unrequited love and make all of us awkward.

I smiled and walked toward Will, who didn't look like he was sure if he was supposed to acknowledge me or not. Constantly shifting rules were hard. I couldn't blame him. "Hey," I said, keeping my voice as normal as I would if we were the Will-and-Hannah of a month ago, before we broke. "You guys going for a run too?"

Will shook his head. "No. Disc golf, but I forgot the discs, so we had to run back to get them."

"Sounds fun," Jay said.

"Jay, this is my neighbor Will and his friend . . ."

"Shauna." The woman smiled, and I liked that she didn't add anything to clarify, like, "Shauna, Will's date." It meant she wasn't threatened. That was a good step toward furthering normal relations with Will. "I'm going to take your word for it that disc golf is fun. I have no hand-eye coordination, but Will says it's a good time, and he promised not to laugh at me, so we'll see."

"I'm not even really sure what it is," Jay said. "I'm giving it the benefit of the doubt because it has the word *golf* in it."

"It's really fun," I said to reassure Shauna. "I used to go with my brother and his friends all the time." I didn't clarify that I meant Will, and his eyebrow lifted at the omission. Too bad. It was time to go while the laid-back vibe still thrummed between us, like running into your neighbor in the hallway should.

"You should come," Shauna said. "I mean, on the condition that you can give me some tips to help me not look like an idiot."

I was about to decline, but Jay jumped in. "I'm not going to lie, that sounds better than trying to look like it's not killing me to keep up with Hannah here on our run." He hooked an arm around my neck and tugged me to him to drop a soft kiss on my hair. Will's eyes darkened, and I hurried to stop us from crashing his date.

"Thanks, but if we don't go on this run, Jay's going to think I can't back up my trash talk."

"I believe you," he said. "So much that I'm going to beg to go disc golf instead where I have a shot at not humiliating myself."

Great. But did I have that same shot with Will around? Trying to test drive our "be normal around each other's dates" plan was way down the road. I tried to figure out a polite way out of it, but Will shrugged and said, "Works for me. I've got enough discs for all of us."

I wanted to make eye contact with him and silently ask, "What are you thinking?" But even more than that, I didn't want Jay to notice that Will and I could have whole conversations without words and wonder why. Or Shauna either. I smiled. "Sounds good. Meet you over there?"

"Sure."

"To the Batmobile," Jay said, grinning.

The drive to the disc golf course was mellow. Jay told me a story about one of his employees who made up increasingly far-fetched excuses about why she had to miss work. I remembered to laugh at the right times. I even meant it. But I could have laughed harder and meant it more if I weren't distracted about how the next two hours were about to go down.

When we climbed out at the disc golf course, we had only a couple of minutes to sit on the grass and stretch before Will's car pulled up too.

"Stretching?" he called. "You guys are taking this hard core. I feel like I need to flex my arms or something, suck in and try to look intimidating."

"I'm not getting my running stretch, so I'm taking it here," I said.

"I'm doing whatever Hannah does so she doesn't get a competitive edge," Jay mumbled to his knees as he worked on his quads.

Will had crossed to Shauna's door and opened it for her, and she followed him to the sidewalk and smiled at us. "I'm ready," she said. "Stretching isn't going to help me."

Will set down the gym bag he'd slung over his shoulder and unzipped it to retrieve the Frisbee-shaped discs. "I'll do my best to match the right disc with the right golfer if you all promise not to accuse me of cheating."

"I'm sure the other expert here will keep you honest," Jay said, nudging my shoulder.

Ha. Will and I were being so far from honest about everything but disc golf right now that it was laughably ironic. But I nodded. "I'm watching you, neighbor."

Will handed everyone their own disc and explained the rules.

"So the rules are basically to get the disc in the baskets in the least amount of throws?" Jay asked.

"Basically," Will said.

Shauna groaned, and Jay laughed. "This is going to go so badly," Shauna said, her voice sad. I had to grin. She was pretty funny.

As we walked toward the first basket, Will stopped to tie his shoe, and I hung back long enough for Jay and Shauna to get out of earshot. I could only think of one way to possibly come off acting normal during this potential fiasco. I stooped down to "tie" my shoe too. "As far as I'm concerned, you're Dave to me today. That's how I have to treat you. It'll work." I jogged to catch Jay before Will could answer.

At the first basket, Will shot first. Jay and Shauna each fell pretty far short of Will's mark. I got pretty close though.

Jay high-fived me. "That was awesome, babe. I don't think this is going to be my new sport though."

The whole course was like that, Will patiently coaching Shauna as she improved slowly and Jay not being that invested in the game. He laughed every time his shots fell short. It wasn't that he was terrible—he had some natural athleticism—but he didn't listen to any of the coaching Will was giving Shauna, so his game stayed where it was. It was totally different from the dozen times I'd played with Dave and Will, who would push harder and trash talk worse than boxers before a big fight.

The change with Jay was nice. I didn't feel an all-consuming passion to shut his mouth with killer shots like I did with Dave and Will. I easily stayed in second place through the end of the game.

I talked to Will only as often as I needed to so it wouldn't occur to anyone to think I was avoiding him. By the time we reached the last basket and watched his effortless win, I was breathing easier. I'd survived. It had been okay. I met Will's eyes on purpose for the first time when we went to retrieve our discs from the basket. "Thanks," I said, finding a real smile and offering it to him.

He only gave me a short nod before he pulled his disc out and headed back to Shauna. What the heck? Why was he being all prickly? We'd pulled it off. We should be slapping high fives.

"Let's grab lunch," Jay said. "It's almost noon, and my stomach is being pretty vocal about it."

"Yes, to food!" Shauna called.

Will reached them before answering, and I trailed him, trying to make sense of the stress tensing his shoulders, but his voice was relaxed when he spoke to Jay. "That's a great idea. Shauna was mentioning a great sushi place."

So that was what he was up to. He was handing me an exit, and I could see as his glance flickered toward me and away again that he was expecting me to take it and run.

Which I definitely would. "Sounds great, but I'm not into sushi. You guys have fun though. I think I'll talk Jay here into beef brisket."

"Oh, we don't have to do sushi," Shauna said. "I like brisket."

"I have my stomach set on sushi now," Will said. "Looks like we're breaking this party up."

I nodded like I was agreeing, but I hoped Will understood that I was offering him a thank you. His tiny smile told me he got it.

"Beef brisket it is, babe." Jay held his hand out, and for me, it was a lifeline.

"See you guys later," I said, waving to Shauna, who offered us a big smile, and Will, who barely nodded again.

Lunch with Jay was good, although I kept losing the thread of the conversation. After the third time, Jay took my hand across the table, smiled, looked down at my half-eaten brisket sandwich, and then looked back up to me. "Whoever it was, he's an idiot."

I colored. "Sorry, what?"

"I'm saying that whoever didn't have the common sense to recognize what he had doesn't deserve you."

The words were designed to make me smile, but instead they spiked my anxiety. "Jay, I—"

He let go of me to hold up both palms in a "stop" gesture. "Don't stress. I know. You're a mess. I'm not misunderstanding the situation if that's what you're thinking."

It was exactly what I was thinking.

"I'm saying what 99 percent of dudes would tell you. You're pretty awesome. So clearly that 1 percenter is an idiot."

The anxiety didn't go away though. Sophie's caution played through my head. "Jay, I have a good time with you every time we go out. An honestly good time. It takes me out of my head for a little while. You crack me up, and you need a trophy for always making great conversation."

"And I'm good kisser."

"So good," I agreed, laughing at his mischievous expression. "But—"

"Don't say it," he said. "Because you're wrong, and I don't want you to regret it. If you're about to warn me about staying casual, don't worry about it. I don't need this to be anything other than what it is, so I mean it. You can relax, have a good time, and not stress about me. I can handle myself."

I wanted to believe him. Badly. Because if he really was getting emotionally attached to me, there was no way I could turn off my own guilt enough to ever enjoy hanging out with him again.

He took a long swig of his drink and set the glass down to grin at me. "You don't look convinced. So I'll convince you. This isn't my first time being a rebound. If I found the experience so bad, would I set myself up for it again? I'm a good guy. I accept your terms. I'm not wired to take advantage of your low ebb beyond having fun hanging out. And making out," he said, the mischief flashing again. "But seriously, it's fine. I've dated girls who are far more damaged than you. I can handle myself. It's fine."

"Damaged?" I repeated. "Is this a habit?"

"No. But after a certain point, is it even possible to find people without baggage? It's not like I don't have my own."

"I guess you're right. Sorry I'm hauling so much with me."

"You've done a pretty good job of not unpacking it all over the place. At this point, I just know you have it and this hazy notion of what's in it. That's a lot different than opening and airing every piece you've got."

"Right again. I'm amazing."

He raised his glass to me. "You're not half bad."

That made me laugh, and my appetite surged. I picked up my sandwich, happy to dig back in. The small knot in my stomach still tightened every time I tried to figure out what Will's deal was on the course today, but I'd get to that later. For right now, it was all about Jay, and I shut the door on Will as hard as I could.

Chapter 21 ♥

JAY DROPPED ME OFF AROUND two. I spotted Will's car so I made Jay let me off in the garage, and we said our good-byes in his Range Rover, where he backed up his "good kisser" brag for a few delicious minutes. But the high from that lasted only until I got to Will's door and knocked, hard and sharp, the glow fading while I waited for him to answer.

It only took a minute. "Hey," he said, opening the door for me.

"Is Shauna here?" I asked, my voice low.

"No."

I pushed past him and squared off, my hands on my hips. "Why are you mad at me?"

He studied me for a long moment before he closed the door and leaned against it. "I'm not."

"Then why were you so weird this morning? You almost gave us away."

"Gave what away?"

I gaped at him, trying to decide if he was being serious. "You know what."

His eyes narrowed. "Tell me."

"That we . . . that you and I . . ." I shoved one hand through my hair. Why was he being so obtuse? "That we have a thing."

He leaned his head back and closed his eyes. "We don't have a thing."

My own head snapped back like he'd slapped me. "I didn't mean it like a relationship. I meant that we have this complicated history, and no one is going to walk in and feel comfortable trying to be on a date with either of us while the other one is around. We pulled it off, but that could have been uncomfortable for everyone, and you weren't helping. Why did you even agree to that? We've never doubled before, and suddenly you're on two of my dates. Here's a new rule: stop it."

His eyes flew open to pin me. For once, I couldn't read his expression. It was closed and tense, and that was it. "I couldn't figure out a way to get out of it without making a big deal about it. Like you're doing now."

"Right now, I need to pick the spaces we share, Will. I need time to hang out with Jay without you around, distracting me."

"I think that's the last thing you need. That guy is not for you, Hannah."

"He's exactly what I need. Anytime we run into each other in the hallways around here and you see me with him, I'd appreciate it if you could think of something important you need to do in the opposite direction."

"You absolutely do not need that guy. He's wrong for you."

"I'm leaving," I said, too irritated to sit and listen to him repeat himself. "I'm sorry it annoys you that other guys see me as a full-grown woman capable of handling myself, but that's the reality."

"You want real? Fine. You said he knows he's your rebound and he's fine with that?"

"Yes."

"Then he's either a player or a knight, and both of those are bad news."

"I know a player when I see one. That's totally not Jay."

"You're probably right. But that makes him a knight, and that's the worst thing for you."

"Do you mean a knight like the rescuing-damsels-in-distress kind? Because I've been in some pretty deep distress lately, so I could use some saving."

"Which would be great if this guy was the right match for you, but he isn't. I've seen his type. He's a fixer, wants to come in and be your shoulder to cry on, distract you with flirting, listen sympathetically. He's not even trying to manipulate you. He's just that dude that feels better about himself when he's saving someone else. And he's going to be super gentle with you, and that relationship is going to be easy for you, and you're going to ease into it until you're two years down the road, bored to death, and looking back on wasted time."

I curled my hands into fists. "Wrong. He's hilarious and fun. We have a good time together. We have great conversations, and he makes me laugh all the time. Stop trying to ruin this."

"I'm not. I'm trying to help you. This isn't me playing Dave. This is me being your friend. Here to help. So listen, please? Please? Because I know this kind of guy pretty well, but I know you extremely well. And I watched him calling you babe today and putting his hands all over you. He's getting attached. What he's getting attached to is being needed. That would be okay with me if it's actually what you needed. It's not. You don't need a guy who tells you everything you do is a good job when you're not even pushing yourself. You don't need a guy who couldn't care less about winning or losing."

My jaw dropped. "Are you kidding me? This is all because you don't like the way he plays disc golf, because the score doesn't matter to him?"

"Sports are a good indicator for how people approach life. You know that, Hannah. I know you know that. Take Shauna. She didn't care about losing, but she did care about getting better as the game went. Jay coasted. And told you everything you did was awesome. You need a truth-teller."

"You're insane," I said.

"Am I? Would you and Sophie be best friends if all she ever did was tell you how awesome you are and did everything you wanted to do the way you wanted to do it?"

"I'm not dating Sophie."

"And you shouldn't be dating Jay."

Anger surged inside me. "Did you hear anything I told you the other night? Even one thing? This is hard!" My voice rose even though I'd fought to keep it even. "It's so hard, and the least you can do is not make it worse. Stay out of this."

He straightened so fast I took a step back. "I heard you," he said, his voice tight. "I heard you the other night, and I heard you two weeks ago when you came in throwing words around like you forgot how hard they can hit. And I kept my mouth shut because that's what you needed. But that was huge, Hannah. Massive. Those were big, giant words you tossed in here like a flash bang grenade and then walked out while I was still trying to see through the flare."

He cursed and shoved past me so he could storm to the kitchen. The skin on my arm burned where he'd brushed against it, and despair flooded my stomach. How long did I have to deal with that heated reaction to him? He switched the faucet on and let a glass fill with water, his hands braced on either side of the sink, his back to me.

When he shut the water off, I cleared my throat. "Sorry." It was barely more than a whisper. I could feel his anger rolling toward me. It wasn't something I'd experienced from him. Ever.

He didn't answer. I shifted from foot to foot, turned to the door to leave, stopped, shifted on my feet again. "Do you want me to go?"

He didn't answer for a long moment. "Maybe you should," he said, turning and settling back against the counter, his arms crossed against his chest.

It was a kick in the gut. I sucked in my breath and nodded, tears pricking behind my eyes. I tried to say, "Okay," but I could tell I'd cry if I talked, so I swallowed instead, nodded again, at a loss to control the jerky movements any more than the Nolan Ryan bobblehead on his TV stand could.

Will watched me, as still as the furniture he'd shoved to get out of my way, and I drew a deep breath that caught in my throat. I turned for the door again, knowing the unsteady breath meant I only had seconds before the tears slipped out whether I tried to talk or not.

He cursed again and had a hand on my wrist before I could even reach for the knob. "Come here," he said, and it was a frustrated growl that rumbled in his chest as he pulled me into a hug.

I leaned against him, burrowing my head under his chin so he wouldn't see the two tears that had escaped. I sniffled hard to keep any more from falling.

"You're right, Hanny. I'm so mad at you." But his voice sounded sad, not angry.

"Why? None of this happened to you."

His arms tightened. "All of it happened to me." He relaxed after a moment and leaned back to frame my face in his hands. "You flipped everything." His touch was soft as he wiped away the new tears that had snuck out to join the first two. "Dave gave me a clear job while he's in Qatar. I don't know what I'm supposed to do now."

"I'm so sorry. I don't know what to do either."

He leaned his forehead down to touch mine. Sophie used to tease me that the reason I had a crush on Will in high school was because he was the only one tall enough to make me feel as dainty as almost every guy at school made her feel with her petite frame. But back then Will had never felt as overwhelming as he did right this second, bent over me. His eyes were closed, and our breaths would have mingled if I was still breathing, but I'd stopped. It would take the tiniest tilt, an almost imperceptible shift, and I could kiss him, like I'd wanted to for years.

But it would set us back even further, and I didn't want to freak him out more. I gathered the strength I would need to step away from him, letting out a sigh so soft I wondered if he could even feel it against his cheek. His hands slid around the base of my neck and threaded through my hair, and he brushed his lips against mine.

I froze. He did it again, pressing a kiss against my mouth, harder, more sure.

"W-Will?"

He only deepened the kiss. I reached up to grab his shirt, lost in a wave of sensation crashing down on me so hard that it drew me inside it and drowned everything else out. It was obliteration. Everything disappeared, including my ability to think. I could only feel—the explosion of heat down the nerves in my arms, the way his lips fit mine so perfectly, and the lurking fear that it was going to end, that I was going to need to come up for air. And I didn't want to, not ever.

I tangled my fingers through his hair to keep him there, and he slid his hands to my back to pull me closer. A split second of panic tore through me that he was going to let me go. But he didn't, only angled his head the other way to drink in more of the kiss.

But the panic terrified me. I had no idea what he was doing, but I bet he didn't either. I pushed against his chest, and he gave me room without letting go of me completely, his eyes dazed. I stared at him, too scared to step away, even more scared to stay there and let this last any longer, to let this become any bigger so that the memory would be impossible to bury.

"I didn't know," he said.

"I know. I got really good at hiding it when you moved in here."

"No, I meant I didn't know that . . ." He trailed off, obviously unable to find words.

"I tried to tell you," I said, pushing against him hard enough that he let go.

"You did. I'm sorry."

The last thing I wanted was an apology, even though I knew the regret was weighing him down. But it couldn't feel half as heavy as the dread spreading out from my chest and into my stomach and limbs. Will's kisses were the one thing I'd never had to hold anyone else up to and watch them fall short. It was the thing that had made Jay better than Will in at least one way, and Will had just stolen that from me and given me the burden of a new impossible standard. He'd turned me inside out, shaking me to the core while holding me like I was made of feathers he needed to gather to him softly so they wouldn't blow away.

I pressed the heels of my hands into my eyes, rubbing them hard, wishing I could sand away my tear ducts and never cry about this again. "Maybe I broke us, but you just ruined everything. Was it worth it? Did you satisfy your curiosity? Did you do that to see if you could?" I spun toward the door.

"Stop it," he said, reaching past me to slam the door closed. "And apologize." His voice was low, laced with a dangerous note I'd never heard in it before.

I put both hands on the knob, tugging to get out. "Let me go, Will."

"No. Not if you're going to leave here thinking I would kiss you out of curiosity. When have I ever been that guy? To anyone?"

"Then why did you do it?" I slapped the palm of my hand against the door in frustration and turned to face him. He was too close, his arm above my head as he held the door shut.

Frustration crossed his face as he stared down at me. He opened his mouth and closed it again. I willed him to give me an answer I could understand, but he stayed silent, a shadow flickering through his eyes. And worse, something I'd never seen on his face before, so I didn't recognize it at first: shame.

Acid churned inside me. "You did it because you're a competitor, Will. First or worst, right? And you couldn't stand that I was suddenly gone, not here to cater to every stupid whim you have, to be your fan girl and stroke your ego. Has it been too quiet without me here to worship you? I'm *such* an idiot."

I shoved him hard and knocked him off balance so he had to take a step back. I twisted to open the door, but he grabbed me from behind and pulled me back against his chest. It didn't hurt, but there was no give in his hold, no chance he was letting me go until he was ready to. "You did this to me. Don't blame me for this," he said, his voice soft. "I didn't make you kiss me back." His breath skimmed along my ear, and I shivered as he let go and stepped back.

He pressed a hand against his eyes, rubbing them, his expression looking a lot like my migraine face. When he looked at me again, I saw pure frustration. "My head is so messed up right now, Hannah. I can't think. I don't know how to solve this."

"Solve this? Because I'm a problem?" That hurt. I couldn't hold his gaze anymore, so I jerked the door open and walked out without a backward glance.

Chapter 22 ♥

"'YOU DID THIS TO ME?'" Sophie repeated when I calmed down enough to call her. "What did you do to him?"

"I don't know. Confused him, I think."

There was a long silence. "How do you feel about that?"

"I don't feel anything except angry."

"I think that's good."

"How can that possibly be good?"

"Because if this were a month ago, you'd be thrilled that he'd quit taking you for granted enough to see you. But you're not thrilled. So maybe it means you're kind of past him a little."

"I'm past falling all over myself to get to him because he smiled at me. I'm past rearranging my plans with anyone and everyone because he texts me last minute to come watch a game. I'm past keeping Gatorade in my fridge because he might come wandering over." I hesitated, not wanting to lower Sophie's new-found respect for me, but we were always honest with each other. "I can't say I'm over him."

"You've loved him for a long time. How could you be? But you're finally recognizing your value in the Hannah-and-Will equation, and maybe things will equal out now."

"Maybe. But the whole thing felt like a disaster."

"He was a bad kisser?"

"No. He's good." That was a mild way of explaining what had felt more like a seismic shift in my personal universe. "That's why it sucks. How am I going to kiss Jay or anyone else without comparing it to Will's kiss?"

Sophie blew out a breath, the sound of her frustration sympathetic and oddly comforting. "That's a hard one."

I was quiet for a minute before sighing too. "I wish you would have said something like, 'You'll have other good kisses.' Because it feels like good is never going to be enough again after mind-blowing."

"Do you think it was mind-blowing for him too? Do you think that's what confused him?"

"Yeah, but not in the same way. It's hard to hide how you feel in a kiss, don't you think? You can tell if it's about lust or like. If it's moving to something more. If he's present. If he's thinking about the Cowboys game. And I think Will finally understood how I feel at a level that my words weren't making clear. I think that before he figured I was going to need a few weeks to cool off and we'd be back to normal. And I have a feeling he finally understood everything I'd been holding back."

"That's a lot to read into a kiss, especially since you're only guessing what he got out of it."

"Not really. He kind of told me too. I said, 'I tried to tell you,' and he said he was sorry."

There was dead silence on the other end of the phone.

"Sophie?" I prodded her. "Did you wince? Because that was exactly what my soul did when he said it."

"I did wince," she said, her voice sad. "That's what he said? 'Sorry'?"

"Yeah."

"I don't even know what to suggest. I mean, ice cream. I don't know. Seems like maybe a good time to take up drinking."

I laugh-sobbed and choked it back, not wanting to set off another crying jag. "I think I'm going to crawl into bed and stay there for a week. Or maybe forever. My heart feels like it has a migraine inside of it."

"This barely happened. Time will make it better."

"Right. You mean the way my feelings for him eventually faded over time."

Silence.

"You winced again, didn't you?" I accused her.

"Yes," she said, her voice small. "I'm so sorry. All-the-way-down-to-my-guts sorry. I want to have an answer for you, but I don't know what to say. Except I'm proud of you. I'm proud that after all the years of trying to make him see that you're perfect for him, you're seeing that it's not your job. You be you. Maybe one day he'll figure it out, but he'll have to live with the fact that he figured it out too late."

A knock sounded on the door. "Hannah?"

My heart thudded harder than the knock. "Oh, crap. He's knocking on my door right now."

"Are you going to answer him?"

He knocked again, louder. "I think I have to. I have a feeling he won't go away."

"Be strong, girl," Sophie said as I hung up.

I set the phone down and smoothed my hair while he knocked a third time, determined to answer on my own time looking totally unruffled. He was knocking again, more sharply, and I pulled the door open and left him with his hand hanging in the air.

"What do you need, Will?"

"We weren't done."

"I feel like we were," I said, starting to close the door.

"Hannah, please. I need to clear something up."

I hesitated and stepped aside. He walked in and waited for me to walk to the sofa before he followed me. I took my corner, and he sat in the opposite one, resting his head in his hands and staring at the floor. "I'm sorry for what happened at my place."

"Which part?"

"Every part that upset you."

"And which parts do you think upset me?"

"All of it. Some of it was just me being mad. But some important things came out the wrong way." He scrubbed his hands through his hair and turned his head slightly to smile at me. His eyes bored into mine, and it paralyzed me. He'd done that a few times since I'd texted after the two weeks of trying to avoid him. It wasn't a look I was used to with him, where I had all of his attention. For as many hours as we'd spent together, it had always been with me as a part of his environment. He saw me the same way he did his furniture or his wall posters. I was woven into the fabric of his life as much as any of the other things he kept close but was well used to.

This expression was different. It felt like having a spotlight on my face. I wanted to hold up my arm and duck, find anonymity from his clear-eyed gaze.

"I never would have taken it where it went today, Will. And now we're here in the middle of quicksand, it feels like."

"Maybe you should have taken it there, Hannah. I think that was the point I was trying to make."

My stomach flipped, twisted, tried to turn inside out. "What are you talking about?"

"I mean, yeah, when you were a kid and you said you had a crush on me, I knew you did. It was obvious. But it seemed like you outgrew it over college. You treated me exactly the way you treated Dave when we went on trips and stuff."

"I had to," I said. "That confession was the most humiliating experience of my life. I needed you to believe it was some dumb kid thing I'd grown way past. But I needed to believe it even more."

"You succeeded. Big time. I had no idea."

"But then you had to go and move down the hall and complicate everything. My alternate reality that I was grown-up and over it puffed away like smoke."

"I don't know if it makes you feel any better, but you totally confused me after that crush thing. You were this gob of emotions all the time. And then you start college and you're fine. You and Sophie are always around, either giggling about guys in your dorm or crying about calculus. And I think, okay, guess she's over it. Cool. And then I graduate, and I see you way less, but you're super chill with me and Dave on our trips.

"Then Dave gets married, and suddenly you're my responsibility, so I take over his lease so I can be nearby and do it right. And I'm seeing you every day, and you're totally pulled together and kicking butt at your job and going out with guys, and it's not what I expected when Dave told me to keep an eye on you. I kinda knew how to do that when you were in college. But polished Hannah? I figured I'd better do what Dave would do. Disapprove of all your boyfriends. Hang out and watch games with you. You seemed fine with it."

"I was trying to be," I said. "You know in that *Nemo* movie where the Ellen DeGeneres fish is like, 'Just keep swimming'? That was me. I'd faked being friends with you for so long that I thought that was all I wanted. And it was working great until you all of a sudden announced that you're on a mission to get married. And I realized everything was going to change permanently. It was a shock to me that I wasn't okay with this either."

He smiled at me again. "I don't get a lot of things this wrong."

I shrugged. "I've spent years trying to humble you and Dave. Figures it would take something this extreme."

He crept forward on the sofa, stretching out until he was lying down, his head in my lap, nestled on the pillow I'd been torturing. "I'm really sorry."

I stared down at him resting there, eyes closed, tension in the crow's feet he was developing. I touched his hair. So soft. He must be using the conditioner I'd made him buy. I ran my fingers through it some more, warm at the roots and cool at the tips. His crow's feet relaxed.

He was quiet so long I wondered if he'd fallen asleep, but his hand crept up, and his fingers laced through mine like they were designed to fit right there. In a minute, I would pull my hand back and make up an excuse to stand and walk away. But I needed that touch for a tiny bit longer.

"Hanny."

"Yeah."

"There are a couple more things I didn't say right before. I need to say them the right way now. Is that okay?"

"Sure."

"Do you remember how angry Dave was after your parents died? He was mad and nothing else. He was a bunch of rage walking around wearing Dave's skin for almost a year."

Will was painting a picture that didn't match my memories, mostly because the months after the accident were a blur. Just grayness. "I don't really remember that," I said, feeling like I needed to apologize. "I was out of it for a long time. Everything I remember from that year is fuzzy around the edges, and the few conversations I remember having with people sound like we're having them from opposite ends of a tunnel in my memory. I know I walked and talked. And I ate. So much. It was the only thing that felt good. Aunt Cindy gave me treats whenever I wanted because it's the only thing I expressed any interest in, I think. And I must have gone to school and stuff. I don't even really remember Sophie too much during that first while." She'd come over. I wasn't there mentally for whatever we were doing physically—playing with Barbies? Getting into Dave's long-abandoned Lego sets? I didn't know. I wasn't ever going to get those memories back.

Will squeezed my hand for a second like he could sense the emptiness that was trying to creep up on me from the dark days. "I'm sorry. I don't want to push on your bruises. But I didn't know how much you remembered about Dave. He was scary. Or I guess I was scared for him, never of him. So I looked up all these articles on grief and anger and how to help him. I even went and saw the guidance counselor at the school a few times to figure out what I was supposed to do."

It broke my heart. This was exactly why I loved Will. As a sophomore in high school, he was doing all this stuff to help his best friend because that was the kind of person Will was. How was I supposed to get over someone like that? I slid my hand from his, pretending I needed to cough. "You've always been a good friend to him."

He pushed himself up and straightened to look at me, and it startled me how close he was. He was nearly as close as he'd been when he kissed me. I could smell his toothpaste. He stared at me before he cleared his throat and spoke again, but he didn't move away.

"I learned a lot about anger that fall, doing all that reading and pestering Mr. Garnet about how to help Dave. And I learned that anger is always a reaction to one of three things: Embarrassment. Hurt." He reached over and touched a strand of my hair, winding it through his fingers. "And fear. Anger is an outlet for fear. It lets you take an emotion that's gnawing you from the inside and turn it around on the world. Or your friends. That's what Dave was doing to me." He let the strand of hair unwind from his finger, then curled it around it again. "That's what I did to you earlier. I was so mad. Everything has been wrong since you told me how you felt, and I was blaming you for it."

I drew my head back, slowly, watching the curl unwind from his finger again, hoping his eyes would stay there too so he couldn't see the embarrassment flooding my cheeks. "I said I was sorry. I don't really want to talk about it anymore." I braced myself to push up off the couch, but the movement tipped me toward him. He leaned forward and kissed me again. Every nerve ending in my body lit up, heat sweeping down from my cheeks and racing along my skin until even my palms tingled.

He pulled me toward him, and he lifted his lips from mine only to brush them across my scorched cheekbone and down to my jawline, exploring, leaving feather-light kisses that burned like fire anyway.

I squeezed my eyes shut, overwhelmed by the sensation. "What are you doing?" I murmured as his mouth traveled back to the corner of mine. "Why are you doing this?" It was a plea to stop wrapped up in a plea to understand, and he heard it, leaning back enough for me to breathe.

"Hannah," he said, and my name was a sigh. "When I kissed you before and said I didn't know, I'm pretty sure you thought I meant that I didn't know how you felt. And I didn't know, until you told me. But that's not what I was talking about. I meant that I didn't know how I felt until you told me how you felt."

My heart stopped, stuttered, and started again, this time racing. "Tell me what you mean because my guesses might drive me crazy."

"I mean that when I say Jay isn't right for you, it's true, but it's also selfish because I'm a jerk who wants you for myself even when I'm terrified I'm not the right guy for you. And because Dave is going to hate this. He trusted me to watch out for you like he would. This is not that." He brushed his lips against mine. "This is so not that. I meant to stay away from you. I did. But I can't. So I kissed you. Again. And again. And again. And I'm going to do it as many times as you'll let me."

I froze, not sure how to even process what he was saying. Will, the boy I had fallen wildly in love with years ago, the man who had captured my heart again despite my best efforts, was saying he wanted me. Loved me? He hadn't said that. But he was as into our kisses as I was, and he didn't want me with anyone else. It was like getting my granted wish, gift-wrapped on a silver platter, waiting for me to open it and make it mine.

I reached out and touched his face, feeling the rasp of his late-day whiskers against my palm, running my thumb lightly across his lips. He was saying he wanted this to be my right, to do this whenever I wanted to, to know with a single touch that he was mine. I had dreamed of this for so long. For too long. And with a tiny sigh, I pushed him away, slid off the couch, and walked away.

Chapter 23 ♥

"WHERE ARE YOU GOING?" HE asked when I reached my front door and it was obvious I was leaving. He didn't sound angry, only confused.

"The leasing office, I think." I didn't even know if they were open so close to dinnertime on a Saturday. But I needed to be out of his space right that second and for every one after that. I needed far more than twenty yards of hallway separating me from Will. I should have done this the day I told him how I felt but that I was moving on.

He vaulted himself over the back of the couch, nearly stumbling when he landed. "Hannah, talk to me. I have no idea what's going on. Please?"

It was the hurt and genuine confusion in the last word that made me turn around. He had no idea what he'd done. He hadn't come in here trying to hurt me. But that was always the issue with him: he never understood the effect he had on me.

"Your point in coming over right now was . . . what, Will? To tell me that you suddenly think I'm hot and want to make out with me?"

His head jerked back. "No. Not at all."

"Then what? Confess undying love? Kiss me as an experiment? What, Will? Why are you here?"

He swallowed, looking so uncertain my heart squeezed before I hardened it again. "I don't know. I wanted to be as honest as you were. You've had the guts to tell me how you feel twice, and I figured it was my turn."

I hesitated and walked away from the door, but not to run to him, not to fling myself into his arms and pretend we were going to start our happily ever after. "Wait here," I told him, heading for my bedroom. I walked into my closet and reached for the top shelf, pulling out a small box I'd made years before at Bible camp one summer. It was the size of a brick but built with cheap balsa, feather light and painted hot pink, my favorite color when I was fourteen.

I walked out and handed it to him. "Open this."

He flipped the flimsy clasp and pulled out the sash inside. Flaking glitter glue spelled out "Midwinter Prince" across the cheap satin. "How'd you get this?" he asked, his fingers grazing the raised letters.

"Your senior year you didn't want to go to the midwinter formal. Do you remember that?"

His forehead furrowed. "No. I went with . . ." His eyes squeezed shut for a second while he tried to come up with a name.

"Emily Scully. But you didn't want to go because you were on the court, and you said that midwinter formal was a consolation prize for the basketball team and that everyone was football crazy and you were tired of being the afterthought. You did a whole rant about how athletes in every sport deserve recognition and you weren't going to be a puppet in the student body's lame attempt to pretend that they treated all sports equally."

His lips twitched. "I barely remember that. I can't decide if I was an idiot or a visionary."

"Do you remember why you ended up going with Emily?"

"No. I think that's the only time we went out. I'm sure I just needed a date for the dance. She was cute, I think."

I pulled the sash from his hands and folded it back up to fit inside the box. "Emily Scully had a crush on you that entire fall of your senior year. And you never even really acknowledged her. She *was* cute. Really pretty, actually, but not in the cheerleader/popular-girl way you liked. She was normally kind of quiet, I think. But she would try hard to get your attention, talk to you, all that kind of stuff. I was always hanging around yours and Dave's lockers. I watched it."

His smile had disappeared. "I don't remember any of that."

"Doesn't surprise me. Do you know when you paid attention to her?"

He shook his head, looking like he didn't want to hear the answer.

"Since midwinter is a girl's preference dance, Emily asked me one day to feel you out and see if you'd say yes if she asked you. But because of my dumb crush on you, I didn't want to help her out. So I told her you weren't going because you thought the dance was stupid. So she said she was going to ask a junior guy instead. Sophie and I were talking about it by Dave's locker that afternoon, and you interrupted, and you were like, 'Senior girls shouldn't be dating junior guys.' And then the next thing I know, that whole rest of the week you're flirting with Emily and inviting her to sit by you at lunch, and by Friday, she'd asked you to the dance."

He leaned against the back of the sofa. "I think I know where you're going with this, but I hope I'm wrong."

"The second you realized you couldn't have her, you went out of your way to get her." The parallels to our situation were so obvious that my eyes stung, tears of stupidity and embarrassment.

"This isn't like that," he said. "It's not even close. I didn't know Emily. I *know* you. I know everything about you, from how you like your nachos to the things that make you sad. And it's been killing me for weeks now that I was one of those things. I hate that. I would never want that, and if I'd known how you'd been feeling, I would have acted much, much differently."

"I didn't want that! I love our friendship. When I realized I'm in your permanent friend zone and nothing would change that, I had to work through some hard feelings, but I realized that I'd rather have that friendship than nothing. That your friendship isn't a consolation prize. It's a blessing. It always has been. It wasn't only Dave you saved back in those hard days."

"Oh, sweet girl," he said, reaching out to draw me into his arms. I nestled my head under his neck again, a moment of weakness where I knew I should push him away but couldn't. "I would have given anything to put you and Dave back together after your mom and dad died."

I stayed there for a full minute, soaking in his warmth and strength, wrapping his soft "Oh, sweet girl," around me before I drew away. "You did eventually." I walked past him and stood at my window. I couldn't face him while I said the next part and have him see into me as easily as I watched what was happening two floors below me at the pool. "But you'll be what undoes me again if I fall into this. You don't love me; you love the challenge. Or whatever it is you think you feel," I hurried to add, not wanting to humiliate myself by reading too much into his kisses. "But I've grown up enough now not to settle for what I can get. If I were to dive into this with you, where would we be in a few weeks? Or a few months. Which would be worse, truthfully."

"What I feel for you isn't going away. It hasn't for ten years. Longer, maybe. But you'll get twitchy again, and you'll go to the next thing, the next girl, the next challenge. And that would rip out my insides. I'd survive. I'm not pathetic. But I don't want to have to do that. I don't want to grieve another loss."

"You're wrong about what's happening here," Will said, his voice quiet. "This isn't me wanting you because I can't have you. This is me accepting truth."

"Accepting truth? What does that even mean?"

"It means that after you wrote up my revised profile, I read it and thought that you'd described a man I've always tried to be, but I haven't always been successful. You wrote about who I am, not what I do, not a list of hobbies that I can crosscheck with someone else until I find a decent overlap. You wrote about my core. And the thing is, I could write that for you. I see you that clearly. I always have."

"But loving someone as a friend is not the kind of love I want. I feel blessed to have that with you, but I have that with Sophie too. If we dated or tried to turn this friendship into something else, the connection between you and me would end; it would have to." I turned away from the window to face him. "It's your nature. I never should have pushed this. Leave it, Will. Please."

"I can't."

"Then I'll beg. Because it's already going to be so hard for us to fix, but now it's on you, not on me. Leave this alone. Leave me alone. Let me put myself back together. It feels hard but not impossible right now. And you're tempting me to give up even that small chance of our friendship with these kisses and hopes, and . . . and . . ." I shoved my fingers through my hair and hunched over. "Go, Will. Please."

"How am I supposed to leave you alone? I live down the hall. I'm going to see you every day and want you every time I see you."

Want. Not love. Want.

"I'm fixing that part. I know the front office won't let me break my lease, but I think they'll let me move into a new unit, maybe in building A," I said, naming the one farthest from us.

"That's it? You're so convinced that you know how I feel about you, what I want from you? You're taking everything I say and using it against me. I feel like there's no way to convince you that I mean what I'm saying."

"Because there isn't, Will! There isn't. And I'm begging you as my friend, as Dave's friend, to go."

He started to say something, and I could feel the hard stab of more tears coming. "Please," I said before he could get the words out.

He swallowed and nodded, folding his arms across his chest, his right hand kneading his left bicep, a sure sign that he wanted to punch something. He'd put a few holes in walls when he was in high school. "I'm sorry, Hannah. I didn't do this right at all."

"You never had a chance," I said with a watery smile, willing him to leave before the tears fell. "I'm too much of a mess, and my twelve-year crush on you is too full of landmines for this to ever have worked. I'm sorry I let my inner teenager take over my common sense for a while. I'll tie her up." The first tear slipped out.

"I hate leaving you like this," he said.

"Then you should know how much I hate having you see me like this. Maybe that will help you jet out of here."

He nodded again. "Okay. Okay. I . . . okay." He closed the distance between us in two steps and pulled me into a hug. "You're always trying to fix and take care of things. But I'm going to do this. I'm going to be the guy you tried to convince the rest of the world I am in that profile. This will be all right. We'll work it out."

He closed the door quietly behind him. I stared after him, timed how long it would take him to disappear into his place. Then I left too, straight to the leasing office to beg for some breathing room.

Chapter 24 ♥

I GLANCED AT MY COMPUTER screen and then at my cell phone. I did the weak thing and picked it up to text Sophie. *Remind me again.*

She sent an instant reply. *You CAN do hard things.*

I set the phone down and scooped it up again to do the first hard thing. I punched in Jay's number. "Hey," he said, sounding delighted to hear from me. Which sucked a lot. But it was the exact reason I had to make the call.

"Hey," I said. "Remember how I was like, 'I'm an emotional mess' and you said that was cool and for a little while we had a good thing going there with our friends-with-benefits situation?"

There was a long a pause. "Had? Past tense?"

"Would you be up for grabbing a meal and talking some stuff over?"

"Does the talking involve you telling me something about how this isn't working for you?"

It was my turn for a long pause. I didn't want to say it, but I had to, and I knew it.

But he answered before I could. "That's definitely a yes."

"Yeah." I sighed, hating the whole conversation already.

"Well," Jay said, his voice tight. "I know you warned me, but I still didn't see this coming. It seemed like we were hitting it off really well. What changed?"

"Nothing," I said, guilt roughing up my voice. "I guess that was the problem. You're so great. Fantastic, actually. And if you couldn't pull me out of my head, I don't think it can be done. It's totally unfair to you."

He sighed. "I can't say this doesn't bum me out, but I'm glad you're saying something now and not a million years from now. This stings my ego, but I'll survive. I think I'm going to pass on dinner or whatever. I've got the gist."

"I'm so sorry," I said, not caring that my misery was probably shining through. "I wish I could clone an emotionally healthy version of myself and set her up with you."

"It's fine," he said, and his voice had that distant quality in it that happened when someone shifts you to their "polite conversation only" column.

"I'm sorry," I said again. "I wish there were something I could do."

He laughed. "You can start by not sounding like you think you've ruined my life. You're pretty cool, but you're not *that* awesome."

I smiled. "I deserved that."

"Yep. And you can do one more thing for me," he said but hesitated.

"Name it."

"Just tell me this: is it Will? The reason you're so messed up?"

"Why would you think that?" I asked, stalling.

"So it is," he said. "There's a crazy energy around you two. Seems like a good guy. Good luck. Is that even what I'm supposed to say here?"

"More like condolences," I said. "That's never going to work. So I'm breaking it off with you because I'm a mess, but I'm definitely not moving onto something else this time. I'm going to load my Kindle with *Eat, Pray, Love*–type books of women figuring themselves out, and I'm going to sequester myself from dating until I make some kind of progress."

That won another laugh from him. "Good luck, and this time I mean it."

I thanked him like a total dork and hung up. I wished desperately that I could go into work, but it was Sunday, and now I had a day to fill with something besides thoughts of Will. Which seemed impossible. I'd wanted to spend the day moving, but even though the leasing office had agreed to let me change apartments, the unit wouldn't open for two more weeks.

Fourteen days of anxiety every time I opened my front door to leave in case I bumped into Will. It would be my outside limit, but I could do it.

The plan after spending an hour on the phone with Sophie this morning was to keep myself as busy as possible to keep my mind off things. Off Will. She'd helped me come up with a list of things to do but not without making me deconstruct the scene with Will twice, especially the part where he said he understood me and wanted to be with me.

"Then why not see where it goes?" she'd asked. As if she hadn't been telling me that he wasn't good enough for me. But she'd brushed away that concern. "He gets it now. And he's a good guy. How will you ever know if you don't try?"

How would I know? Because I'd had a lifetime to study him. And I could see the breakup as easily as I could see the early days full of infatuated kisses. And in the time it took to go from one to the other, I'd end up collecting a whole bunch of new memories it would be impossible to purge when we ended.

Sophie had dropped her argument and helped me make my "keep insanely busy" list. At the top was to limit all proximity to Will so I could try to think about him less. At least I had a move in the works. But I still had lots of other spaces full of Will to clear out somehow. Delete messaging threads; unfollow him on Twitter, where he was documenting his Gatorade bottle castle; unfollow him on Instagram, where he posted adventure pics.

How do you quit someone cold turkey when you can't remember when they weren't a part of your life?

I pulled up HeyThere and logged in, needing to deactivate my profile too so I couldn't suck anyone else into my drama. But the second I clicked the button to hide my profile, my fingers zipped over the keyboard on kamikaze autopilot, typing in Will's screen name and trying to destroy me.

Nothing popped up.

I straightened and tried a few things, but no Will. I punched in every possible search sequence that could find him, but he wasn't there. He'd scrubbed himself and the beautiful profile I'd written off the website. I took a couple of virtual tours of other websites he'd mentioned when he'd started his experiment, but there was no trace of him on those either.

Okay. What did that mean? He was giving up on the online thing? When had he done this?

It didn't matter. What mattered was that it made things a tiny bit easier for me, and I'd take it.

I picked up my cell to delete our message threads, but it buzzed in my hand. It was him. *Your heart is bigger than Texas. Don't tell Sophie I used that cliché.*

I stared at the message, then typed, *Thank you. But what was that for?*

I waited several minutes, but he didn't answer. *Will?*

Still no answer. I left the message thread alone for the time being until I could figure out what that last text had been about. Instead, I got up and worked on the second thing on the keeping-busy list and spent an hour rearranging the spices in my cabinet and listening to a science podcast about bee-colony collapses. I'd had better Sunday nights, but that project plus six *Friends* episodes was enough to keep my mind at a low rev instead of a flat-out race until it was time to go to sleep.

I didn't have a set bedtime, but for the foreseeable future, it would be when I thought I was tired enough to lie down and drift right off without spending any time in that vulnerable place where I could feel how hard I was already missing Will, where the weight of everything that I was losing could smother me.

My phone went off as soon as my head touched the pillow. Will again. *There is no better friend to have than a Becker.*

Great. Except I'd screwed up even that. I stuck my phone in my pantry so I wouldn't hear it, then went back to bed, but sleep didn't come for a long time.

He texted again almost as soon as I fished my phone out of the pantry the next morning, and I startled when it buzzed, dropping it in the sink, where it narrowly avoided landing in the oatmeal bowl I was soaking.

You always see the best in people, and you expect more from them than they expect from themselves. It makes me want to be better. It always has.

I couldn't stand it. Not one more message. *What are you doing?!!!*

He didn't answer.

I mean it. Tell me. What's up with these messages?

The phone vibrated. *Come down here and ask me that to my face.*

I didn't respond. I left for work a half hour before I knew he would. I didn't normally walk into work happy to discover that we had a massive bug to sort through, but today, if I could have found the bug, I would have hugged it for semidistracting me until midafternoon when Will texted again. I hated that I hoped it was him the second my phone went off. I hated that I wanted it to be another compliment. I hated that my fingers fumbled to pull up the message.

If we could figure out how to harness your determination and convert it into fuel, it would be more powerful than fusion. Your willpower is amazing.

But not my Will power. That was totally weak and fading fast. I set the phone down and walked back to the conference room to work through the broken code my team had finally found. At least here I had problems I could solve, unlike at home where I only made them worse.

I could only hope we had an equally nasty batch of code to debug tomorrow because even with work taking all of my concentration, Will was stealing thought after thought.

I didn't respond to him at all for the next two days, despite five more texts. He told me that he admired my relationship with my brother, the way I loved what I loved, like *Friends* marathons, even when other people like him teased me for it. He told me that I had the quickest mind of anyone he knew and that he loved the way I cooked, even when it was rabbit food. But it was the fifth one that pushed me too far. It came in right as I got home on Wednesday. *You've always taken better care of me than anyone. You are so good at that.*

Because I love you! I wanted to scream. *Because I would have done anything for you. Because I still would do anything for you.* So why couldn't he give me this one thing? It had been three days since I'd watched him walk out of my place, three full days where I didn't feel one bit better, one iota more hopeful that I would get through this.

Stop it. I pressed send. If I needed to beg, I would, but this had to be over. And yet my phone vibrated in my hand.

Make me. Right now.

It was a game to him. A freaking game! I stomped into my bedroom and tore off my suit, skinning into my running gear as fast as I could. I'd outrun this. Him. My anger.

Because he was making me very angry. Furious.

I tore open my front door, intent on hitting the running trail, but I stopped cold. A package sat on the doorstep topped by a card with my name on it in Will's handwriting.

I scooped them both up and dropped them on the table. The box was dense, maybe a couple of pounds, and it made a loud thunk when it hit the table. I ripped the envelope off the card. There'd better be an explanation inside. And an apology. And a promise to respect my boundaries.

It wasn't a card at all but a piece of printer paper folded into fourths, and when I opened it, his scrawl filled the page.

Dear Hannah,

I'm sorry things are wrecked right now. You keep taking the blame for it, saying it's your fault for telling me how you feel. I've never been great with words like you are, but I've never been bad either. I've tried explaining this to you a few times, and I screw it up. I'm going to try again here, in writing, to see if I can make it come out right and if I can stay out of my own way.

It's hard to say these things in front of you. I lose my train of thought, and I don't want to talk. I just want to . . . never mind. You're distracting. In a good way. Let's leave it at that.

So here goes: when I read the profile you put up for me, it lit my brain on fire. You saw me like I want to be seen, and you know me like I want to be known. I don't know if you know how that feels, but if you don't know, you need to. It's a gift—one you deserve. It's amazing to be understood and accepted anyway. And that's how seeing your words made me feel.

I could date a hundred women a hundred times each and never find one who will know me like you do.

But I know you like that. I know you think I see you as my responsibility because of Dave. But that responsibility to Dave is different than what you think it is, and maybe you'll be willing to ask me about it. Because I want to explain. But that's not what this note is about. This is about you. Those texts were to tell you that I see you. I do. I see every single part that makes you who you are.

This is the part I screw up when I try to explain it to you. I say it, but I don't think you hear me, because maybe I'm not saying it the right way: I have always seen you. Since you were seventeen, a long time before you told me you had a crush on me and I laughed at you to save us both.

These words aren't coming out right. I think I'm giving up on words. But I'm not giving up on trying to tell you at all. Open the box if you haven't already. Maybe it will say it better. And if you don't understand it, come find me.

Love,

Will

To save us both? What? What did he mean, he had always seen me?

I tore open the box, so full of anxiety I was on the verge of puking. He'd shoved a dark-blue towel inside. I scooped it out, gasping when I unwound it. He'd finally carved the cocobolo block.

The piece was beautiful, maybe as long as my forearm, a sinuous design that moved in a few clean lines through space, and I smiled. He'd made me an infinity symbol, the curves flowing into beautiful straight lines that sloped and curved again. The wood was gorgeous, almost warm beneath my skin.

I loved it as soon as I saw it, even more when I touched it. But I still didn't know what it was supposed to say that Will's words couldn't. I stared at it for a couple minutes, trying to figure out the message.

I set down the wood and picked up my phone. *It's beautiful. Does it explain everything? Or even anything?*

I wanted so badly to fake a psychic connection, to believe that I could read his mind, that I could perfectly understand what he was telling me because I knew him so well. But I told the truth. *I'm lost.*

I sat down and looked at the wood again. It was strange to see a finished piece from him. So often he whittled something that almost matched his vision but not quite. When that happened, he put it aside. It wasn't worth sanding something that wasn't everything he meant it to be. So he'd abandon it.

But this slid like polished stone beneath my finger. I couldn't resist touching and tracing it, noticing new patterns in the grain with every pass.

A light tap sounded on the front door a second before Will's head poked through it, swiveling until he spotted me at the table. "May I?" he asked.

I nodded, and he stepped in, hands in his pockets. His eyes caught on the note he'd written me. It lay face-up waiting for me to study it again for new patterns too.

He cleared his throat. "How did you find the guts to march into my place and tell me how you feel? This is hard."

My stomach clenched. "Why? What do you need to say?"

He laced his fingers behind his head and stretched. A minute ticked by. He stayed where he was, holding his own head up, staring at the ceiling.

"Will?"

"I don't want you because I can't have you." It came out in a rush. "I want you because I've felt that way since you were seventeen years old."

The world exploded. My entire understanding of everything Will and I had ever been to each other peeled away and collapsed around me, like watching someone demolish the exterior of a skyscraper, leaving behind a steel skeleton that suddenly had no context as the only thing standing.

Will let out a shaky breath and leaned over, putting his hands on his knees, still not looking at me. He looked like he did after a hard run.

All that came out of my mouth was, "What?" A vacuous, stupid-sounding word, but I had no other ones to give him.

"Yeah. That's not a confession I was ever going to make. 'Hey, when you were seventeen, I was a total creeper at twenty, digging my best friend's sister.'" He straightened and met my eyes finally. "But I'm confessing it anyway. I don't even know what's happening to me anymore."

I gaped at him, mouth open, too stunned to even blink. "When I was seventeen? How could you like me? I was fat and awful."

"You were bigger, yeah. But you've always been you. I mean, you're happier now, maybe. But your personality is the same as it's always been. And you're gorgeous. You know that, right? Even with the extra weight, you've always been gorgeous."

It was the last thing I'd ever expected to hear from him. Finally I swallowed and licked my lips so I could make them form words. "Why didn't you say anything when I told you how I felt?" But I couldn't sit still while I processed all this.

I touched the sculpture again, a tingle traveling up my arm. He had made it, had turned this over and over in his hands, and I wanted to feel that same touch so much that it was distracting me to the point of driving out coherent thought.

He watched me closely, apprehension around his eyes as I turned a full circle in the kitchen, trying to figure out what to do next. I could only replay his words. *I've felt that way since you were seventeen.* My brain was glitching, and I didn't care. I could listen to that forever.

I stood and crossed to sit on the couch, staring blankly at the coffee table in front of me. *I've felt that way since you were seventeen.* "Do you still feel that way?"

I didn't turn around to watch him as he answered, but it didn't matter. He didn't say anything anyway. I heard him move to the table, then back toward me on the sofa, stooping to set down the infinity sculpture before settling into his corner and leaning back. "Yes. I still feel that way. That's what the carving is about. I think I'm always going to feel that way. I want you to know that."

I stared at him, dazed. He finally unclasped his hands to look at me, like he couldn't figure out why I wasn't saying anything. I didn't even know what to ask, but I was desperately trying to come up with questions so I could understand.

"I'd come home for a holiday that weekend when you told me you loved me," he said. "Presidents Day, maybe. It was a Thursday night. I was back at campus by Friday noon. I was so freaked out."

"Why? Because I was young?"

"Because I thought the way you felt was my fault. I'd kind of figured it out that fall, that you were not Dave's little sister anymore. That you were separate from Dave. And, yeah, maybe a lot of the boys around the neighborhood were too dumb to look past a few extra pounds, but enough did. Didn't you ever notice guys checking you out? I saw it happen two or three times. You didn't?"

I shook my head. Never.

"The first time I noticed was the first time I started to see you differently too. But I could laugh at myself. I chalked it up to me being kind of a typical guy, paying attention to anything with nice hair and curves. But Dave noticed guys checking you out too, and it made him so mad. It brought out that protective streak in him, and it bothered him that he had to be gone during the week for school, that he couldn't stick around and keep an eye on the guys sniffing around."

"Nobody sniffed around!" I said, exasperated. "I never even had a date until senior prom, and that was after I'd lost about half my weight."

He shrugged. "I'm telling you, guys have radar for this stuff. But for me, it didn't matter. I felt weird about being attracted to you already, and when I saw how much it bugged Dave to see other guys paying attention to you, I felt worse. So I slammed a door shut on the whole idea and figured I'd be around you so much less from that point on that it didn't matter. Then you had to go and confess all your feelings a few months later. Geez, Hannah. Talk about killing me."

He sat forward, elbows on his knees, and turned to face me. "I was afraid I'd unintentionally sent out some kind of signal you were picking up. But there was no way I was going to cross Dave. So I laughed it off and figured it would fade for both of us."

"You crushed me," I said.

"I'm sorry," he whispered. "I thought it was a high school thing. I thought we'd move past it." He rubbed his palms up and down his thighs. "It honestly seemed like you did. So I did too. It was easy when I wasn't around you that much, to dismiss you as being young and dumb and let it go."

"I did get over you," I said. "Finally. A high school crush is a stronger force of nature than you realize. But I did it. That's when I started running. And when I got to college, I decided I needed better hobbies than eating my feelings, and the rest of the weight came off."

He nodded. "When you got to UT, every time I saw you, you were full of stories about guys and dates and stuff with Sophie. I was happy for you. I'm not really clear on . . . I don't know what happened over the next few years. I mean, I saw you when you were over at Dave's. Then you started tagging along on our trips, but that was cool. I was glad whatever had taken over my brain when you were a senior had gone away."

"I don't think that's right at all. I think you've seen me as seventeen for the last eight years. Why else would you think you had to move in down the hall to babysit me? I was fine, Will. I was totally fine until you showed up."

"When Dave said he was marrying Jessica and heading out to Qatar for work, he asked me to keep an eye on you. I think he meant check in on you from time to time, like over the phone, be available if your car ran out of oil or something."

I glared at him. "You idiots taught me how to change my oil before Dave would teach me to drive."

"Right." He scrubbed his hand over his hair, leaving a few strands poking out. "I know that. I knew that you could take care of yourself, but at some level, I worried because he worried. I could tell how much it stressed him out to leave, and suddenly I was volunteering to take over his apartment lease. I thought it would be fine. It seemed fine. It seemed like everything was normal between us until . . . until it wasn't."

"You mean until I ruined it all with another confession."

"Yeah. I mean, no. It was just that I'd convinced myself I was here on Dave's behalf even though that was way more than he'd asked of me. And I was so shocked when you told me the truth. I mean, I'd been feeling myself getting so used to having you around that I'd decided the best thing I could do was go on a dating streak—"

"Wait, *that's* why you did it? That's why you came up with the marriage plan?"

"You were getting into here again," he said, squeezing his eyes shut and tapping his forehead. Then he pinned me with his stare. "I needed you out. Maybe you understand how that feels."

"But why didn't you say something? Or put a signal out? Why didn't you confess something when I ran into your place babbling like an idiot weeks ago? I was dying inside, Will. Your dates were killing me."

"Because I didn't want to get on Dave's hit list!" He groaned in frustration. "There is no going back now. None. I can't be just friends with you. And he's going to think I moved into his place for this, to seduce you while he was away. And he's going to kill me."

"Don't get ahead of yourself," I said. "On any of that."

He flushed but nodded. "You see what I mean? I screw it up every time I try to explain to you."

"And the carving?" I asked. What did infinity mean?

"Our histories are so wrapped up together. I don't know when exactly my feelings started. I don't think they're ever going to end. I don't want them to. I'm not going to fight them anymore."

I fell. All the way off the edge of sanity, down, down, down. "What about Dave?"

"This might be the unforgivable sin, to mess with his precious Hanny."

"Is that what you plan to do? Play and move on?"

"Is that what you think?" His eyes flashed. "Is that what you're getting out of all of this?"

I shook my head and scooted toward him on the couch, resting my hand on his forearm. He tensed beneath my palm, and the falling turned to floating, but my stomach stayed wild, churning, flipping. "No. That's not what I'm getting out of this at all."

He met my eyes, his gaze steady, a challenge creeping in. "Then what are you getting out of it?"

I brushed the sculpture and let my hand fall back into my lap. "A gift. This. But more." I slid closer and threaded my fingers through his hair, pulling him toward me. "So much more." His pulse pounded at his temples, and I could feel it against my wrist. My breath sped up to match it, afraid to believe him but wanting to with everything I had in me. "It feels like I'm getting everything I ever wanted. Am I?"

He didn't wait for me to kiss him, dipping his head and pulling me toward him in one move, the kiss saying everything that he thought his words hadn't. Joy exploded through me.

"I'm so sorry," he said. "No one's ever handed me a greater gift than when you stormed in and told me how you felt, and I set it aside. I freaked out."

"I'm going to let you work that off," I said, rising to my knees so I had some height on him. He grinned and pulled my head down for more kisses, and I gave them out and drank them in, delirious with living out the daydream I'd had a thousand times, dizzy with how much better the reality was.

When I finally pulled away, I framed his face in my hands, a perfect snapshot of all I would ever need. "You're better with words than you think you are."

He pressed down on my shoulders with the lightest of touches until I was eye level with him again. "I didn't give you all my words yet. I owe you a few more." He took a deep breath and ran his fingers through my hair, combing it out of the way, pulling it back to spill around my face, then brushing it over my shoulders again. Finally his hands stilled, his thumbs feathering along my jaw. "You drive me crazy. You push me hard. You make me think. And laugh. And feel." He touched his forehead to mine like he had the first time he'd kissed me. "I love you, Hannah Becker. Even though your brother is going to kill me. I love you."

"It's about time," I said, kissing him with all the happiness sparking through me, the crazy fireworks ricocheting through my rib cage and inside my head. "I love you too. But you're telling Dave."

Epilogue ♥

"I CAN'T SEE YOU BOTH," Dave said, staring at the Skype screen. "I'm getting half of each of your faces. One at a time, y'all."

Will answered by lifting me onto his lap and tilting the camera to capture both of our faces. "Better?" he asked innocently, and I pinched him. He only grinned.

"No," Dave said, crossing his arms. "What's going on?"

"Ummmm," Will said, and I slid my hand into his, knowing how much he was dreading Dave's reaction. "I'm in love with your sister. She's infuriating."

I elbowed him but kept my eyes on the screen, where Dave's blank expression stared back at us. "Sorry. I think the camera glitched. What did you say?"

Will groaned, but I knew Dave too well to buy it. "He said he loves me. I love him too. Deal with it."

Dave's expression didn't change for almost ten agonizing seconds, and then a slow grin spread over it. "And how long has this been going on?"

"Years," I said, and Dave's grin dropped.

"We just didn't know it yet!" Will said, scrambling to smooth things over. "We only figured it out a couple of weeks ago."

Dave smiled again. "Y'all are both kind of dumb, then. I figured it out a long time ago."

My eyes flew wide, and I stared down at Will, who looked equally surprised. We both turned to look at Dave.

"You did?" Will said.

"Yeah."

"So you're not mad?"

Dave's smile faded. "I don't know. That depends. What happens next?"

"Dave," I snapped. "We haven't even had a month to get used to this. We have no idea what's next."

"That's not true," Will said. "Hang on." He fished something out of his back pocket and held up a ring, a simple band carved out of cocobolo that he slipped on my ring finger. "I'm all in, Hannah. I'm replacing that with gold. And diamonds. Or whatever you want. But I'm all in."

I stared at the band, up at Dave, down at Will, then grinned before I threw my arms around his neck and let my kiss say yes for me. And the last thing I heard before disappearing into the haze of Will's kisses was Dave's groan and the beep as he killed the Skype connection.

"I love you, Han."

"Always, Will."

<<<<>>>>

About the Author ❤

MELANIE BENNETT JACOBSON BUYS A lot of books and shoes. She eats a lot of chocolate and french fries and watches a lot of chick flicks. She kills a lot of houseplants. She says "a lot" a lot. She is happily married and living in Southern California with her growing family and more doomed plants. Melanie is a former English teacher, who loves to laugh and make others laugh. In her downtime (ha!), she writes romantic comedies and cracks stupid jokes on Twitter. She is the author of ten other novels from Covenant.

10 Facts about Melanie ♥

1. My husband bought me an e-reader before they were cool because he couldn't handle bringing a whole suitcase just for my books on our trips.

2. I once gained five pounds in a month from eating sea-salt caramel gelato.

3. My paternal ancestry is Cajun, and I make a killer jambalaya.

4. I e-mailed my now-husband on a dating site because I was impressed by his book list.

5. I'm a roller coaster fiend—bigger, higher, faster, but no dead drops!

6. I'm a sci-fi nerd: books, movies, TV shows—I love it all. Well, the good stuff.

7. I'm fluent in ASL (my parents were deaf).

8. I'm weirdly lucky. If there's a raffle, chances are I'll win.

9. I always get the best parking spots but pick the worst checkout lines.

10. I'll eat anything if it's made from potatoes.